William Barry

Sporting Rambles and Holiday Papers

William Barry

Sporting Rambles and Holiday Papers

ISBN/EAN: 9783337299361

Printed in Europe, USA, Canada, Australia, Japan

Cover: Foto ©Andreas Hilbeck / pixelio.de

More available books at **www.hansebooks.com**

SPORTING RAMBLES

AND

HOLIDAY PAPERS

BY

WILLIAM BARRY

AUTHOR OF "MOORLAND AND STREAM"

LONDON & NEW YORK

GEORGE ROUTLEDGE AND SONS

LONDON:

PRINTED BY J. OGDEN AND CO.,

172, ST. JOHN STREET, E.C.

CONTENTS

———◦•◦———

PART III.

ESSAYS ON SPORT.

PART IV.

NOTES ON SHOOTING.

PART I.

SPORTING RAMBLES.

THE MOOR OF MONBRAHER.

THE LITTLE DOG WALLACE.

MUCH bewildered is the little dog Wallace at the first head of game he flushes on the Moor of Monbraher. Wallace is a rather obese clumber, whose sporting experiences have been hitherto confined to pheasant coverts and the turnips of the English counties, and he has never before wagged his tail over an Irish moorland. He comes to a dead halt opposite a great bunch of withered flags rising from a black ooze of peat and water. Wallace does not know what to make of it. There is something there, no doubt : and with a heavy sigh as though waking from a gloomy dream, a man suddenly rises in the reeds and confronts the dog and his master. This figure will stand for the very genius of ague and of Monbraher. Though bent with cramp, he stands six feet high in the ragged bandages which are swathed upon his legs to serve as moccasins. His face is livid, a thin hoar-frost of beard fringes his jaws and lips, and his hollow eyes glitter. In his lean hand he clutches a reaping-hook, and on his back is the reward of his toil—the withies and other stuff which he gathers for fuel or for manufacture into coarse matting. Has not a poet told us of beauty born of murmuring sound passing into the face of a woman ? On the countenance of the ague-stricken matmaker the desolation of this landscape has impressed its hungry gloom —its separation from the world of culture or intelligent interest— its abandonment to birds that do not sing, but

cry with painful, querulous notes when the chill wind
scatters their squadrons, or when the fowler surprises
them.   Wallace so far recovers himself as to bark,
and then to sniff at the lean shanks of the Monbraher
matmaker.   "Have you seen any snipe or duck?"
Yes, but 'tis late in the day to come for them.   There
are four or five heavy duck, he thinks, pitched two or
three hundred yards, but his honour had better be
quick, for Lame Carey the tailor is "stalin" down on
them already.   And, indeed, Wallace is fated this day
to meet more than one curious product of Irish moorland existence.   With stealthy jerks of a crutch, and
with a long single gun in hand, approaches Lame
Carey the tailor, a well-known character in this wild
district.   Advancing to meet Mr. Carey (who has furnished the end of his crutch with a flat piece of wood,
to prevent it sinking so deep in the soil that he would
be staked to it or unable to pull it out again), a parley,
and an offensive alliance against the birds, are entered
into with him.   We agree to come at the spot indicated by the matmaker from different sides, so as to
have a better chance, and the manœuvre is not unsuc-
cessful ; one bird goes down to Mr. Carey's score, and
two to that of his temporary confederate.   It was impossible not to admire the skill of Mr. Carey in
shooting under difficulties.   His gun was fastened to
the stock with twine, and though furnished with a
nipple, it had no lock.   The manner, then, in which Mr.
Carey discharged his piece of ordnance was this : He
put a cap on the nipple, took a large stone from his
pocket and gave the cap a sharp blow, whereupon the
gun went off.   Wallace never saw any weapon similarly
treated in Bucks.

Lame Carey is an invaluable guide.   He knows
every inch of Monbraher.   He retires from sport himself after his one shot at the duck, and begs to be invested with the bag.   His performances with the
crutch are astonishing.   When a drain is to be crossed,

he turns half round, and then swings himself by an indescribable wriggle off the ground altogether, and, making a kind of spread-eagle in the air, he is at the other side in an instant. The feat calls to mind an odd mode of transit over this very moor adopted many years ago by an athletic minister of the Church, who officiated every Sunday at a little parish on the edge of the bog. This reverend gentleman, finding the highroad tedious, and having a taste for muscular exercise, procured a pair of stilts after the fashion of the peasants in the Landes, and stalked to service on them. After awhile, however, he considered this system of travelling rather slow, and he substituted for the stilts a huge leaping-pole, and with white tie and spectacles and a tall hat, might be seen bounding like an ecclesiastical kangaroo to church, returning home in the same manner, a distance of three or four miles. But this is a digression. Lame Carey points to a field full of dry barren grass, and says he is certain quail have settled in it. Carey is right. Wallace no sooner puts his foot on the spot than he shows evident tokens of game of some kind being about, and in a few moments a quail is added to the bag, and two others marked down. Wallace does not like snipe-shooting. He has not been brought up to the work, and is too quick and impatient; nevertheless a very fair number of snipe continue to accumulate in our collection, when upon the hill at the southern end of Monbraher—a hill most appropriately termed Mount Misery—a cloud suddenly descends, and a chiding sough of the wind, heard all over the moor, warns us that what Mr. Carey terms a "dhrop o' rain" is approaching. The dhrop o' rain is a steady downpour, in the midst of which we trudge for shelter to a cabin or shieling, the upper half of the door of which is open, allowing volumes of thick smoke to rush out. Lame Carey, with the usual salutation, unhasps the lintel and disturbs a group of poultry from the threshold, the fowl

cluttering with a tremendous pother to the rafters, the
dresser, the top of the bed, and other customary
roosting-places. Three women are sitting round a
huge potato pot by a bog-oak fire. Lame Carey
plunges his pipe into the red ashes, and inquires if
Thomasheen is any betther than he wor. A shake
of the head from the eldest of the women signifies
that Thomasheen is very bad indeed, and rising from
a wooden box that has served her for a chair, the
bare-legged dame goes over to the foot of the bed,
where a cradle has been deposited. Covered with a
dirty rug, but withal warm enough, is Thomasheen
(Little Thomas) himself, undergoing the ordeal of
measles. His cheeks are round and plump yet, his
bullet head is covered with a thatch of golden curly
hair, and it is to be hoped that Thomasheen with
his dark blue Celtic eyes will weather his complaint;
there is the stuff and stamina of half a dozen London
children in him, at any rate; and yet Thomasheen has
been reared on the same dismal swamp of Monbraher
of which our matmaker above-mentioned was a native
and an illustration.

Out into the open once more with Lame Carey, we
find the rain has cleared off, or rather there is no more
for the present where it came from, and our route requires us for a time to take a road, or what passes for
a road, through the moor. "There's sure to be some
tale (teal) in there, sir," remarks Mr. Carey. "You
had better let me hold the dog, and creep in behind
the furze." Wallace submits rather ruefully to an
embrace from Lame Carey, who sits on the ground
and puts his arm about his neck, puffing villainous
tobacco at the same time into the nostrils of that
gentle and clever dog. But Wallace is a perfect gentleman, and submits to the restraint and to the rude
caress without a murmur. There is nothing to be had
for the adventure, however; the teal had either departed before our arrival, or had never been there,

and so we must seek our quarry elsewhere. Wallace, released, skips and frisks in so friendly a style around Mr. Carey, that he gazes at him with fond admiration, and surmises that he is worth his weight in gold, and can do everything but " spake."

We arrive now at a more civilised district of Monbraher. A few cabbage gardens and potato fields have been reclaimed from the moor ; they require to be fed with sea-weed, and the ocean odour they emit is strong. Women are at work here, with bare legs and feet, and scanty petticoats, and Lame Carey has a joke or a greeting in Irish for each and all of them. They tell us the golden plover were on the ground about early in the morning, and in fact we can see a huge stand of them in the air, but miles away, and exhibiting no sign of alighting. Further on we meet with considerable quantities of snipe, and Wallace, with some mild—very mild—correction, begins to understand the peculiar kind of sport to which he has been introduced. He has not yet got accustomed, perhaps, to being so very wet. His master has made a vain effort to escape one of the penalties of fowling in Monbraher, by bringing with him from town the most scientifically constructed boots and leggings, warranted proof against damp. At the very first " gulch " into a Monbraher moss-pit the patent everdry boots were charged to the brim with Monbraher particular, the only advantage, if any, derived from the elaborate construction of the renowned boots being that the person in them was accompanied by sobs every step he took for the rest of the day. They retained the water admirably ; and when they were removed in the evening they were proportionately as full of bilge as the carcass of a heavily-insured coffincollier. As for the waterproof leggings, they were also a snare and a delusion. They smelt abominably of creosote or gas, or india-rubber ; and despite the various and mysterious nastiness in which they were apparently steeped, or with which they had been anointed, they were as limp as wet brown paper at the close of the day.

Resisting Lame Carey's suggestion to remain on the edge of the moor until duck-flight, Wallace and his master prepare for a good three miles' stretch to home. The last stage of that march is by a path on a sand-cliff over the sea. The grey evening dies in a dark sulk, but the night is very beautiful, with all those tender ornaments of moon and shining stars, which never seem so lovely as when they glitter upon the waves of the tide. The beach is fringed with white half-phosphorescent foam, and from the tumbling surf comes a constant boom along the coast away to where the light-house lamp is gleaming across a reach of wet sand. A schooner in full sail passes almost within a stone's-throw of the road we have now arrived at beyond the cliff; you can hear the voices of the sailors on board, and the hail from the pilot-boat that offers to convoy the vessel across the treacherous harbour-bar on which the sea-horses are tossing their manes. If you listen you can catch the whistle of the wild-duck in the sky bound for Monbraher, the calling of the curlew, the occasional croak of a heron. Wallace is weary, and rubs his head against the wet waterproof gaiters as though to hint that dalliance with scenery at such a time is cruel to him, and so the pace is accelerated, and the welcome town twinkles at our jaded feet, where Wallace shall rest, for that night at least, upon a soft rug.

THE "KIRKEEN-THRAW."

THE sea, which no doubt formerly flowed over this waste, still growls at one side of it, and then an arm of the tide runs up for a mile or so inland, where the

water privilege has been used for canal purposes. On
a keen frosty day some good wild-fowl shooting may
be had by taking a post at the opening of the creek,
or by following its course in a boat or on the path.
A great lumbering lighter with coffee-coloured sail
creeps along, its huge oars manned by peasants in
flannel jackets, and the tiller held by the captain, at
whose feet a woman sits smoking a short pipe. The
barge she reclines in does not exactly suggest the
golden burnished galley of Cleopatra. The *Kirkeen-
thraw* has no perfumed lug to make the winds of
Monbraher love-sick as it fills the patched and ragged
canvas; the oars move not to the tune of flutes, but
groan in the rotten rowlocks while the noble craft
makes her mile an hour, breeze and tide permitting.
It occurs to the fowler that a short voyage in the
Kirkeen-thraw would afford an opportunity for an
opening at passing plover, red-shank, or duck; and as
the *Kirkeen* halts to take in a stray passenger at a
rough quay, she is boarded by the fowler and the dog
Wallace. The captain—who goes neither by the stars
nor compass, but who steers his boat by such simple
landmarks and unseamanlike memoranda as " keepin'
her head aist of Tim O'Brien's farm," or " standin' off
from where ye see the workhouse, God help us ! on
the top av the hill miles away, for there's always a bit
of a neddy tide (eddy) near the bank "—is not so
occupied with his duties as not willingly and cheerfully to enter into conversation. He reports intelli-
gently on wild-fowl, and does not promise much sport
until we have a harder spell of frost. His wife, the
lady who has been smoking, presently gets up and
disappears into what serves at once for cabin and
kitchen of the *Kirkeen-thraw*. She shortly returns
and says something in Irish to her spouse, who re-
peats it to his valiant crew, who at once suspend their
hard labour at the oars and allow the *Kirkeen* to move
by sail alone. A couple of fellows now dive into the

recess which the lady had explored, and emerge bearing between them a pot of smoking potatoes. It is, in
fact, dinner-hour on board the *Kirkeen*, and although
kindly and respectfully pressed to the banquet, the
fowler and his dog retire to the bow of the ship on the
watch for birds.

There is a cheerless expanse of mud on either side,
but the sky is a lovely intense blue ; the brown moor
looks almost pleasant with its myriad ponds and pools
blinking in the sun, and the peaks of the mountains in
the dim distance are capped with snow. Thousands
upon thousands of sea-birds are calling to each other
from reedy aits and islets, gulls of a hundred varieties,
some making an odd sort of piggish whine, others
screaming and croaking. The red-shanks, swift as
snipe on the wing, dart by with a clear flageolet
whistle ; the wily whaup, who already seems to smell
powder, gives a plain note of warning to the entire
feathered community ; a little clutch of teal are
coursing round and round within a narrow circle of the
air ; a cormorant waddles ashore and flaps his wings
to dry them, with a mechanical movement and an
ungainliness of aspect which reminds you of the owl
in the diabolical scene of Weber's famous opera ; three
gaunt herons stand as solemn as Grey Friars at the top
of a still lagoon, which reflects them like a mirror ;
but nothing can surpass in wonderful unanimity of
evolution the performances of the little water-fowls
whose Irish name has been given to our barge.
Literally, the kirkeen-thraw means "the little hen on
the strand or of the strand," and the bird signified by
it is that known in England as the sea-lark. It would
be impossible to convey a notion of the number of
these birds in one of the divisions shimmering over
the verge of Monbraher moor. "Shimmer" is the
word—for the light glances on the cloud of quivering
pinions as upon a polished surface ; but these huge
aerial armies are constantly altering in shape of out-

line, although they invariably preserve a perfectly symmetrical form : and they seem to stir in this strange, free, unwearied fashion from a mere instinct of joyousness. There they remain depicted against the sky for an hour, taking vast sweeps and curves, contracting and expanding, rising in a globe until almost lost to sight, and then growing into view as a glittering fan, and then, all of a sudden, as though time were called, the mighty host breaks up into little, darting, piping detachments, one half of which flickers into the low sea-line where the breakers are rolling and muttering, while the other lodges upon the stubble-fields, seeking, perhaps, a change from constant fish or sand-worm diet. All these sights and sounds, however, afford no real work for either Wallace or his master. Nothing will come within shot, and the fowler limits his operations to wild-duck, either widgeon or teal, to curlew, plover, or red-shank. The kirkeen-thraw is certainly not worth shooting for any culinary or ordinary purposes, and it is so horribly tenacious of life when wounded, that the circumstance adds to the wanton cruelty of firing at it "for fun." The captain of the barge having assisted his wife to remove the tokens of dinner from his quarter-deck, and the crew taking their places at the oars, we begin to move briskly—comparatively briskly—for the next hour, and then we sight our destination. The *Kirkeen-thraw* is to make a return voyage with the ebb-tide, and the captain agrees to take the fowler in for that venture, wishing him good luck to fill the bag in the meanwhile.

And as the day was growing old, and as yet not a barrel discharged, it was necessary indeed that some-thing active and immediate should be done. Luckily, bold Mat Savage approaches — Mat Savage, who shares with Lame Carey the honour of being the greatest and most expert poacher in the country, Mat, recognising the limp aspect of the sportsman's wallet, offers to fill it off-hand with snipe which the cunning rascal has caught with hanging rods. This proposition being rejected, Mat leads the way to a bog, which he enthusiastically described as alive with 'em ; and so it was. No sooner did Wallace put his paws into it than the swamp appeared to explode snipe in every direction ! They got up in wisps ; they started in couples, and for a good twenty minutes it was a matter of fire and load as quickly as possible. Wallace was utterly startled and frightened. He simply looked on as a spectator, occasionally retrieving a bird, but with quite an absent, distraught air, as though the place and the business we were about suggested problems to him he was unable to solve. "An' we'll not lave it widout a hare," said Mat, when nine brace of plump snipe had been lodged in the netting ; "only last Sunday I put up a puss in the corner beyant ; " and Mat's statement was verified by the circumstance of a hare being now put up in the same spot, whose next appearance in public will be as soup. "A tidy shot enough, sir," says Mat, critically, "though you might have let drive wid your left at the wather-hin." It is difficult to persuade Mat that the wather-hin, as he calls it, is not worth shooting, especially as Wallace has testified to the bird being game, by paying a remarkable attention to its haunt. Mat Savage sticks by the fowler until the bag is a serious weight to carry, and then proceeds to accompany him to the wharf from which the *Kirkeen-thraw* is to depart upon her return journey. That gay barge has already hoisted her grimy sail, though there is not a breath of wind to fill it. The dusk is already coming on when we let go the painter and proceed to drop down with the current. The captain again assumes his place at the helm, his wife sits at his feet as in the morning ; but on this occasion, instead of smoking a pipe, she is crooning over an infant. In half an hour it is quite dark, and Wallace, curled at the feet of his master, is asleep. We have no oars now, and no one apparently on board save the captain, his wife, and baby for crew, Wallace and his master for passengers. But there must be some person to tend the big sail; and so there is, for a word from the commander brings to his feet a slumbering giant who has been stretched in the now vacant hold. When the moon is visible she first shows through the bars of a shattered breakwater, and then the light streams down upon us; and our galley, the wet sides of which are silvered with it, does not look quite so unlike the barge of Cleopatra as it did in the morning. The woman's wild Irish lullaby is now mingled with the distant sullen boom of the sea. The water washes and gurgles about the blunt prow of the *Kirkeen*, and as we pass a peninsula of withered flags and rushes, the reeds creak and whisper, though there is no palpable breeze to aid us on our voyage. But we do get to the end of it at last, where the captain is hailed on turning to his wharf with a hearty shout of " Deos meurahuit " (God be with ye), and gives the expected response, " Deos meura agus Phadhrig dith" (and the same to you, Paddy), while the kindly mariner roars a safe-home to the fowler and the sleepy Wallace, who trots at the heel of his master with a semi-conscious, som-nambulistic gait. We pass another day in the *Kirkeen-thraw*, with the wind blowing hard from the sou'-west, a dirty sky, the water churned into wreaths of foam, the birds flying madly, as though in distress, through the mist; Monbraher wrapped in a fog, the waves thundering on the coast, and casting high on the shingle the tangled weeds torn from the sunken rocks. When this flotsam and jetsam of the deep appears, a hundred hands are busy to snatch it into safe heaps, that it may be used to force the miserable soil in the district to grow a pallid, dropsical potato. The *Kirkeen-thraw* labours in the turbulent stream, and, knowing that her cargo consists of such dead-weight as manufactured bricks, the fowler would perhaps feel a trifle uneasy at every successive squall that came howling up the bleak river, but from being quite confident as to himself and Wallace being able to swim to shore in the event of an accident. And, as far as sport was concerned, this wild-weather excursion in the *Kirkeen* was far more interesting than the voyage undertaken in a milder season. The duck fled low, almost skimming the water, and the dog of the captain of the *Kirkeen*, a tough Irish water-spaniel, divided with Wallace the pretty hard work of bringing on board the dead and chasing the wounded. Wallace made friends with this willing brute at once, and contrived to get him in cunningly enough for more than his share of the duties which devolved upon both. We had to bring up the *Kirkeen* often enough to try the temper of the most patient sailor, but our captain was in no hurry, and the manœuvre was effected without very much difficulty. The only mistake made by Wallace was when we came opposite Tim O'Brien's. It happened that Tim's flock of geese were taking their daily swim to an oozy pasture-ground of theirs at the opposite side of the stream. Wallace was on the look-out for a job at the moment, and, before he could be stopped, had leapt into the midst of the unsuspecting fleet and made an attempt to seize the gander. The gander stoutly resisted Wallace's efforts to capture him for a few minutes, but at last succumbed, and was piloted by the neck to the *Kirkeen*. This unlawful proceeding was regarded waggishly by the water-spaniel, who never took his brown eyes off Wallace during the whole time the incident was occurring. The gander, it may be mentioned, was returned to the place from whence he had been violently taken, only the worse by a fright and a few ruffled feathers.

FROST.

AT the close of a raw day the wind dies off the moor, and the brazen cloud-wracks which overhang the sea take odd and fantastic shapes ere they fade into night. The stillness of the spirit of frost is upon everything, until you think you might hear the pools and the ponds hardening in the dark. But the wild-duck of Monbraher are not to be had at duck-flight without a little patience and even fortitude. The keen eyes of Lame Carey are peering from behind a stack of turf into the dreary wold, drearier and more lonely for that populous and busy aspect of the innumerable stars. Lame Carey opines we shall not have a chance at the duck until moon-rise, but it is better to be in time at our posts. Perhaps it is; but even through a series of wrappers which, if worn by an Esquimaux, might enable the savage to go with half his allowance of seal-oil, this vigil is numbing every drop of warm blood in the body. Besides, if the duck did arrive, just now shooting them would be out of the question, though Lame Carey again thinks otherwise, and pretends, at any rate, to be able to see in the confusing no-light with which we are surrounded. The silence of the moor is at length broken by a red flash from the hill-side, and the sullen boom of a piece of wild-fowl ordnance owned by a sporting farmer in the vicinity, who gets what he calls "an amplush" at the haunts of golden plover every other evening. "Bad luck to him!" is the muttered and emphatic ejaculation of Mr. Carey, as the sound comes crashing towards us; "may the next shot murther him." So adds the now ungentle Mr. Carey, who turns a ferocious look in the direction of the disturbance, as though his scowl at a mile or so off would prevent

Mr. Martin Hannigan from again discharging his
untimely weapon. The moor is noisy enough for a
minute or so after this episode. The peevish call
of the pewits sounds like a remonstrance for being
awakened and having to take their tufted heads
from under their wings; the snipe bleats, the whaup
whistles; but gradually these voices of the moor
cease, the curlew having the last word, after a sulky
grunt from a heron and a thin, frightened scream
from a sea-lark. "No opportunity now, sir, for half
an hour at laste," remarks Mr. Carey, as he refills a
short pipe known in this quarter from its dimensions
and from a convenience offered by its proportions, as
a "jaw-warmer," and proceeds with vigorous efforts
to make the pungent weed burn into a glow that half
illumines his shrewd, deep-scored Celtic face.

It grows colder and colder. A meteor sweeps
down through the wall of blackness which seems to
inclose the moor. Surely the moon is due by this
time, and does not mean to disappoint a couple of
eager wild-fowl shooters. But now across the fen a
breeze, suggesting the wave of a wand which will
curdle every liquid thing to ice, precedes a green-
yellow glimmer which grows into a radiant haze, and
we have a proof that the calendar we consulted for
our expedition did not mislead us. Now we can at
least see to some extent what we are about. "Steady,
sir, they're comin'" "Where?" "Ready, sir, are
you?" "Yes; but——" Crack goes the stone against
the nipple of Lame Carey's gun—the stone that
serves him instead of a lock. "What was it, Carey?"
"The ducks, to be sure, sir;" and up he starts, and
hobbles with his crutch twenty yards or so, returning
with a couple of plump mallards. "Your honour
isn't used to the light." Another long wait, during
which Mr. Carey's companion gets rather impatient
with a sport which involves a complete abstraction of
caloric from the system and a very small, or at least a

very limited quantity of excitement. Hark! The severe weather is upon us in earnest, for we distinctly catch the chime or clang of a string of wild-geese, but there is no prospect of our getting a shot at them. They will in all probability pass along the moor into the high, wet reaches of the mountain. And so it is decided to hold our watch on Monbraher for another half-hour only. A sudden rustle, or rather swish, resembling a thunder-downpour of rain. " Now, sir, let fly ! " and this time Lame Carey is not unassisted or unaided in his attack. We have made a fortunate " vacancy," as Mr. Carey terms it, into a large flock of teal, and pick up nine. Every limb creaks under the ordeal of the march home. Lame Carey hops to his cabin on the edge of the moorland, and the fowler creeps into the shelter of the warm, sparkling hearth as quickly as his half-frozen limbs will permit him to move, there to enjoy the pleasures of a thorough thaw.

Next morning the moor of Monbraher has put on a robe of quaker-gray from end to end. The pools are sheeted with ice ; the ground is frozen hard. Not a single bird is to be seen upon or near the entire waste. You might perhaps find a few snipe or a teal in the green springs sparsely scattered through the fen, but we have other and better sources of sport to fall back on in the district. That line of hills at one side of the moor is intersected with numerous gullies and glens, and down every one of these we shall find running streams, and no doubt some means of adding to the contents of the shooting diary. Then the sides of the hill are sure haunts of both the golden and the green plover. And so, full of hope, we take the field, the frost in the air giving that exhilarating impulse to activity and exertion which contributes so much to the thorough physical enjoyment of exercise. Wallace is apparently subject to the same atmospheric impression, for he has a roll in the frost-covered ferns, and exhibits a kittenish weakness unworthy of so accomplished an animal for playing a game with his own tail. A word, however, reduces Wallace to an obedient and business-like gravity, though he will not be expected to work over-much during a day of the kind. And now we come to " Piper's Glen," so called from a piper having fallen into it returning from a wake at which he had been professionally assisting. The ghost of the piper (for he became a ghost on the spot) is frequently heard playing upon his ghostly instrument, to the terror of rustic strayed revellers ; and hence the name of the place. Piper's Glen has nothing of the awesome in its appearance. It is wonderfully pleasant and lively in the frost. The great rocks, which tease and fret its little rivulet into all sorts of frantic gurgles and expostulations, are gleaming with spears and beads of ice ; banks of brown, withered fern are on either hand, here and there enriched with cones of fairy coin, the blossoms of the golden furze, or the scarlet berries that the chuckling blackbird delights in breaking with his beak. There is a " Holy Well " in Piper's Glen, with its rude wooden cross ; its thornbush shedding odd flowers and leaves in the shape of votive rags and ribbons from believers ; at the end of the gully is a picturesque, dirty cabin, with a chimney on one side, like a rakish, battered hat ; and with the chorus and prattle of the stream there comes from the cabin the constant clink, clank, clankadillo of the blacksmith and farrier, whose forge is attached to the modest domicile. And on this bright afternoon there is as much real sport to be had in Piper's Glen as in many carefully tended preserves. The snipe lay in the soft moss by the stream, in the flags, in the sedge by it ; and a pretty sight it was to see them darting off, until they were obliged to stop at a peremptory " halt " from a straight-held gun. For this diversion Wallace was not of much service, and

seems to think so himself, for he is on a beat of his
own (well within call), and is nuzzling and scampering
round the ferns and furze, and has something, too.
" Steady, Wallace ! " and a cock springs from under
Wallace's nose, a woodcock plump and russet, and
an ornament in the netting of the game-bag. The
game-bag at the moment is in charge of a young
volunteer, who for the honour and glory of carrying
it, and receiving a trifle in the shape of backsheesh,
has neglected his legitimate farm-occupation, whatever it may be. The habit of the attendant is to
flatter, even when flattery was embarrassing and expressions of condolence more or less impertinent.
Thus, when a second cock was found who managed
somehow or other to avoid being hit by two barrels
discharged point-blank at him, Master Flavin roars
out, " O begor, sir, his leg is hangin' to him," as if
that circumstance was proof of skill or design on the
part of the fowler. " Av you didn't hit him in, you
made him lave *that*," was another consolatory phrase
of Master Flavin's, when a snipe miraculously baffled
the aim of a—well, of an experienced snipe-shot. A
hare bolted from a bush in the glen ("was covered by
the gun as dead as ever a hare was covered"), and
yet bounded off with a speed that might test the pace
of the late Master McGrath. When this occurred,
Master Flavin, after watching the flying course of
the hare for a full minute with much gravity, turned
round and says, " Faith, thin, sir, I wouldn't be surprised if that ould divil of a hare was onaisy in herself
this minnit ! " Master Flavin has a sense of humour
that may get him into trouble.

As the hours waned we passed from Piper's Glen to
the high ground, and then commenced an entirely
different kind of shooting. The plover, however,
were not very plentiful ; at least, not so plentiful as
might have been expected from the severity of the
weather. The pewits made the other birds exceed-

ingly wild and difficult to approach, but Master
Flavin was of use in frightening the birds towards
points of ambuscade. From one of the hills the bag
was more than agreeably weighted for Master Flavin
by two broadsides into a stand, and the knocking
over of a couple of rabbits. But the December day
is short, and already the Monbraher fen at our feet
has its gray, still face flushed with the red light of the
sun, and again the clang of the wild-geese sailing
inward from the tide shows that the cold grip of the
frost is not yet to be taken off the land.

KILLVULLEN-BY-THE-SEA.

IT is something to be a monarch in Thule. I have been elected, I think, by universal suffrage to that exalted position in Killvullen from the mere fact of being a stranger, in much the same fashion as the islanders of a burlesque theatre fall on their knees and do homage and service to the tight sailor who is wrecked amongst the savages on a hen-coop. Killvullen is a very retired nook on the Irish coast. It has no trade to speak of: the grinning fangs of the rocks, with the white breakers snarling round them, show in front of the bay in order to warn off the ships. When the tide is out there is a wonderful hunting-ground for the naturalist or the marine botanist along the shore. The Killvullen crabs are of gigantic size, and I used to wonder at the courage of the girls who went to gather dillosk at low-water, in venturing with bare legs into the shallows, where the mammoth crustaceans might be noticed backing and waltzing into the huge coils of sea-weed. Killvullen boasts of a national school, a chapel, a holy well, and a coastguard station. The school is on the edge of a cliff, and the buzz and purr of the academy can be heard on the shingle. The master is glad to meet a strange face. Poor fellow! it is a weary task for him, trying to educate his flock of white-headed little Celts on a salary of about £35 per annum. His only recreation is fishing, and you observe his lines twisted round the square frames hanging over the door to dry in the hot August sun. That ridiculous figure in whiskers, with a short jacket, broad stern, and spy-glass, sidling into the path

that skirts the sand-hills, is appointed here by Government to capture smugglers or to report the coming of
an Armada. The main (and only) street of Killvullen
is at present in the occupation of a flock of questing
geese.   They are marching quite proudly up the
thoroughfare ; and when Billy Walshe, my landlady's
heir, runs out to try and start a game of some sort with
an elderly gander, that demure fowl makes a neck
and a hiss at him that sends Billy scuttling into the
shelter of the Hotel Walshe.

Very comfortable am I in the Hotel Walshe. Our
cuisine is limited, to be sure. The *chef* consists of
an octogenarian female, of so pious a turn that she
gave warning when I ordered a bird to be cooked
on Friday. We cook fish, however, excellently at
the Hotel Walshe, and we bake and manufacture a
delicious tea-scone out of butter and potatoes. Mrs.
Walshe is a widow, and as strict a worshipper of
cleanliness as a Dutch housewife. The only object
not polished and scrubbed on the premises is my friend
and walking companion in ordinary, Master Billy. His
mother is so fond of him that I think she refrains from
touching him up, on the principle that an affectionate
antiquary refrains from furbishing some darling relic in
his collection. Let us pay a pilgrimage to our holy well.
We pass to the landward side of the village, into a grove
of elms, now powdered with white dust, and at the end
of a grove turn into a field of yellow grain. In the
corner of this field there is an aged, gnarled thorn-bush,
almost covered with fluttering rags of all sorts and
colours.   A hutch-like edifice, thatched with moss,
stands by the dreary tree, and shelters the waters of
the sacred pool. The well is so clear and limped
that it seems empty but for the trickle into it of a rill
from a spring without. Every year in this month of
August there is high festival held on this spot. The
water has a wonderful repute for healing qualities. It
has worked miraculous cures for the last five, six,

seven—how many centuries?—ever since, in fact, the great Saint of Killvullen flourished in the parish. The inhabitants have vague, though reverential, notions of the date of Saint Killvullen's existence. That he was of foreign extraction would appear to be proven on the testimony of a boulder which lies on the beach, and on which it is stated the blessed Killvullen voyaged here direct from the well-known seaport of Rome, with a commission from the Pope in his hand to convert the Irish. To wriggle under a cavity in this stone and come out on the other side is an infallible remedy for the lumbago. I have seen an afflicted farmer, too stout to crawl through the hole, rubbing his back against the miraculous slab, with an expression of mingled credulity and doubt on his countenance which it was hard to witness with gravity. The remains of a very old church are also supposed to testify to the reality and celebrity of Saint Killvullen. There is, indeed, no doubt of the immense antiquity of the ruin. Over what is left of a door is the ancient Irish hieroglyph of the Saviour. The diminutive chancel is full of tall grass, and through the framework of a rent in the northern wall is a picture of the sunny blue sea, with a yacht as small as a sea-bird with folded wings resting upon it. It is a favourite perch of mine, to mount on the wall into a perfect nest of cool, aromatic ivy. Here, if you please, I bring a book and a pipe, and spend hours of complete delicious idleness. There is an unbroken prospect of sea-scape to send your thoughts wandering over when the book wearies; and if you only turn on the couch of leaves, you look beyond Killvullen into a valley dotted about with picturesque Irish cabins, and on its furthest edge the shadows of a mountain famous for the number of land-agents shot in its neighbourhood from time to time. Of course there is a gap in this mountain, supposed to be made in a single bite by the devil. There is scarcely an eminence in Ireland out of which the demon has not devoured a sample ; and a traveller counting over all the devil's bites, and devil's gaps, and devil's punch-bowls in the country, must be impressed with the curious appetite for granite, peat, and brushwood evinced by the demon.

I am occasionally called off my post of observation and reverie by Billy Walshe, who reports for me when he sees a flock of pigeons by the cliffs. Then do we both—I with the gun, and Billy proudly bearing the shot-bag—sally forth on a day's campaign against the blue-rocks. These are none of your Hurlingham doves, but birds native to the wild sea ramparts, bred in the storm-seamed clefts of the head-lands. We trudge for a couple of miles before we come to our ground, the path sloping upwards, until the surging of the tide sounds at a dizzy distance below us. Hundreds of gulls are flying about, and the gaunt cormorants are fishing in sullen loneliness in the numerous creeks and inlets. Now we have arrived at our preserve. We keep strict silence as we approach it, and I move as close as I can, with gun on full cock, to the edge of a narrow gully, to look into which and see far down the swirling water is rather trying to the nerves. It is the office of Billy to fire off a small piece of brass ordnance at a signal from me, and at the instant a bevy of the pigeons spring as quick as light from the gulf, and try to make, some over the water, some across the field into the shelter of the other cliffs. I succeed in tumbling one into the ferns which grow on the opposite side of the spot where we are, to the intense delight of my assistant, who has the bird picked as bare as a billiard-ball for the spit by the time we arrive at his maternal hostelry.

"Och ! yere a grate sporter intirely !" ejaculates the female Francatelli, who meets us with a solitary piece of game (call it game) at the entrance of our lodging. These pigeons taste best when eaten fresh killed, and so I request that Mrs. Donovan will be good enough to prepare the fowl for dinner. I suggest that it may not be boiled, with a touch of irony in my voice which is quite thrown away on Mrs. Donovan, who is deaf to every remark not formally delivered at her through her mistress, Widow Walshe.

As I lie down for a rest on a sofa from which the kitchen-yard is visible, I perceive the *chef* calmly smoking a dhudeen as she scrapes the potatoes for my banquet. I daresay Mirobolant used to consume a cigarette in the intervals of composing his lyrical entrées; and Mrs. Donovan has an equal right, surely, to burn Limerick twist as a solace to her culinary exertions. My landlady is away to the nearest town, and has promised to bring my post with her, for letters do not come to us here. The quiet, indeed, and remoteness of Killvullen is its chief charm. But now Mrs. Donovan enters to serve, as she calls it, my dinner, and breaks the thread of serious reflection with which I had been occupied. The pigeon was done to a cinder, and when I venture to call Mrs. Donovan's attention to its condition, the good woman smiles grimly, and then soliloquises audibly in the passage: "The Lord be merciful to us! He thinks of nothin' but his —— "

OUR ELFIN MYTHOLOGY.

IT was my original intention, when setting out for Killvullen, to pursue the interesting study of Marine Algæ. For that purpose I bought a handy book on the subject, the composition of an erudite German, which has received the compliment of an English translation, and which leaves nothing to be said on the *cosmarium margaraligerum amphitctras antediluviana.* But I meekly abandoned my useful design for quite a different branch of inquiry. I discovered that genuine Irish fairies still existed in the neighbourhood of Killvullen. Through the medium of Billy Walshe I was introduced to Tim Foley, who combined the accomplishments of angling and story-telling to perfection. Tim was a shrewd old fellow enough in most things; but when he talked, in a low, earnest voice, of the good people, with his dark eyes looking with an odd stare as if into an invisible world which he feared to disturb with even a whisper, it was impossible not to yield to the notion that he firmly believed in the reality of his quaint fancies. Tim would give a wide berth to certain districts of Killvullen supposed to be haunted by the elves. He would think, if he could not say, with Mr. Allingham :—

> Up the heathery mountain,
> Down the rushy glen,
> We daren't go a-hunting,
> For fear of little men.
> Wee folk, good folk,
> Trooping all together,
> Green Jacket, Red Cap,
> And White Owl's Feather.

He had seen the court of Don Fierna, the King of the Munster Pixies, within the grass-grown interior of Ightermurragh Grange, one night last summer, as he was coming home from Maurice Hennessy's wake. The moon was full and bright at the time, and shone over the walls of the grange, and " as sure as God made little apples " (this is his own language), " there was the great Don, with his cocked-hat and sword and wig, surrounded with hundreds of ladies and gentlemen, futting it like winkin' in the ruins. The musicianers were perched in the ivy, and when Tim accidentally knocked a stone off the wall, whist! the company vanished, though he could hear a noise in the air of the flutterin' of water, for all the world the same as the sound made by the stare (starlings) flyin' in thousands to the twigs on the banks of the Dargan, when the sun drops over Knockmealdoun in December." Don Fierna, or Fiernach, means Don the Truthful, and the fairy monarch, from what I can gather, is altogether a beneficent potentate. Before St. Killvullen arrived in the parish, the Don was a familiar apparition, who expectēd suit and service from mankind to be paid him. But the Saint shut him up in a hill, together with his subjects, and it is only of an odd time the Don is permitted to revisit the open ground. Only whistle to him, though, from outside his residence, and he will answer you. Blow a blast of a bugle at the unseen portal of his palace, and you can hearken to the response, at first loud and challenging, then faint, and thin, and distant, as the elfin trumpeter retires to the remoter hollows of his furze-roofed barracks.

"Is it true that the fairies can blight the limbs of people they don't like, or steal their children from the cradle?"

"Thrue! to be sure it is. There's ould Jack Ahearne is but a boccogh (cripple) ever since nothin' would do him but to go in the dark wid his gun into the bog beyant, where there niver was anything good seen yet. He was standin' there wid the water up to his knees, waitin' for ducks, when themselves begin to hop about him in the shape of little blue lights. In the mornin' ould Ahearne felt his legs as cold as a stone, an' that day he tuk to his bed, and unless he can be cured by makin' his rounds at the next pattern of Killvullen, 'tis small use shoe-leather will be to him ever agin."

"And what about fairies stealing the children, Tim?"

"Well, sir, of late 'tis few of 'em is worth stalin'——"
And here Tim, who has a weakness for controversy,

diverged from fairies into politics ; and into this latter region I shall not follow him at present.

Perhaps Mrs. Donovan, the pious cook, may contribute to my budget of fairy lore. She ought to be what they term a " knowledgeable woman," as she has certainly lived long enough to be wise. I enter the apartment where dishes undreamt of by Soyer are conceived, and ask Mrs. Donovan straight off if she has ever seen a fairy. *" Did I ever see the devil ?"* is the irascible and scornful rejoinder, delivered with such desperate emphasis that I retreat from the presence of Mrs. Donovan abruptly, to seek elsewhere the materials for a bouquet of legends.

I have been so far successful as a collector of elfin anthology that I can now, with pipe in mouth, lie on the heather on a Killvullen cliff and distribute my fairies at will over the landscape. The best time for the purpose is the gloaming of this hot August day, when everything is hushed save the deep-toned muttering of the sea on one side, and on the other the song of an unwearied lark, who is transfigured to a ruddy speck as he rises on a level with the sun. The light fails gradually from the dark, far-away mountains, which seem to move into the purpling dusk until a single star is fixed upon the crest of the tallest, and the evening comes with a rustle of the wind from the land as it passes over the dimmed fields, brushing with soft wings the Hill of Doona, where Don Fierna lodges. I hope the Don will bring out his elves for a festival in the grange when the moon rises, a couple of hours hence. The grange lies below me, a gaunt and desolate, a gray, ragged ghost of building, with sepulchral eyes. As I look at it, an owl sails from his home there, and makes off for the fairy hill ; and no doubt the echoing hoot that reaches me is his signal to the elves that the coast is clear for them. It is my conceit to think that the owl is over-early in summoning the fairies. They must have their moon : all poets insist on this part. But the owl continues his hoot-hoot, until at length the broad face of the planet confronts him—not Dian's car, or any other pagan invention, but a real fairy moon, with a sly, cunning countenance, and a wink upon it of humour, as though it were ready to give the most grandfatherly encouragement to the gay pranks Don Fierna may choose to engage in with his court.   I think I have seen a portrait of this Irish and fairy moon by an artist somewhere, and I recognised the truth of the picture at once.   I now get up and saunter down to the grange, with a faint hope that I might be as lucky as Tim Foley in having a glimpse at the King of the Munster Fairies.   But I am not so fortunate.   Ightermurragh Grange receives no elfin guest within its crumbling walls this evening ; at least none that I can see.   A couple of bats are flickering round it, and another owl is snoring, exactly like an apoplectic old gentleman, in the solitary tree which stands before the battered entrance where there was once a door.   And so I resolve to wend my way quietly towards the Hotel Walshe, calling, however, first at the Hill of Doona.   Perhaps Don Fierna might be induced either to allow me to enter his subterranean mansion, or to hold a review, in order to oblige a literary traveller, in the grange or in the dell at the foot of his residence. I am irreverent enough to blow a dog-whistle at his gate.   Hark ! a hundred sportsmen are calling dogs within the hill, and far away over to them to other hills, and the effect is so strange and weird that I am not surprised at the manner in which the phenomenon was regarded by Tim Foley.   And now, as Don Fierna makes no appearance, I am vulgar enough to shout stale jokes and wild ironical sayings, merely to have them flung into the air and back to me in the oddest melancholy of tone.   The cadences of the merest trash sound inexpressibly sad.   The laugh rings cheerly for once into your face, and then the heart is taken out of it; it speaks with a chill mockery, a fleshless, uncanny manifestation, not of mirth, but of its opposite in ghastly disguise. I call my own name to the Hill of Doona, and the reverberation of it sounds a threat or warning; implies again a sentiment of profound compassion, which almost induces a feeling of terror. One repetition of my name struck me, I know, with that odd, creeping sensation which may be experienced when a mirror suddenly fixes for us a peculiar, unthought-of expression of our own minds— the revelation coming from the reflection of our features within the glass at an unprepared moment. But I must not forget what is due to the monarch of the elves. *Good-night, Don Fierna.* The "good-night" is duly taken up by the hills, and said over and over again. *Good-night, Don; good-night.*

The fairy moon wears, I think, a rather reproachful air now; possibly blames me as a disturber of Don Fierna and other midnight friends of the planet beloved of elves and pixies. Entering the Hotel Walshe, I am encountered by Tim Foley, who, it appears, has rushed into Mrs. Donovan to tell her that there was awful goin's-on at the hill to-night, and that he had heard them calling my name, an' he hoped no harm would come on it. I was able to reassure Tim on this score, while Mrs. Donovan was good enough to remark in my hearing that she wished them luck with me if they had me, and perhaps I wouldn't be so particular with my "vittles." The woman was growing intolerably familiar, not to say impertinent; but it is necessary to humour her. Her contempt for Tim Foley and his folk-lore is unbounded. She regards my concern in these matters as a proof of downright idiocy. "An' isn't it a sin an' a shame for ye to be grinnin' and sneerin' at laygends of the holy and blessed Killvullen (the Lord keep his soul in glory for iver, amin), an' goin' about the country with a fool of a bliggard the like iv Tim Foley, listening to nansinse av fairies an' pishogues that everybody knows wor banished be the saints whin they convarted us. Mebbe ye'd like to have a horse-shoe on the door, or a sprig of ash in yer bed, to presarve ye from the good people. Baithershin! Ugh! me back is broke wid thim for omlits. An iligant fresh egg taken from the hin won't sarve your turn unless I cook it as you tould me. I'll spake to Mrs. Walshe to-morrow." And here Mrs. Donovan became more or less incoherent from want of breath. Now I say nothing, but unlock a box on the table, and hand Mrs. Donovan a cake of aromatic, rich cavendish tobacco. This attention, bribe, or whatever it may be called, changed her mood at once. She made a sort of rheumatic obeisance, and pocketed the bounty with the most profuse thanks and blessings. Shure I wasn't a bad soft, afther all. She had a crass timper, an' hoped I would forget her palaverin' "Yes, sir, the supper will be ready for you at wonst, an' good-night and God bless you for the bit of backy that'll comfort the ould woman that has but little left to comfort her now after the sore thrials she has gone through."

ROUGH ANGLING.

ROUGH indeed! No friendly Thames bank in sight, no familiar ait or wimpling shallow or chiming weir-fall, but a plain of green, undulating water, with a desolate beauty of its own, as it heaves softly as the bosom-swell of a sleeping maiden under the hush and glimmer of the red-frosty dawn. Our baits are not derived from book or feather-artist. A pile of silver sprats, a heap of amorphous mussels, a lot of ungainly claw-twisted crabs, with soft backs, lie at the bottom of our boat. No punt this boat, but a thick-ribbed, solid, six-oared craft, able to live in bad seas and wild weather, tarred and scarred and tested even as her crew have been. Her crew at present reduced to three hard-visaged salts, who do a little piloting, a little fishing, and a vast deal of idle sauntering from out the port of the little town, which lies a couple of miles astern.

We have got amongst a fleet of murres, small divers, that when put up, fly as swiftly and as strongly as driven partridge. At present they are all afloat, and calling, or rather purring to each other, and plunging like dabchicks at the splash of the oars. And now the rosy-fingered dawn is speeding away; the sun, fully awake, bursts in a blaze of light upon the sea, but no lark salutes him from the rolling meadows of the tide, although a matin croak of welcome sounds in the air, like the jangle of a loose piano-wire hastily plucked. The performer of the hoarse music is a gannet, with an eye from aloft for fish for breakfast. And gulls follow our wake, coming, as it were, out of space. Fling a sprat overboard, and three are down upon it, with the squeal of street Arabs scrambling for coppers. The lucky finder is sheering off with his treasure; he drops it, when, lo! a sullen, heavy splash, and the watchful gannet, whom I thought incapable of seizing any meaner quarry than a live herring, makes for the morsel; and as the huge gray robber starts off with his booty the gulls whine dolefully and shrug their wings in a despairing, bewildered fashion, as though they would say "It can't be helped, it can't be helped."

We arrive at our "pitch" at last, and have it all to ourselves. The lines of stout twine, packed round square wooden frames, are prepared. We have lines and hooks for hake, for codling; lines and hooks for gurnard and for sea-bream. The hake-lines and hooks are much stronger than those for the gurnard, but the latter are stout enough, and would look like hawsers side by side with that delicate thread you rod-angle men cast into the beck with its lure to stir the red-spotted trout. I bait me with a wedge of sprat, and —by way of a tid-bit—a gelatinous clot of mussel, and over go two links—two hooks, charged with this delicious composition. Our prey is to be had five or six fathom deep at least, and so, after sounding with the lead for ground, we pull up the line a height of eight or ten feet from bottom, and then, with the reel or frame secured by a hitch round the rowlock, with forefinger on hemp, we wait patiently for a bite. Not in this style, however, do our briny companions proceed to work. They hope for hake, and prepare accordingly. They bait with the same stuff that we do, but they use it in larger quantities, and add to it what they term a "lash," *i.e.*, a sliver from the skin and flesh near the tail end of a conger. Instead of waiting on the line they keep moving it see-saw, drawing it in and letting it out a foot or two. Ha! a tug for us! Haul on steadily, hand over hand; take heed that your line coils neatly at your feet. Peep down now, and you perceive swimming up perforce a brace of gray gurnard—easy—slap them not against the side of the boat, but catching the thick line a little above where the links are attached to it, heave them in steadily. There you are! and in truth a fair beginning. And the fun now commenced does not slacken until the bottom of the boat is a weltering mass of fish. You weary of the sport in the end, for though the slaughter is immense, the work is rather monotonous, and after a time uncomfortable. Despite your suit of oil-cloth you feel wet and chilled, and your hands and fingers are shrivelled like a washer-woman's thumb. Still you stick to your graplin until the day dies in a glory of green and purple clouds. Now, boys, give way, for the dusk draws on apace, and we have only the fag end of the tide to help us homeward. Already the beacon to sailors shines

D

from our familiar lighthouse, and the friendly twinkling stars of the night have been set their watches,
while from the land comes the hollow roar of the surf
on the beach, and anon the quick snort and snuffle
of the restless steam horse who brings news and mes-
sages to us from the world of London.

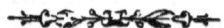

START not, O reader, at the title of this article! Picture not from it a miserable gull-potter recklessly blazing into flocks of harmless sea-fowl. In or out of close time I object to the wanton destruction of the fisherman's friend, who takes but scant toll for his friendly pilotage to the waters in which the silver sprat is found in myriad shoals; who helps the sailor in the treacherous fog by his warning shriek of rocks ahead; who in the day tempest flashes with wings of gleaming white against the purple cloud-rack of the storm; who—but a truce to poetics, as old novel writers used to say when prosing. Enough, that in our cliff-ramble you will not be invited to the death of the bird whose conversion into an article of diet resulted, according to a legend, in young natives of St. Kilda being born in pin feathers.

We commence our ramble along the shore of heavy shingle. The tide is far out; and calm as the sea is now under the frosty sky, the big green waves tumble heavily and noisily on the fringe of weed-covered stones which marks the low-water level. Skimming in glittering squadrons across the black reaches of the remains of an antediluvian forest—the yew and ancient oak in compact burial blent—are hosts of sand-larks, red-shank, scooting and whistling in council, with the warning pipe of curlew and the whine of the gray herring-hunter. But quarry such as this shall not tempt us; for, indeed, the birds will be impossible to approach.

And now, by gradual ascent, we enter upon our journey over the cliffs of Ardglah. A gillie or gossoon carries the rifle, while I bear a trusty muzzle-loader.

We moreover take a couple of terriers, warranted good rabbit chasers, and their office comes into play full soon.   Before the cliffs assume that seamed and iron face with which they look upon the yeasting waves, there are milder gullies and clefts warmly lined with brambles, with golden-blossomed furze, with banks of soft clay—containing many towns and villages of those four-footed earth people, the conies.

"Hie in there, Jack! in there, Peg, old lass!" There frisks a bonny brown brute, but, alas! in such propinquity to the skull of Jack that a shot might be fatal to the dog.   Another and another; but in sooth I am not skilled in the art of "Snaps," and before I have made up my mind to pull, nothing is visible, nothing stirring, save Jack and Peg, who are so brisk and eager in their ministrations.   At length, however, Jack manages to hunt a rabbit across the path up from the bank, and this rabbit's days upon cliffs are numbered.

The path grows so steep that it rather tells upon our pace.   Steeper yet, and a peep over the edge shows us no longer brakes of briar, bramble, and furze, but grim hollows of rock.   Now we approach the first great gully of Ardglah.   We look right over at a perpendicular wall of stone far beneath.   Though the tide has dropped so far off the shore behind us, here the sea rolls in and breaks out of sight in a profound murmur; and then, with sad repetitions and verberations in the numerous caves which pierce the gaunt hills, the curling billows are heard soughing and groaning like some ponderous living beast in a flurry of pain and death.

Spinning quick as thought from the twilight of the gulf came a clutch of blue-rocks.   "Bang, bang!" The noise awakens an angry clap and growl from the startled solitude.   One of the pigeons tumbles into the grim pit; but, as luck would have it, the other, hard hit, falls on the top of the big eminence before us, and can be picked up by going round. The report of the gun has brought out hundreds upon hundreds of other blue-rocks, but they keep well from range ; and, besides, it requires a head better educated to the work than mine to stand at the extreme edge of the precipice and perform a shot with either accuracy or resolution. The pigeon is in plump condition, and, though smaller in size, feels quite as heavy as a woodland relative of his knocked out of a fir-tree a few days ago by the same gun.

The second great gully of Ardglah. It differs from the first in this, that its sides are not quite so perpendicular, and there are even signs of a thin brown thread of path, winding to the broad tabular rocks, which seem laid out for the open-air banquets of mermen and mermaidens at the bottom of it. They come here resting after such unhallowed deeds as Scott ascribes to these briny personages :

> From reining of the water-horse,
>   That bounded till the waves were foaming,
> Watching the infant tempest's course,
>   Chasing the sea-snake in his roaming ;
> From winding charge-notes on the shell,
>   When the huge whale and sword-fish duel,
> Or tolling shroudless seamen's knell
>   When the winds and waves are cruel.

" Billy, give me the rifle ! " At the sea entrance to the gully is a sort of pillar supporting a kind of flat slab, the whole arrangement strangely resembling a gigantic petrified mushroom. This place of vantage is occupied by seven cormorants—I was going to say in holy orders, so clergymanlike and solemn do they look upon the rude platform. The ungainly fowl converse not : the congress of sootinesses is as motionless as a Quaker's meeting. They are, these cormorants, carven uglinesses. Forgetting that your cormorant can be brought up by hand, and made to angle for your pleasure, the slave of a ring, incited to violence by an æsthetic revolt against the squab-beryl-eyed creature that sulks its inodorous life in weird and desolate spots, I took the rifle from Billy. Crack!

"Lord, lord!" as Mr. Pepys would remark, what a plump, scatter, and squash was there! Every Dan Cormorant of the lot cast his swag belly on the tide, and then flip, flap, flop, flop, winnowing the water with its vans, tries to put steam up for flight. The bullet has only frightened the dingy conclave, and not frightened them so much either, for when they have scuttled away eight or nine hundred yards, they settle on the calm, rolling sea, plunging at different times under it, as though to dodge any other offer at their lives.

Rara avis : if I could only have a chance! "'Tis only a jackdaw, sir," remarks Billy; but no, Billy, 'tis the crow with the red legs I am sure—the chough of the Cornish coast, the cardinal of cliffs in stockings of scarlet! They have been reported to me often as seen in this locality, but they afford no opportunity for a shot. They plunge down into the gully, and then skirt the outside corner of it into the next recess.

Meeting a peasant-man a little further on, I learn that the pigeons often lodge in the open fields back of the cliffs, and that if I station myself immediately behind the hedge, I shall probably get what my peasant-man terms "a vacancy" at them. I act on this advice, and I am sorry to confess that I did not make as good use of the "vacancies" as I expected. The rate at which these pigeons flew—rather say swept—to the cliffs was something that puzzled me altogether. A whisk, a blue gleam of wings with a glint as of sun in them, and you fired behind, and had nothing but a "vacancy" for your pains. Once, indeed, I let drive on speculation, and positively knocked over two, to my own astonishment. I believe I may have wounded a few others; for these birds so far resemble their relatives the woodquests

as to carry off the best part of an ounce of lead in
their bodies now and again, without flying the worse
for being thus heavily handicapped.

Once more to the cliff edge. Beneath is a sort of
bay, famous in summer as a resort of seals; indeed,
about forty or fifty years back quite a little business in
seal-oil was carried on in the adjoining parish, the seal-
hunters also contriving to combine with the trade a
small commerce in brandy kegs, tobacco, and French
lace. The picturesque smuggler, however, is extinct,
and I saw no trace of the seals. The water in this
bay, or rather fiord, is of the loveliest colour and of the
clearest complexion. Even from the heights you can
see so far into its green depth as to note the long
waving serpentine tangles of what grows in the sea
gardens, and you think some day of approaching the
place in a boat, taking a perch on yon rock, and
angling for the gaping fish that are doubtless lying
mute and staring from out the gelid brakes of brown
oar-weed.

The cliff-march alters in ground, and we are knee-
deep in withered fern and gorse. "Clutter, clutter,
clutter." Who could help it, though it is late in the
season? The covey have been evidently untouched
before; they are birds of a roaming and vagrant
quality. "Billy, my boy, put that brace of partridge
in the bag."

An interval for luncheon and a pipe, during which we
are gravely reconnoitred by five majestic gulls, whose
wings are large enough to cast big shadows on the ground.
Our walk is then resumed and carried on until the
sun dies in the west and the stars break out in shining
points, but the bag is not heavier. We reach in goodly
time the little village which crouches at the remote
end of the cliffs, and sleep for the night within sound
of the surging cry of the waves, mingled with the
bawling of a lot of drinking boors, who are celebrating
a return from a fair in the tap-room of the inn.

ON a still morning, with frost glittering on the tiles, I can see from my bedroom window a sea calm as a tropical lagoon, and green as a shaven lawn in the spring. Here at its full the harbour tide is locked in, save at a narrow outlet fenced with round-shouldered hills, and at its ebb there are vast flats of mud covered with noisy squadrons of sea-lark, curlew, and red-shank. But these latter wild-fowl tempt me not. I might contrive, and have contrived, to compass them, to surprise them, to lie in ambuscade for them; but it vexes me to think that yon immense fleet of floating widgeon, extending for a good part of a mile in close order, have utterly defied my efforts to approach them. I have put in practice every device I could think of, tried all I knew, and still the brutes invariably beat me. I have endeavoured to drift amongst them in a punt, and, without showing the least alarm apparently, they have steadily swum out of shot, whistling (I think) derisive comments to each other on their perfect position of security. In the course of this manœuvre I have been stranded, or rather "mudded," with the option of either remaining for hours in an ooze swept with a nor'-easter, or of leaving my craft to her fate and walking some furlongs knee-deep in the slush. I have adventured upon the widgeon in a fog, and found that they could hear in that condition of atmosphere much better than I could see in it, and that they left me here awa' and there awa', showing through the misty cloud like Wandering Willie, while they executed flank movements and retired at will, always within my hearing-

distance of that tantalising, ironical pipe of theirs, con-
veying a sense of irritating superiority to guile as
manifest as that indicated by the gesture of the sacristan
in the "Ingoldsby Legend," who put his thumb to
his nose, and spread out his fingers when asked to
believe a pious tarradiddle.

In sheer anger I have armed me with a rifle, and
sent a bullet scattering amongst the flock at three
hundred yards. How they escaped, I never could
guess ; but how the crew of a peaceable barge escaped,
I was afterwards informed by a volley of curses from
the men—perhaps not unnaturally put out of temper
by hearing a pellet of excellent penetrating qualities
bury itself in their boat. A survey of the locality
proved, indeed, that a repetition of the rifle-practice
would never do, the chances of the lead ultimately
lodging in a peasant or a flounder-fisherman being
quite equal to the odds that its mission would be concluded and spent in the body of a duck.

The arm of a sprat weir extends in one direction of
this widgeon haunt, and I was advised that, if I were
to tether my shallop alongside this at the gloaming, at
a certain hour of tide, the birds would probably give
me a shot at them through the stakes. Not they !
The giant Fee-Fo-Fum had not apparently a keener scent
for supplying his larder with stores than the widgeon
had for the presence of a gun and a man at the end of
it ! Fate, however, at length put the solution of this
difficult and perplexing problem in my way, and thus :

I happened to be shooting snipe in the reeds at the
edge of the upper part of a creek or pill when the tide
ran from the widgeon quarter. Here I enlisted a bag-
carrier, supplied by a friendly farmer in the neighbourhood. After walking a little distance, my assistant, a
ragged, rakish, well-built youngster, stopped a moment.

"Mebbe yer honor would like a wadgeon !" I
thought the query referred to his bringing me down,
as we say, on some odd bird that might be about the

place ; and so it did, for, while I followed the fellow,
gun on full cock, he went to a bankside close to us,
hauled out a stone, put his hand into a hole, and drew
forth what he was pleased to call " a wadgeon ! "

" You scoundrel, where did you get that ? " The
bird had only been some hours shot.

" Well, yer honor, I don't mind tellin' you that I
have an ould ' piece ' under the thatch, and now and
agin I has a twist at say birds an' the like. 'Twould
play the divil entirely wid me av it was known, for
sure a poor man as meself couldn't pay for a licence."

" Oh, Jack, your secret is safe enough with me ; but
you must. tell me how you shot the widgeon, and put
me up to your plan for the purpose."

" 'Tis aisy enough, sir ; an' niver fear, you will have
a turn out of 'em for wadgeons that yer honour will
be plazed with."

In accordance with a plan of campaign then and
there laid down by Jack, I find myself a week later
standing with that ingenious personage midway up the
creek. It is night time, and a worse night for playing
upon a guitar in the open air never came out of the
heavens. The old moon likes it so little that she
turns in very early, and leaves us much more in the
dark than otherwise. The wind from the sou'-west
roars up the pill, driving the rain before it, and shouting in the most abusive fashion of stormy language,
as though charged with the conveyance of a thousand
witch-ridden broomsticks. Although I am muffled
from head to toes in a shapeless but comfortable garment, I feel, to put it mildly, that there is a great deal
of weather about. Jack Bride accepts the situation,
however, not only with patience, but with cheerfulness.

" Did you hear 'em, sir ? Listen agin ! "

Nothing but the lapping of the water, a howl in
the breeze as though a demon superintending it had
raised his voice in pain and anger, a sudden lull, and
then " *Bang* " from Jack's venerable weapon, and a

sort of rasping sound in the air. " *Hie in Coaley !* in,
Coaley ! after 'em, boy !" roars Master Jack to the
semi-starved water-spaniel who accompanies him.
Coaley, brave brute, is into the water fast enough, and
is out again with two ; in again, out with one ; in yet
again, away for a minute, and returns with a winged
cripple, and would be off for a fifth time but that his
master prevents him.

" Be ready the next time, yer honour."

But I was not, although Jack was, and knocked
down four ; at least, we got four, and doubtless quite
as many escaped the aquatic industry and research of
the spirited Coaley, who, never daunted by wind,
wave, or weather, dashed after his game the instant he
heard the report of the gun.

" The night is beginning to clear now, sir, and
perhaps you would be able to do better."

Better I might do, worse I couldn't, for I had not
done anything, though, thanks to Jack Bride, we had
already a pile of slain at our feet.

The night, as Jack says, clears. The rain ceases,
and, though the wind is still high, of a moment there
is a wondrous rent in the clouds, and, with a single
attendant star, the moon comes out, this time with
kindly light, and with a radiant countenance that
would put to shame the cleverest imitations of her
beauty in a theatre. There is now no great difficulty
in distinguishing the birds who rush by, flock after
flock, and we only drop the sport when Coaley, poor
wretch, is almost ready to collapse with fatigue, though
I verily believe that he would to the last gasp endeavour to perform his duty to us.

I simply hesitate to put down the weight of the
bag, but I must enter this much against our success,
not one of the birds was fit to eat. Of all the tough, un-
savoury, barren morsels I ever put a fork into, the slice
from one of these widgeon's breasts was the most un-
savoury and disagreeable. I anticipate contradic-

tion on the point—I should have had proper sauce,
and didn't keep the birds hung up long enough, and
all the rest of it.   Now I am cunning in sauce, and I
gave the widgeon every chance-—made several trials
of them in various culinary forms ; 'twas all the same.
What say you to a *salmi* composed of old chamois
gloves steeped in the preserve oil of an imperfectly
soldered sardine-box?   Think you should like such
a delicacy?   Then proceed to shoot your widgeon
and to eat him.   Have you an Esquimaux on a visit
who would desire something at table to remind him
of home?   Give him a roast widgeon for dinner.
Faugh ! 'tis neither fish nor fowl nor good red
herring ! The widgeon is a gross impostor, passing
for a duck, and possessing for the *gourmet* none of
the affectionate interest which is reasonably lavished
upon the mallard, the canvas-back, or their barn-door
cousins.

IF the weather were a little hard or a little wild, something might be done. The snipe will not leave till the end of March; but in this soft, warm, balmy noon it is vanity and pure vexation of spirit to try and fill a bag. The sun is positively hot, and what looks like a veritable summer mist is spread over the bog from end to end. No sooner do you place your foot on good ground, than up, far out of shot, start hundreds of the longbills, bleating madly. From reed bed to reed bed, from dyke edge to dyke edge, from spring to spring and ooze to ooze, they call each other, and skirl to a vast height into the sky—at such a height, indeed, that their singular piping appears to come after awhile from the depth of the soft white fleece that rolls under the blue dome. You gaze on this sight with a feeling of bitterness, if not of anger and disgust. There, in a crash as it were, your hopes depart; and yet, with that sanguine impulse of expectancy which should always form a portion of a sportsman's temperament, you beat the quarters carefully with steady, egg-walking old Rap.

But Rap, quite as well as you, knows the meaning of the sudden emigration of birds he has witnessed. He gazes at wisp after wisp departing, with as mournful an expression of countenance as the face of a dog is capable of wearing. Yet he does not refuse to comply with your wave of the hand, and he proceeds to work, but in a perfunctory fashion. Were Rap a tyro at the snipe-shooting business, you would have trouble enough with him now. He would commence to draw, to pull up, and to petrify at where they were, until your patience would be utterly exhausted. As it is, he creeps; now and then he is quite couched, like an heraldic lion, on the very peat—a sure sign that you will not be balked of a shot.

C-r-r-r-r! a quail! An odd bird to find here, certainly, at this season of the year; and yet, if you turn back to your diary, you find you brought a couple down on the very same spot this time twelve months ago. You are so used to Rap's manner, that by the mode in which he indicates his discoveries you can guess what is before him. He would never, for instance, lie down before a snipe; he will before a water-rail, a water-hen, a partridge, a cock in fern, a quail; snipe he stands to, and points in the orthodox manner.

Now we unearth, or rather ungrass, a jack, and miss him out of haste, and follow him to where he alights a hundred yards off, and hit him again with such haste that all that is left of him is a pulp of blood and feathers, and not much of that.

Saw you ever such hosts of lapwing? Vast clouds of them bourgeoning across the moor, acrobatic trios of them squeaking and tumbling, solitary pewiteers performing the most frantic evolutions all around! A few of the golden plover are mixed with their dissimilar cousins, and you can easily detect them by their sanity and symmetry of flight, as well by a hawk-like practice of sailing on outstretched wing occasionally —a manœuvre in which the pewit never indulges.

Is this February or May? As I live, on the skirt of the moor, in a sheltered mossy nook, above a clear, beautiful well guarded by a venerable thorn-bush, I find a primrose—a real primrose! It had its beauty all to itself, and was a very shy-looking flower indeed. And, to render the simulation of spring still more perfect, the birds are not merely chirping, but singing. They, too, I think, must be deceived to some extent by the day. I find my clothes desperately heavy, and my gaiters uncomfortably warm. However, we trudge

again into the marsh, and Rap, old boy, with a knowing
wag of his tail, leads the way into a miserable potato
garden, where, to paraphrase the saying of Douglas
Jerrold, "the turf had been tickled with a hoe, and
laughed—at the husbandman."

Rap and I may not be altogether disappointed in
an accidental product of it, though.   Steady, Rap,
steady ! I couldn't help it ; besides, there are no
greyhounds in the neighbourhood, and I might as
well have that hare as know that it would be mobbed
to death with terriers the very next Sunday ! A plump
hare, too, but a hare, intended by nature not for roast-
ing, but for soup—age being good for soup.   A solo
on the dog-whistle brings helter-skelter over the bog
the lithe and agile figure of Jim Roach.   Jim is made
to carry the hare, and is further invested with the game-
bag ; light enough, worse luck !

Jim tells of "grey" plover in his father's "bawn"
field, and to the paternal bawn acre we turn our steps
accordingly.   Sure enough, there is a pretty little
stand of "golden plover" in the bawn field, but the
birds are exactly in the centre of it.   The only thing
to do is to send Jim to the opposite side by the hedge,
and get him to pop over it at a signal; the chance of a
shot at the birds on the wing might then present itself.
Depart, then, James, on thine errand ; but gently,
gently—show not thy shock head above the briars until
the proper concerted moment.   Now, good James !

Right into my face in a long line the birds come, and,
for the only instant that I oughtn't, I fire—first barrel
at a plover that seems to be hurled at my forehead,
second at the lot generally, five yards over the top
of the gun, staggering meanwhile from a lost balance.
Not a feather touched ! It *was* a stupid proceeding
—one of those execrable blunders which a sportsman
hesitates to recall.   For half an hour afterwards I left
my gun unloaded, and sought respite and nepenthe
from the pangs of remorse and regret in a pipe of

mixed cavendish and bird's-eye. There is a sort of homœopathic fitness in the consumption of bird's-eye by a fowler. Psha! the wretched joke is only put in to divert your attention from the thoroughly bad shot I have felt bound to confess.

No sign, no vestige of teal, of wild-duck. Three snipe in a dry rushy field, and a wounded widgeon bagged from a clump of withered reeds—a worthless brute, evidently suffering from a severe cramp or rheumatism when he tried to escape—this makes a very bad day indeed. Nor is there much prospect of mending matters. Everything apparently has been put up. Even the pewits have disappeared; but from the sea-shore, which the tide is rapidly covering, quantities of curlew commence to arrive. Would it be possible to stalk a few of the wary whaups? How carefully the fellows keep out from yonder straggling fence— from every point that might be for you a place of vantage. And, besides, you may wager anything they have a sentinel on the wing, besides numerous out- posts on the ground. However, for the hundredth time, you make an attempt to surprise the curlews. A cow, to make an Irish bull, serves you for a stalking- horse (the confusion of this sentence is worthy of Sir Boyle Roche). The cow, endeavouring to find some- thing more succulent to devour than the bitter marsh grass, is wandering towards the field now occupied by the whaups. You march stealthily by her lean and leathern hide ; you approach within a hundred yards of your quarry ; and then an observant bird who has been watching your every movement for the last five minutes from over your head, where you never thought of looking, gives a shrill and peremptory note of warning, which is instantly obeyed by his companions. Farewell, then, to all hope of adding a curlew to the day's bag.

Once more you send Rap on the search ; but Rap, as you do, wearies of it at last. Not one of the snipe

flushed in the morning has yet returned to the moor;
but they most probably will come back in the night.
You say to yourself, noting the lengthening evening
and the soft wind, that, if a late frost is not in store
for us, the wild-fowl shooting hereabouts is over : but,
then, our climate is so variable that even already, in
that flush of high colour over the sea in the west, you
may read the promise of such a change of weather as
would make the fen once more a desirable resort for
the snipe-following sportsman.

TWO IRISH REMINISCENCES.

THE BALLYVOURNEY REGATTA.

COMING back from Cowes, where young Blenkinsopp has been entertaining half a dozen of us in his yacht, supplying that craft with the best viands, and being sensible enough never to trouble about racing, but content to drift in the Solent under delicious awnings, I find on my table a circular, requesting a subscription for the annual Ballyvourney Regatta. The request brought to my mind some scenes which I witnessed at a former festival of the kind, which may be thought worth a passing record.

Ballyvourney is on the Irish coast. It is rather a dull place in the winter months, the rain every other day coming in with the tide, and leaving a fog after it until the heavy downpour returns with the flow of the sea. The town of Ballyvourney itself is not like a centre of industry. You might often fire a rifle down the main street without running any risk of making a job for the coroner ; and, except on pig-market days, even the public-houses do not seem to do much business. But all this is changed once a year. At the end of July the Ballyvourney Regatta is first heard of. It is so serious an affair for the locality that the authorities of the borough debate the preliminaries in council, and elect a committee to solicit subscriptions for the occasion. The genial mendicants go from house to house, followed by a crowd, to whom they announce the amount they have succeeded in levying from each resident, and according to its proportion the mob cheers or groans over the result of the requisition. A Ballyvourney Regatta costs something. It must be advertised in the county papers. There must be a ball after it, or attached to it, and one big prize must be offered to draw the yachts into the harbour. Then fireworks are absolute necessities, and fireworks are not to be had for nothing. Bang goes five pounds in a shower of rockets before you know where you are. Now, the difficulty the committee of management of the Ballyvourney Regatta principally experienced lay in the disposition of the inhabitants to indulge in a class feeling in the matter. The Protestants and the Catholics of Ballyvourney were pretty equally divided ; if anything, there was a preponderance of numbers towards the latter ; but the former made up for this by better organisation and system. The first bone of contention at the regatta parliament would be the appointment of a man to discharge a cannon at the commencement of every race. The discharge of artillery was a feature of the Ballyvourney aquatics. A shot was fired at the start, another when the first boat came in, another for the second, and two when the pig was taken off the pole which hung over the water, with a union-jack waving about the grunting porker, in order to give a maritime kind of excuse for this apparently unregatta-like diversion. Now, there were two gunsmiths and gunpowder-sellers in Ballyvourney ; one went to church, and the other went to mass ; and the inhabitants bought whatever they wanted of Curtis and Harvey or Pigou (both "glazed and blasting") from their respective co-religionists, purveyors of explosive compounds and meerschaums. The Protestant gunsmith was ulti-mately appointed, and when the morning of the regatta dawned his piece of ordnance was seen mounted on a platform over the sea-wall ; and a lively place Ballyvourney was then ! The Scullahone boys, from the Scullahone River, in flannel jackets, arrived to contend for the second pulling-race. Against them, and at mortal feud with them, the heroes of a neighbouring headland, called Drumvarrig, were to contend. It was necessary to have a boat full of policemen between these gentry until the word or the signal was given for the start, and across the police-boat they kept up the most fearful war of words in Gaelic, with constant fluency and virulence. The prize was only five pounds, and for this amount they were obliged to pull out to sea, almost out of sight, round a flag-boat, and back again. The Protestant artilleryman stands to his gun, and off it goes with a tremendous report, leaving the ears deaf, and in the air the most awful and depressing stench conceivable. The Scullahone boys got the best of the start. With three-quarters of an hour's pull before them, the rival craft are already making the water smoke with their exertions. Drumvarrig bumps Scullahone, and in an instant a mutual boarding takes place, about three hundred yards from the quay, and Scullahone and Drumvarrig are having a naval engagement of the most fierce and bloodthirsty character. The police-boat tries to interfere, and a large oar, skilfully levelled by big Jack Murphy of Drumvarrig at the peelers, stretches three of them "hors de combat" at the bottom of their vessel. With immense difficulty a truce is established, and Scullahone and Drumvarrig are brought back to the starting-rope, and again the artillerist of the Reformed persuasion fires his cannon.

This time they are made to give each other a wide berth, and pull fairly enough until they reach the flag-boat. Here they are seen, by the aid of a glass, to have fouled again, and there is a general impression that Mickey Donovan, who is in the flag-boat, will be murdered between them. A magistrate and a priest pursue in the police-boat, and only arrive just in time to pick up the crew of the Drumvarrig craft, whose sides have been staved in by the Scullahonites. The latter, having their antagonists in the water, are trying to hit them on the head as they float about. A rescue is effected by the authorities. Meanwhile, Mickey Donovan, who had been anchored in the flag-boat, has disappeared, and so has his boat. Mickey is fortunately descried on the edge of the horizon, drifting in the direction of the United States, having cut the rope of his graplin in order to prevent his complete demolition by the faction oarsmen.

Nobody cares for the yacht-race. The yachts are of small tonnage, but there is one owned by a gentleman of the locality who is regarded as a desperate, rake-helly personage by the people. He is, in fact, more than half mad from drinking raw whisky from morning until night. It pleases him to call his wretched cockle-shell of a boat the *Coffin*. He mounts a death's-head for a flag, and has cross-bone buttons on his jacket. He is a desperate miser, and lives on a leg of mutton, a box of biscuits, and what fish he can catch, for a week. His crew consists of a boy from the workhouse, whom he has trained to considerable dexterity by kicking, and starving, and cursing him for the slightest blunder. This rollicking seaman is an important personage at the Scullahone Regatta ; he is the proprietor of a rotten brick-barge, which he will lend for the pyrotechnic display at night.

Shall I describe the regatta ball? The wonderful business-like fashion in which dancing was done! None of your slinking into corners and looking compassionately at the people bothering themselves to waltz, but being in it everywhere and all night yourself, until the day-streak. Then comes the second day's regatta. Billy Bolly, the town fool, is to perform in a punt-chase. This, as you may know, consists in a single man in a little handy boat dodging and escap-

ing from a six-oared ship's boat. Billy Bolly is such a
fool that, before he can be well prevented, he strips
off all his clothes, to the discomfiture and instant
retreat of the ladies, with whom the punt-chase is
usually an event of interest. Billy being restored to
decency, and made to understand that he is expected
to take to the water clothed—if not in his right mind,
reluctantly prepares for the chase. He succeeds
admirably in baffling his pursuers, who can never turn
swiftly enough to catch him. In the end they do,
however ; but he slips from their fingers, and dives
like a duck into the tide, this being part of the game.
They wait for him to come up, but they wait in vain.
The spectators grow uneasy. Billy Bolly, to be sure,
was only a fool, but it is awkward that he should be
drowned at the regatta ; and so the temperance band,
which had been discoursing something between a
waltz and a dirge, ceases, there being an impression
that the music was inappropriately gay. The excitement
increases. A drag is sent for ; two sailors dive. Billy
is given up for lost, and is suddenly discovered holding on to the chain of a yacht, where he has been for
the last quarter of an hour, like a thorough fool, enjoying the anxiety of the wise people on his account.
The fireworks at night were not very artistic ; but when
you saw the green, calm sea-water lit up with a red
flash, the hills starting out of the darkness at a signal
from a blue rocket, the surf on the distant beach
shining and rolling for a second at the twinkle of
a violet flame, the sight was, no doubt, interesting.
All through the fireworks the Protestant artilleryman
gave us something more than a taste of his powder.
He was to be paid according to the quantity he got
rid of, so it is not difficult to surmise that he was not
economical of his ammunition.

By lodging a pound or so of blazing wadding in a
newly-painted, fortunately empty boat, which was
floating under him, the artillerist succeeded in adding

an unexpected firework on his own account to the exhibition. That night the town of Ballyvourney was the scene of a final tremendous battle between the boys of Scullahone and the boys of Drumvarrig. The combat raged until morning, when both sides fell upon the police. Nothing more came of it, however, than a few broken heads; and a Scullahone or Drumvarrig head took a great deal of breaking before it was past mending. The gunpowder bill of the artillerist was discussed with polemical heat and temper when the estimates for the festival were brought in ; but it was, of course, settled in the end, and Ballyvourney Regatta remains an institution quite different from anything known to members of the Royal Yacht Squadron, or to Sybarite yachtsmen like Blenkinsopp of Cowes, who puts to sea in order to have an appetite for French cookery and opportunities of luxurious travel and hospitality.

THE GREAT KILLOOLY COURSING CLUB.

WHEN I look back through what sentimental writers term the mist of years, I see through the agreeable fog of a cigar a group of very jolly fellows indeed assembled for the first time to arrange matters for the organising of a Coursing Club in Killooly. The congress was held in Sullivan's Hotel, and was continued from dinner-hour until cock-crow. Four of the gentlemen who attended the gathering remained where they fell under the table, others who had to drive home were taken care of by their horses; but the only real drunken man of the party, perhaps, was Bill Morgan of Tullogh, who nearly murdered the ostler, in trying to harness him between the shafts of his gig instead of the pony.

To tell the truth, this auspicious opening brought the club into ill-favour with most of the ladies whose husbands joined the confederation. They prognosticated openly that it would turn out badly. However, the members went actively to work. The club was composed of representatives from every degree in the Irish social scale. There was a sprinkling of county magistrates, a couple of priests, plenty of respectable farmers, two or three solicitors, a few shopkeepers, and a doctor. The first thing to be done in organising a coursing club is not to catch your hare, but to get your dog. At the start almost every member thought it necessary to provide himself with a greyhound, and I never shall forget the collection that was exhibited on the side of Clearsach Mountain at the first meeting. Dogs lame, dogs halt, dogs blind, dogs with bull terrier written on their countenances, and dogs with lurcher plainly expressed in their noses. They had been picked up in all parts of the country, and were, in fact, the refuse and mistakes of studs that had been saved from the pond by farmers or servants. Every other man had his hound in a slip, and, as no recognised arrangement had been come to, when a hare was put up—the first hare coursed by the great Killooly Club—at least fifty dogs were seen tearing after her. Not only did the dogs but the members run at the hare, which would probably have escaped, but that Andy Murphy, a boy employed to " bate " on the occasion, could not resist firing a stick, with a charge of lead in the top of it, used by Andy generally for service at fairs, at the animal, with such effect, that he smashed its skull as it was clearing a ditch. Despite the remonstrances of a few gentlemen present as to the informal character of the whole proceeding, it was voted a highly successful inauguration of the club by most of the members, and flasks were produced and emptied, while the noble dogs, many of them with bits of fur sticking to their maws, were being gathered in by the peasants of Andy Murphy's degree who were in attendance on the "sporthers." It was settled, however, that at the next "so-ho" better order should be observed, and Andy Murphy was told not to make such brilliant play with his cudgel, and to confine his exercise with it to searching the tufts and bushes. Two dogs were put in proper fashion into the slips, and the rest were to be held in if possible. Bill Morgan was the slipper this time, and was supposed to be an expert at the business from the fact of his being an excellent snipe-shot. The connection between the accomplishments is not quite apparent, but it seemed to satisfy the Killoolyites as reasonable and distinct. Clearsach Mountain did not abound in hares. It would be curious if it did, as it was open ground, and on Sundays was examined by troops of gentlemen like Andy Murphy, who would mob a month-old leveret without the slightest remorse or hesitation. Well, Bill Morgan was ready to slip, and at last a hare was put up, and Bill loosed Lightning and Fag a Ballach, the respective chattels of Father Clancy and Doctor Ryan. Fag a Ballach ran for about thirty yards, stopped as if blinked, though the hare was in full sight, and, amid the execrations of the entire company, ran off in the opposite direction, as if his life depended on his exertions to escape further work. Lightning (a brute with as much breed about her as a dog in plaster on a suburban villa doorstep) cantered in an easy fashion after the quarry, which would have reached the form unhurt, but for the cunning agility of Cæsar (pronounced Sayzar), a terrier belonging to Declan Hoolaghan, who was lying in wait for puss in a ditch, under the evident instructions of Mr. Hoolaghan, who was on the spot almost as soon as his dog.

Dinner in pic-nic style was to be served at six o'clock in the house of Declan Hoolaghan, who was what is called a strong farmer. Each member had dispatched a contribution of comestibles and liquor to Hoolaghan's, the host undertaking to supply potatoes for the symposium. The room in which the banquet took place was evidently the only apartment in the mansion, save a roosting place, reached by a ladder, in which, it is to be hoped, a few of the dozen members of Mr. Hoolaghan's household slept at night. The banquet was not marked or distinguished by any special features ; but I do remember seeing Mr. John Casey, gentleman attorney-at-law, a very large, fat man, creeping upon all-fours in the moonlight outside the door of the cabin. When I saw him he had just reached the top of the pig-sty, and he looked for all the world like a huge tom-cat travelling over tiles. Mr. Casey was making tracks for his outside car, and had adopted this mode of progression after a series of experimental proofs that he could not maintain an upright position with comfort. But one circumstance of the finish of the first meet will dwell upon my mind as long as I live.

I sat on a car—the invariable outside—with Joe Baynes, of Kilmavrogue. We were balanced by Ned Dogherty, the gauger, and Frank Hannigan, the stipendiary magistrate. Joe Baynes was in that stage when a man who has neither voice nor ear feels inspired to sing, or rather "bay" as loud as ever he can, and as we were coming to a road crossing our own he was in the middle of a stave, when the driver, with a dreadful yell, dropped from his seat to the ground. "Yerra, yerra ! O the Lord presarve us ! an' save us ! Look ! gintlemin, dear, look ! look !" and he pointed over the hedge towards the cross-road. Joe Baynes was the first to take a peep, and he reeled back with his hand to his forehead. "Am I awake or asleep ?" said Joe. "Who before ever saw *elephants* on Clearsach ?" "*Elephants !*" We all ran over, and sure enough, coming up the round, the big, clear moon shining behind them, were two enormous elephants. We gazed at each other in dumb dismay and fright, but Tom Carty, the valiant driver, jumped into his seat, and crying "Begor, I'm not goin' to be ate be sperrits," gave his horse a lash of the whip, and, before we could stop him, was out of sight. Meanwhile, the elephants—elephants, mind—advanced towards the road where we were. We all stood our ground. When the first of the huge beasts approached we could see that it was accompanied by a man. A few words, and the phenomenon was fully accounted for. The elephants belonged to a travelling menagerie, the waggons of which were coming up, and the keeper was giving the animals an airing at a time when their exhibition would not, from a trade point of view, be injured by the fact. We came home that night, or rather morning, in one of the menagerie waggons, the only further incident of our journey being a slight dispute between the incorrigible Baynes and the proprietor of the show. Baynes commenced shrieking the "Cruiskeen Lawn," and woke up the laughing hyena, or some other beast in the caravan, who resented the disturbance to his rest in a most emphatic and unearthly noise, between a yelp and a howl.

Alas! the great Killooly Coursing Club is now a thing of the past! Though we never sent a winner to Waterloo, we enjoyed ourselves in our own fashion thoroughly, and after a time managed to kill our hares with sporting propriety, and contrived to come home without encountering either elephants or menageries.

PART II.

HOLIDAY PAPERS.

WHY does not some artist paint a picture of the old red palace from the bridge in the white light of the spring, with a trembling phantom of itself suggested, rather than seen, in the Thames? The place is quiet and tempting, these days, the Cockney boating season not having yet set in. By the banks, indeed, the pleasure-skiffs are lying in dozens, the proprietors either ruminating in that cow-like fashion peculiar to their tribe, or indulging in an elegant sort of wit best understood by themselves. No fishing-punts are visible, the only quarry open to capture being a trout, a rare visitor, who must be rather besieged than angled for by the patient Waltonian. Turning down to the gates of the Court, you see the signs of strict military discipline maintained in the royal residence, where so many well-connected people are lodged, and where a bed is always kept ready for the use of a queen or a prince. The bugle gives out a war-like challenge to the crows, the peaceable crows, who answer it defiantly over the tops of the trees; the soldiers at the door of an equine canteen drop off one by one at the tootle of the instrument, and leave the yard undefended save by a lancer, who reminds one of a Battle of Waterloo signboard, and who, on his beat, is solemnly attended by a brown retriever, tired of yawning in the sun. Within the walls are the familiar faces of the silent beauties that Lely painted so long ago. Note the wonderful family resemblance between them all, the ripe lip of Countess Frances, her full dark eyes, her bust being repeated in the Countess Sarah. It is only wearisome to linger here,

with high noon in the gardens below. The grass is
of the brightest green, and so smooth, that when a
sparrow twirls like an autumn leaf out of a tree upon
it, he seems both large and important. Under the
shade of the yew that in the peacock days was carven
and clipped into so many odd shapes, you can hear
the voices of the love-making birds both far and near.
The hoot-hoot of the cuckoo is borne on the soft
west wind from the Home Park, down from the sky
itself falls the song of the lark, within the heart of an
elm a blackbird is piping a sweeter tune than Pan
ever played, thrush is calling to thrush from a hundred bushes, while the whistle of the robin sounds
an octave over the rest, and the little musician puts a
great deal of feeling into his treble notes. Our spring
orchestra contains other performers besides. We must
not leave out the caw of the rooks, nor the interval
rustling of leaves, nor the purring of invisible pigeons,
nor even the anachronistic shout of a cock in a far-
away farm, who is making up for lost matins ; nor
the chime and toll of a bell, that rings as if the sound
came across a strip of sea at night. Not to the ear
alone does the spring reveal itself. In the pool
beyond, the gold-fish are keenly alive to the comfort
of gelid, instead of half-frozen, water ; they scuttle
about at your approach like sparks from the anvil of
the smith, and they are almost as vivid in colour as
fire. A few of the shoal are bronze in complexion,
a few more are of a deep azure, and they remind you
at once of the story of the people made fish in the
Arabian fables. That black, swooping object was a
martin swallow, coursing flies ; a bee sails along, close-
reefed, and ready to drop anchor in the first flower he
comes to. A cloud moves athwart the sun, and as
soon as the shadow is sensibly felt, note how fully one-
half the birds cease singing, and how, when the, cloud
passes off, the whole choir bursts out again more
joyously than ever. The garden has few visitors.

There are two young ladies teaching a dog to beg like a man on the centre walk, two windows of the palace are framing the faces of a couple of pretty maid servants, who are evidently admiring the gentleman in costume (of the police) who is entrusted with the care of the peace on the ground. Even the maze is deserted, save by four children and a governess, who evidently use it as a lounge, and to whom it is no mystery at all. The difficulties of the contrivance are adventured by another person, who has to invoke the aid of the royal official, who takes a penny fee for his ministrations, in order to get out and see the spring elsewhere.

Bushey Park is as pleasantly deserted as Hampton Court garden. Here the Crow connection is very strong, and family affairs in the trees are conducted in a noisy, almost boisterous manner. You can easily distinguish the scolding fathers from the obstreperous children, who must be now very good for pies. No doubt there are neglected wives in those umbrageous towns also, but the nurseries are unquestionably full. In the midst of the clamour, a crow, with an aged head, perches on a tree a little apart from the rest, and gives the tumultuous wigwams a warm Spurgeonesque lecture. This discourse evidently enrages the multitude more than ever, and there is a sudden sally upon the preacher, who escapes with a clever dive, and betakes himself to another quarter of the colony. The long avenue is empty, the spaces between the trees fold in a sort of cathedral dusk and coolness; the deer flit and whisk in the open glades dumb and soft-hoofed; the ornamental water with its gilded statue has its fountains aspout, and the whole show has but a solitary spectator. This, indeed, rather adds than takes from the interest of it, for the love of fair scenes is ever a selfish humour.

By the awful cataract of Moulsey Lock, which really makes an exceedingly respectable pother, considering the means at command, there is a comfortable pen-

F

insula on which to smoke. A riparian philosopher haunts the spot, who is profoundly learned in everything connected with eight or ten miles of the Thames. He knows of a Bill or two touching the river in the House, he "hears on" every distinguished fish in the neighbourhood, he has an opinion concerning the piscicultural labours of those who are trying to raise trout and salmon in the stream. He circumstantially discovered that a most industrious angler was in private life a writer of screaming farces, and he came up himself to scream at one of these compositions from the pit of the Haymarket Theatre. He gives this information, and more, without an eye to beer, and is a sturdy independent old fellow, whom it is a real pleasure to meet. He passes some of his leisure in firing stones at an empty bottle placed on a stick, and is so expert at the game that he must contract for the bottles. Opposite the lock is a charming cottage with an apple-tree in front of it, rich and comely with blossoms of the most delicate, pink-white. An old goat is dozing in the sun-glare, while the goatling tumbles gleefully on the sward, which is flecked and powdered over with daisies. The end of the garden overhangs the stream, and here a group of ducks are alternately bathing and making their toilettes ; the latter process involves much fuss and bridling. A canoeist from Ditton shoots through the bridge, and with a dextrous twirl of his paddle comes to land with quite an acrobatic finish. There is a gipsy cart on the towpath hung all round with wicker goods, while from the interior two ragged children issue to demand toll on the curiosity of the passing stranger. The gipsy man—an evil-browed, grimy ruffian, who is cursing from habit at a cur dog, comes from behind the vehicle, and roars viciously at another of his mendicant flock, who has so far forgotten business as to go prancing after a big yellow butterfly in the neighbouring field. Once more on the bridge, bound for dinner, and no bad dinner either—a salmon, steak, duckling, and very fair Moselle, at a moderate charge. Before that meal is over, grey clouds have thickened heavily aloft, and there is a chill northerly whiff in the wind. A boat runs past with a brace of water-nymphs for a crew, and a helms-girl at the stern in a pilot jacket and straw hat. That concert we heard at noon is entirely concluded, except for the steady cawing of the rooks, who are from time to time roused into a fury of contention by the bugler of the well-guarded palace. As the train takes us from the spring into town, where the beautiful season is choked in her prime and disfigured by the soot, the sun once more shines on the waters and grounds of Hampton, and again the Thames reflects the walls and chimneys of the sleepy and almost silent Court.

IT was a good omen to meet almost the first thing, on a walk in search of the Spring near London, a right merrie masque in the rural district of Hammersmith. A day to be given to fancies could not have been better begun than with the sight of a splendid procession of gods and goddesses. What though the mummers were merely circus people advertising their show to a sluggish public, the spectacle brought to mind in an idle mood the olden time of Maypole pranks, and so left a little colour of that Arcadian era in the feeling through which one afterwards gazed from Kew Bridge upon the Thames and saw the river, the hue of the cat's-eye jewel, floating off into the mist. The Green is all asleep. The tea-arbours are silent—no solicitous waitress stands at the door to tempt the traveller into the mild refreshment of which hot water for twopence forms so important a constituent; no merchant of nuts or shell-fish bawled his tariff of prices with competitive energy. The Rose and Crown was as still as though its inmates were petrified. The houses, with blinds drawn, refused to gaze on the lovely spring noon, and a cow in the centre of the grass plot was the only living creature to be seen—a cow munching on that steady, persevering fashion, which suggests that eating is more a business with it than an appetite. And so until the gates of the garden are reached, where there is no token of as much as a beadle abroad. A slumbering giant rouses with a groan from his hutch, however, on hearing footsteps, and apparently satisfied with an owlet sort of inspection, finishes his interrupted snore as he retires once more to his bench. It is

indeed curiously warm and drowsy for the month of
the year. The carefully tended, smooth-shaven acres,
with the brown walks, and the glittering domes of
glass, stretch out before you. But for the absence of
the lines of border flowers you might imagine that
June had arrived. As you rest for a minute on a seat
within a stone's throw of the entrance where the Royal
arms blink upon the portals, the air seems balmy, and
the sense of repose is rather induced than disturbed
by the songs of the birds, the short piping of the red-
breast, who is watching you with a beady eye from the
holly-bush on which the coral berries are still blushing;
the mellow flute of the blackbird, whose busy wife has
just dashed out from yonder pile of rhododendrons ;
the loud, bold challenge of the thrush, and the very
far withdrawn chuckle of a rook, who belongs to a
colony of his tribe over the river.

But you have many visits to pay here, and first
offer your respects to the tropical tree ferns close at
hand. You slam the door after you, and in a second
you are in the midst of a hot climate, surrounded by
natives of Australia, of India, of Brazil, of Jamaica, of
Trinidad. Some of the glorious fern-leaves waver to the
rays of the sun and you see through them and in them
every vein and vessel and network of their economy.
You walk down an alley of these and the stillness and
heat is so oppressive that it is a relief again to slip out
and saunter in the open. Why here is a tree in full
May blossom, white as the snow, and with much of its
wealth of bloom sprinkling the ground beneath it.
You think it resembles an old prickly friend, but it is
tabulated with an inscription appointing its origin to
a foreign country. And not far from it is a cedar of
Lebanon holding dusk itself as it were in the mid sky,
and with its harsh gloom setting off the tender white
of buds on the branches of its homelier neighbours.
In the vicinity is a diminutive Crystal Palace, and
peeping through the panes you sight a wonder of tints

caused by the glass being coloured green, while the sun rays pierce through it and touch a clump of small ferns that have just been drenched with water. The trembling drops on the fern absolutely appear to flame with an emerald light, but the delusion vanishes when the valet in attendance on the plants crosses the place. Further on the treat of the day is in store for us. A door inscribed "Greenhouse" lies invitingly open. Here on the threshold you are saluted with a welcome of perfumes, and every shelf is loaded with living flowers. They seem to keep no season ; they are as beautiful,. as ample in their charms, this March noon as ever you have met them at later horticultural displays. And they appear so much more naturally in this home of theirs than when on view for prizes like stall-fed cattle. Narcissus, azaleas, tulips with Batavian nicknames, and hundreds of others with their common garden titles disguised in nurseryman's Latin, appeal to you gracefully for admiration, and have flourished hitherto without it as their brethren do in the tropical forests where no human sight has ever beheld their glowing revelations of the spirit of love and comeliness that pervades the unknown as well as the known portions of the globe. And we are not without music—a complete orchestra—in our unfrequented flower-show. Not merely the "mute aerial harmonies" which the poet tells us arise from the beds of the roses in the exhaled perfume ; but we have an absolute concert more appropriate to the situation than any waltz or jig of military music-master. 'Tis neither more nor less than a chorus of bees. Here they are singing at work gaily as the reapers in an opera harvest, and having their fill of nectar from the flower bells in the meantime. When a basso profundo has sounded his deepest note and finished it off by a pedal effect, procured by buzzing against the glass for a moment, he plunges into a flower which rocks with his weight, and his hundred companions keep up the performance. A new tenor with a distinct quality of voice arrives from without, and before commencing business recitatives all over the place until he contrives to find a promising plant to loot. And from the garden itself comes the piping and whistling of the feathered minstrels, many of whom, by the way, would think little of garrotting a gorged honey-maker who was carrying more than was good for him home to his house under the dovecote in the farm-yard.

By the margin of the pond sit two rather rough-looking visitors, who watch the water-fowl with an expression derived from a frequent contemplation of the same objects enjoyed as a relief from horse-play in St. James's Park. "That 'ere swan now must be a tidy age," remarks one of these gentlemen to the other, as the graceful bird moves out of the way of a pebble flung at it. The swan sails to the other side, where he is loudly hailed by a little man in black velvet and red stockings, who entertains him hospitably with part of his private luncheon. The great palm-house is suffocating. The great palms have an aspect of being condemned to solitary confinement for life. They have an obese swollen appearance; their broad crowns are pressed by the roof; they must miss, you think, the jewelled birds that flashed amongst their leaves, the odours of the tropic tide, even the crash and roar of the tropic storm. Here there is no room for them to budge; they exhibit symptoms of vegetable elephantiasis. Bending our steps towards the hideous Nankin tower, our pilgrimage so far is ended, and we trudge into the dusty road for Richmond. The Spring has not yet come to the river. The trees are still bare, save those on the stream islands, and they are only furnished with pale-green leaflets. The water is almost inanimate as far as boats are concerned. As we take the tow-path to Kew, the Thames is quite deserted. Even the swans are few and far between.

A barge is pulled up by a snorting tug, followed
by another dragged by horses. The mariner at
the helm of the latter is conversing with the old salt
who steers the horses on shore, and the language
of both would have suited our army in Flanders,
although the subject of the dialogue is the innocent topic enough of a boat-race. A slight wind
stirs up from the east and rolls towards the falling sun
a huge cloud of fog, and quite suddenly it grows cold;
the west deepens to blood colour, and the tops of the
glass-houses in the gardens resemble the great car-
buncle in the legend. And with this fog—a chill apparition born in the Essex marshes and swathed in a
mantle of London soot—the beauty of March and of
the Spring is chilled at once to death. The birds
cease to sing, the gardens are muffled in brown holland, the river turns grey, the picturesque houses are
blotted from the landscape, and when you reach the
railway station you have to confess that the swallows
are right in not putting faith in the treacherous climate
in which every weather is possible within a round of
the clock.

IT is not given to every one with a taste for angling to haunt the beautiful rivers of Wales in the spring, when the trout are ready to take the coloured fly, or to wander, rod in hand, to the distant brooks of Ireland of Scotland, where the brown waters foam round the rocks, and the heather-covered shoulders of the hills are interspersed with the groves of dark fir. And so it is well for a brother of the pastime to incline, in compulsory circumstances, to its humbler divisions, to become catholic and liberal in his piscatorial tastes, and no longer to despise the punt artist of the Thames, the watchers of the quill and the float, the real patient descendants of honest Izaak, our good teacher, who, in fair and foul weather, continued perseveringly to illustrate the triumph of hope over experience. Was it not in a tavern, the Nag's Head, that a famous theological celebration was reported to take place, which up to this hour is discussed by people interested in the topic of episcopal succession? And a tavern as far away from the river side as the Liverpool Road is selected for the introduction of an anxious Pupil to the mysteries of London angling. The ceremony is not attended with any great bodily peril, but the chamber in which it is performed is in itself a curious ichthyological museum, intended to excite the ambition of the tyro. For on the walls, enshrined for ever in glass cases, are various notable captives of the "Club." Mr. Brown's pike, caught in the Scamander, and big enough to swallow an ordinary-sized infant, without making two bites at the cherry, Mr. Smith's roach, &c. These dead, mute, glistening objects all wear a comic galvanised grin on their countenances, as if they were nocturnally diverted with the stories in connection with their species, of which, with tobacco, the atmosphere is redolent.

But the secrets of the brotherhood could never be practically applied in the Liverpool Road, and so one afternoon the Pupil finds himself in the fast-falling of the eventide on a dusty road in Herts, bound, with simple wallet on back, for a stream which for reasons may be disguised under the name of the Scamander. It was cold, the wind whistled with a dreary sough through the elms overhead, and though the sun was not yet down the birds were silent in the fields, and round the edges of the day-ghost of the moon was a ragged fringe of vapour betokening a wet day on the morrow. The pilgrim is quite new to the spot, and has to depend for directions on a scrap of paper obtained from the Master, who has preceded him to the banks of the Scamander many hours before. Three miles of a trudge, and the village of Rickholme is reached, and then the chart directs that the traveller is to proceed to the " Fisherman's Home," by Bob Gray, where the anglers are furnished with entertainment and shelter. The path to the Fisherman's Home lies partly through a churchyard, and then over a picturesque bridge, underneath which, on the banks of the canal, within a stone's throw of the Scamander, close to a mill-stream, the hostelry is situated. Raising the latch of the Home, the Pupil is cheerily welcomed by the strongest smell of cheese that ever proceeded from a mouse-trap, and finds himself then at once in a bar uninhabited by either maid or pot-boy. The Home is silent and deserted. A robber might have his will apparently of anything in it. The Pupil, not a little weary and athirst, calls, " What ho, there !" or something equivalent to that theatrical shout ; his voice rings with a hollow echo through the Home, and appears to faint off in a garret, and then return like the repeating chuckle of a ventriloquist. Stamping and

kicking, kicking and stamping, at length with the jerk
of a demon from a stage trap a short, strong, bullet-
headed, grizzled man stands before the pupil. " This
is the Fisherman's Home, is it not ? " " Yes." " Was
Mr. Gray in the house ? " The bullet-headed grinned
to introduce himself as Gray. "Was the gen'elem
a member of the ' Club ?' Then, sir, follow me. To
remain here until Monday ? All right, sir. Mr. Horner
(the Master) is on the water, and was a expectin' of
you, sir. There he is, sir. You can find your way to
him straight over the foot-bridge."

By this it has grown dark, or nearly so, and as the
Pupil approaches the Master he beholds a quaint and
striking object. Mr. Horner wears his trousers in
Mackintosh coverings ; on his head is a huge sou'-
easter ; what can be seen of him over the edge of an
Ulster coat, into which he has got as a sentinel might
into a hutch, is blue. A huge rod stretches from his
feet across the water. He greets his Pupil in a tone
of affectionate heartiness, a little impaired by the
chattering of his teeth, and by a quivering in his voice
suggestive of general misery and disappointment.
" What luck, mine honoured Master ?" At this query
the adept swings round a huge canvas sack, capable
of holding a few brace of bottle-nosed whales ; and,
after feeling about in various compartments of his
enormous wallet, produces therefrom what resembles
a sardine, the knocker of whose aquatic residence
should have been tied up in a white glove, and a sprat
of stewed appearance, mottled with the bread-crumbs
of his prison. The Master admits his quarry not to
be in the best condition ; the Pupil is dutifully silent,
but rapidly chilling ; and pleading his long walk and
an appetite, suggests a cessation of slaughter for the
occasion and a return to enjoy that ease which is to be
found at an inn. Mr. Gray is at his door. smoking
his pipe. The Master asks him if his beer is good.
" Well, I don't think much of it myself, sir. You see,

I'm givin' hup the 'ouse, and the brooar he sends a'most any stuff." A trial glass of the liquor is brought, and a trifle of it proved that a great deal might be thought of it indeed in connection with tobacco and salt. "I suppose you have some whisky, Gray?" "No, sir, I don't want to keep a stock, because——" "Have you any soda-water?" "No call for soda-water 'ere, sir;" and the Master ascends, with his Pupil, in dudgeon, to the best room, and descends in desperation with a stone jar under his arm, to forage for ale through the village. After an interval of eggs, fried ham is laid on the table with something of a flourish by Mr. Gray, who has put out his pipe to wait. A mouthful of the meat causes an expression of mutual anxiety and alarm on the visages of Master and Pupil. They gaze upon one another silently. "It ain't a bad 'am, mind," remarks Mr. Gray, anticipating condemnation, "though it's what I call a 'ammy 'am, and many gents prefers a 'am as is a little 'ammy." The 'ammy 'am is ordered off, as being too highly suggestive of a pig who had escaped the knife by dying a natural death—but sportsmen must put up with hardships. A big fire is contrived, and a forgotten bottle with materials for hot grog is unearthed by the Master; the wind howls and screeches outside, and shakes and searches the Ricketty Home, and the Pupil receives an oral lesson in angling until it is time to retire for the night.

With the roar of an absolute gale, the Pupil is roused this spring morning to see the air charged with driving sleet and the clouds black and bitter, to descend to the shabby best room, with the white ashes of last night's fire in the grate, with the breeze coursing copies of newspapers round the table, and a black cat, with bottled anger in her green eyes, in possession of the sofa. The Master enters, and an effort is made to put the best face on things. An overture on the bell, continued for ten minutes, has the effect of conjuring Mr. Gray from the basement of the noble fabric whose hospitalities he so gracefully dispenses. Well, his attempts at breakfast are not so bad. But how is the day to be got through ? There is apparently no chance whatever of the rain ceasing. The sleet, indeed, has discontinued, but the rain descends fiercely, and the clouds show no break, no token of relenting. All of a sudden a change takes place ; the sun dashes out with a perfect burst of triumph, the clouds clear off, opening out glimpses of azure and silver, and a complete chorus of larks rises up from the meadows as Pupil and Master ramble to the stream. And the cold has departed on the instant. Swarms of swallows are hawking on the very surface of the Scamander, now and again brushing it with their wings, then darting through a thin plantation of osiers, than flitting through a long reach of yellow buttercups. This transformation scene is complete. Spring has asserted herself in the most determined fashion, with the very grip of the untimely winter at her throat. For the music of the meadows is almost distracting in variety and strength. The jubilee for warmth and sunshine is celebrated in every bush and briar and hedgerow, in the covert, on the hill yonder. And the Master hereupon takes out his bag of live worms, and selects one for his hook. A perch, he thinks, might come to it, mayhap a dace, perchance a roach, nay, a trout might, only for certain mills on the Scamander, the refuse from which disagrees with the more delicate fish. The Pupil grows recalcitrant and inattentive, and is in a holiday humour to be wooed simply by the sights and sounds about him. The Master extracts another victim from his worm-bag, and impales him with deliberate skill. Perch, however, come not, dace keep away, roach are not to be beguiled, the Scamander trout is in all probability as much a myth as the " sargus " fish described by the veracious Du Bartas, that occasionally saunters on shore in order to flirt with billy-goats, but nevertheless the Master

angles perseveringly, and sternly refuses to be occupied
with landscape reflections.   The weather has now
another surprise in store for us.   The larks stop singing
and come down like so many falling meteors in an
August evening, and with a grand drum-roll in the sky
a thunderstorm sets in and the hail-drops pelt Master
and Pupil pitilessly.   There is nothing for it but to
cross the Scamander at the first bridge, and to pass
through the village to the Home.   And the folk in the
porches of the doors and at the lintels of the numerous public-houses laugh at dripping Master and dripping Pupil.   And remembering the quality of the Home
ale, the fishers furnish themselves with bottles of Bass
at the " Lion," and thus laden, journey in the midst
of thunder and lightning and broad grins to their
hostelry.   Mr. Gray has a leg of mutton for dinner,
and his guests are grateful indeed that it is not what
Mr. Gray might term a muttony leg of mutton of the
same character as his 'ammy 'am.

And is the Pupil cured of a taste for angling within
the London circuit and of visiting Rickholme?   By
no means.   He intends to stick to his Master.   The
season was against angling, the time not propitious;
but the fisherman must of all things be patient, live
in hope, accept his failures philosophically, and try
and convert them into account by observing the wonders of the animal kingdom with which he will come
into contact, including Mr. Gray and his 'ammy 'am,
and the native politeness of the rural English, to say
nothing of the advantages of pleasant companionship
in every stress of weather and bad sport.

THE scene is a meadow, golden with yellow buds, and shining with the pearls of the rain hung in the ears of the cowslips. The larks are piping in hundreds, a mill plays the big drum, and there is a murmuring chorus from the river, while clang, clang goes the holiday peal from the bells of the church, and a cow joins in with a single, solemn " Moo ; " and in the middle of it all the odd effect of a slang march performed by the Rickholme town band, and, Heaven be praised, far enough removed to render the sounds of quavering cornet and halting trombone only faint and irregular. And then comes the sudden sigh of the wind crossing our little two-mile prairie ; and the crack of the rifles of Volunteers, who will defend us from invasion, but who are preparing for the enemy at so great a distance from here, that the birds never stop to wonder at the noise. A new pastoral symphony might be written in this scene. And the composer should leave nothing out, but score, if he can, between his five lines and four spaces, in his sharps and flats, and majors and minors, adagios, and prestos, and fortissimos, the odour of a hundred wild flowers and water-mints, the blue of the sky, what Wordsworth calls the " vernal impulse " of the wood, the croon of pigeons, and the sense of peace over the sleepy land. Perhaps the sleepiness extended to the fish, for they did not rise. When you have tried your gentle, essayed your scoured worm, impaled your live bait, mounted your flies, spun your minnow, and nothing comes of it, to what must you put down your bad luck. The Master, oblivious of landscape observations, and assisting his amazing faculty of patience with a small pipe of birdseye, searches through his vast store of lures and cheats, natural, artificial, and purely tackle-shopical, in order to demonstrate the reality of his art by a dace, a trout, or anything, for his angling conscience has grown callous under disappointment, and he is now threatening murder against everything with fins, independent of the honourable considerations of season. And the Pupil, the meek apprentice, after watching with fervid interest the extraction of a vivacious minnow from a piscatorial aquarium in the form of a tin can, and the subsequent operation of passing a hook through the jaws of the creature, and then casting it into the stream· as a tit-bit for trout or perch, leaves his lesson for a time, and knee-deep in the grass, wends his steps towards a series of water-cress beds. These are laid out in exact parallelogram form, and are being raked by a stout peasant, who plies his implement with a cheerful sailor-like song to the work. Looking on at him is an old gentleman in a smock and leggings, whose face is positively dusty with age. The voice of this antique (he appeared to have no more life in him than a cameo) sounded as though it were underground ; his lack-lustre stare gave one a chill to meet. His talk was of the anguish he suffered from that portion of his economy which it pleased him to call " his insides." Did he reside in the neighbourhood? He pointed with a skinny trembling finger to a wooden hut on the edge of a canal above the Scamander, and then walked towards it, followed by the curious Pupil. The hut or hutch was close by a lock. Over the door was written laconically " Ginger Beer."

A dame of possibly greater age still than the poor dreary hind in the gaiters stood inside the hotel of ginger beer. She was dispensing a tumbler of the frothy liquid to a canal-boat captain and his wife, while two other Paddington mariners from the barge, one male and one female, were basking in the sun by the porch or entrance. The wife of old " Insides "—

who was coughing with his back to the wall, in a
manner suggestive at every hollow sob of the rattle of
the ceremonial earth upon a new coffin in a church-yard
—wore a wooden leg, which peeped gracefully from
beneath her gown when she offered ginger beer to her
customers. There being nothing specially attractive
or interesting about these premises, the Pupil glancing
at his Master still occupied in managing his float in
the stream below, ascends a hill leading to a beech
grove ; and here he confronts a pair of evident lovers
in that shy stage of silence and awkwardness in which
the gentleman walks several yards apart from the lady.
In this instance the lady was followed by an idyllic
pet in the shape of a tame lamb, who stuck to her heels
like a dog, and whose personal attachment to his
mistress was ascribed later on by the Master to the
fact of her having a bottle of mint sauce in her pocket.
The swain bore a bunch of wood flowers, and altogether
the picture was a pleasant one. But the Master has
brought a fish on shore. The Pupil is duly hailed to
witness the process of landing the quarry, and he
obeys the signal with diligent submission. The perch
is skilfully played, cunningly guided into a shallow
bay, and then deftly whipped flopping on the grass,
his jewelled eye gleaming with rage and surprise, the
spines on his back fiercely erect, the copper
bronze of his scale armour glittering like a red
winter sunset upon an ice-pond. The master is cool,
as becomes an adept. He exhibits no trace of in-
artistic enthusiasm or excitement. He compels the
perch to surrender the hook, and then he constructs
for him a cradle of dock-leaves where he reclines,
heaving yet with astonishment and perhaps suffering
slightly, say from nervous irritation, at not being
able to breathe. The perch, according to Father
Walton, quoting one of his favourite and reliable
naturalists, " have in their brain a stone which
is in foreign parts sold by apothecaries, being

G

there noted to be very medicinable." But the Master
does not bear out this anatomical statement. The
Master fishes and fishes and still fishes—worm, gentle,
minnow, stone-loach, gudgeon ; minnow, gentle, worm
again, and there moves no fin towards his angle. And
so the Pupil ultimately petitions that the rods be tied
up, for the evening is beginning to fall. But there is
a stay until the nightingale commences vespers, which
she does as Master and Pupil sit and smoke by the
water-cress amphibious plantation. We speak not, so
that a brown rat creeps out of his burrow to stare at us
fixedly, and, in the very middle of the nightingale's
jug-jugging, an owl gives a solitary good-night whoop,
so hollow and remote in tone that it appears to sound
as a trumpet summons to the elves to meet in the
glades of the now dusky woods above us.

Rickholme is thinking of sleep when the march to
dinner is adventured by Master and Pupil. And a
dinner it was, as dinner ought to be at a stout, cosy,
unpretentious country inn. Toothsome cutlets gar-
nished or equipped with slices of smoke-cured ham,
the mealiest of mealy potatoes, beer clear as amber
and honest in quality, a rhubarb pie made to perfection, a table-cloth white as snow and odorous of sweet
herbs, a clear fire before which our slippers were carefully toasted, and after our humble repast a placid and
silent pipe or two. Master and Pupil are obliged to sleep
in a large double-bedded room, wainscotted, and filled
with quaint Elizabethan carvings ; for our inn is of
immense antiquity, and was a hotel probably during
the Wars of the Roses. Its ancient garden is visited
at cockcrow, and there, amidst his own vegetables,
blooms our fresh-faced landlord, a burly Yorkshireman,
with a peachy cheek, a hazel eye, and a jovial paunch.
It is quite pleasant to exchange a greeting with him,
and pleasanter still when his good wife leads us in
to a breakfast of fresh eggs, cold beef, pigeon-pie,
water-cresses, carefully prepared toast, dry and

buttered, until the Master growls with hungry satisfaction while he informs the Pupil that we must not
forget business because we can linger over cream
instead of chalk and calves' brains, and sweeten our
bread with something more palatable than Thames
mud or railway grease. And we are shortly again at
our stations, fortunate again in a fine day, and also in
full creels. Even had our success been less, our
enjoyment would scarcely have been inferior. The
Master may, indeed, feel a tender pang when his
minnow dies without a fish of quality or boastful proportions nibbling at the hook ; but even he, absorbed
in sport as he is, cannot be insensible to the charms of
the country, and to the aspect of the myriad rural
things, glad for mere existence, including old "Insides"
and his wooden-legged wife, to whom the angling
season brings an annual promise of mild weather, and
an increase in the consumption of ginger beer of their
own bottling.

DOES not the goddess send us, according to the poets, the most attractive messengers to distribute her pets? Blind angels, who speak lyrically, or open-eyed sylphs of the most peaceful and fascinating mien? Here, guarding her basket redolent of the odours of Spring, and sucking a short, black pipe of Limerick twist, behold one of Flora's April emissaries. At her back is a mound of gleaming ice and a fish wearing a yellow lemon in his mouth, but the good-natured fish-monger who owns the stall does not disturb the Tipperary flower-girl from her post. And it is evident she prefers tobacco to primroses. At sixty, perhaps, with a little hunger and a touch of rheumatism, even violets will not bring up tender and absorbing fancies. In an hour or so the mature nymph of the cheap bouquets will get upon her feet; and if you follow her you will find her make for a neighbouring street, in which stands a large house with an open door. She pockets her pipe, and puts her basket in the porch. There is no one to buy from her on the spot, but she kneels before the shining lamp of the altar, and perhaps as far as her mind can think, it has of a sudden brought her even above the lark's flight. These very humble servants of Flora keep within easy trudge of their Roman Catholic Chapel. They are mostly Irish, and a turn at prayer seems to refresh them more than fifty pinches of snuff.

What sweet shepherd is this with the fur cap, the grimy face, the torn jacket, who stands opposite our window, crowned with a hundred wild and garden flowers? Crowned, perhaps, is not the correct word, for the superb regalia is in a wicker casket: but then

some of the leaves nod over his brow, and, if you did
not recognise the costermonger, might suggest a Roman
diner-out. There is nothing pastoral or arboricultural
about this gentleman, however. He has gone into
scarlet geraniums instead of red-herrings, that is all.
He is troubled on account of the ephemeral character
of his investment, and is very eager indeed to dispose
of his wares. You never observe him straying into
churches, but he has a corner in his heart for a bull-
pup, and enough of religion to derive pleasure from
cursing. " All a blowin', all a growin';" and on being
asked from the area the price of a plant, he lodges his
stock on the ground, and holding the flower-pot in
one hand, he uses the other to give gesticulative force
to a blasphemous certificate of its value and cheapness.
It is a wonder how he contrives to keep alive the
geraniums or more delicate azaleas in the awful lodg-
ings to which he retires at night ; and yet they survive
apparently for several days, and may in the end have
the honour of meeting death at a dinner party under
the gaseliers, or in the bouquet that lies upon my lady's
table.

Shall we find the traditional flower-girl in the neighbourhood of a railway station? Scarcely. Where holi-
day-bound folk largely congregate, troops of worn,
wretchedly-clad girls may be seen offering flowers for
sale—but not as in the ballet. They are but unfortunate mendicants in disguise. Unconsciously (to a
few), the flowers serve for begging purposes for these
girls as effectively as if they were furnished with
crippled children. Poverty and flowers you think
ought not to be seen together. The hungry, pinched,
wistful face appears more hungry and pinched when
associated with the happy gathered children of the
gardens and the fields. And so, from an instinct of
compassion or sentiment, you give an alms to the
flower-girl which you never thought of bestowing on
her when she was in the fusee and cigar-light business.

She makes up pretty things for the button-hole of honest little Jones, who has escaped for a day from his office, and who has a necktie that would put the hottest poppy that ever flamed in an August corn-field out of countenance.   Flora's Alley in Covent Garden does not either present you with any Nydia illustrations. The ladies in charge there remind you perhaps of the Rose of Sharon, and many of the names over the doors will contribute to the same idea.   But you are oppressed with the riches of the place.   It is Oriental in its aromatic spiciness and colouring.   The sacrificial combinations to be employed at wedding obsequies are distracting to all but possible brides or bridesmaids.   To what picturesque uses will these specimens of the art of bouquet making in yonder window be put?   That bunch of gleaming flower-jewels in the corner may be flung at the feet of Zerlina, of Marguerite, of Maria, at the Opera ; may be placed in front of a private box at—— But this kind of speculation would lead us into districts of thought in which the more fragile interest of our subject would perish.

Flora in the windows of Belgravia is showing herself in neat form and loveliness these genial afternoons. The majolica vases and troughs are bubbling over with scarlet and blue, and green and yellow, and creamy white.   Pendulous nests of moss contain cunningly-mixed tints brighter than the breast of the humming-bird, or the plush of the featherless canary who helps another gentleman's gentleman to lounge against the portico of the window-gardened mansion.   And in more modest fashion Flora has chosen to deck for us an acre in the midst of brick and mortar with almond blossoms and leaves of dark and light green, and has sent birds to sing there within rattle of omnibus and van.   And Flora has stolen into Hyde Park and Kensington, honouring these spaces even before the country.   In Kensington you might almost

think the May had come already—the May that
Calderon the poet was weary waiting for.

We alight upon our transcendental flower nymph at
last. She is retained at the establishments to which
those resort who would not think they were dressed
without a yellow rose in the coat. She is handsome,
but with no special type of beauty. She no more
gathers flowers than she digs potatoes, and she contemplates them with as little sentimental regard as an
apothecary entertains for a Spanish fly. She must,
however, practise a certain amount of fascination in
order to draw customers to the shop, and as this has
to be done for the most part upon a good set of
men, who are not cowardly in talk to a woman, the
task comes easy to her. There is a considerable
amount of competition amongst different bouquet
establishments. They charge generally from a shilling
up to three shillings for a button-hole flower, but two
shillings is the average tariff. With care, a man may
dine in the flower he has worn in the Row; but the
ferns round the flowers are exceedingly fragile. Some
of the bouquet shops have adopted the plan of sending
a dozen or so of prepared little bouquets to the hall
porters of the clubs. The hall-porter disposes of them
at a considerably reduced figure; but then it is supposed
to be a different affair altogether to have the decoration
attached to your lappet by an obese functionary in a
scarlet waistcoat, and by a damsel who takes your
florin after that service with a smile as though she
loved you.

Of the flower-shows enough has been perhaps often
written, but the theme becomes to some extent novel
every year. The only remarks that may be made
on the score of these exhibitions is, that, out of
the thousands who attend them, a very small proportion take the trouble of visiting the ostensible objects
for which the gatherings are held. For this disposition
there is no cure and no remedy. It has been noticed

that what are known as nice girls hover round the bands at the flower-shows, and the—well, the plain girls—linger round the geraniums. I shall not attempt to give any explanation of this phenomenon.

TROUT MURDER.

I SHALL, in connection with early fishing, describe to you a deed which I have blushed to witness, and which my ink almost turns carnation to record. A gravid salmon has by means of an unlawful spear been secured, and its interior deprived of the entire quantity of that material suggesting magnificent possibilities of future fish. This orange stuff is put into a bowl, and well soused and carefully manipulated until the particles composing it are definitely marked out, and the gelatinous substance liquified off. Then the unhallowed bait is placed in a strainer and water poured upon it, and subsequently dried delicately and tenderly in a soft cloth. Finally, it is sprinkled with salt, and after a short time is bottled or boxed, and use it as ye may. I crave my readers' forgiveness for even chronicling an atrocity of the kind. Only on one occasion did I myself condescend to bait a hook with the villainous and murderous compound, and that was not until my patience and fly-book had been exhausted.

Trout fishing on the 1st of February is usually anything but the pleasant and idyllic pastime that the sport becomes later in the season. The weather may be, often is, muggy and dark, but that you may be prepared for. You must be content to forego all pastoral expectations. The trees are yet bare, sensible birds are silent, flowers there are none, and the whole riparian landscape looks cold, silent, and indifferent. But February has still a worse mood for the eager and the early angler—such as I shall attempt to depict when mentioning the circumstance

of having condescended to bait a hook with—a name-
less compound.

I agreed to accompany a pair of veteran enthusiastic
anglers to a river on the First—let us call it the Wobble
—seven or eight miles from the town in which I was
residing. My companions are to fish for salmon,
while I am content to try what I can do for
trout. We start at seven in the morning, night's
candles are burned out, but the day, anything
but jocund, stands tip-toe on the mountain-top, pre-
ferring a matin penance in a white sheet of fog.
However, things brighten up a little by the time
we arrive at the edge of the Wobble, and my
friends proceed to work. But as it brightens it
hardens. A wind springs up with a chill in it that
makes the appearance of an artificial fly a miserable mockery and transparent cheat. And yet in
the midst of a squall Tom Hackle's reel gives out
the music the fisherman dearly loves, and Joe Mullet
is ready with the gaff. It is but a six-pounder for all
the row made by the brute ; but is the maiden quarry
of the season, and so his capture is duly celebrated by
a drink.

Meanwhile how fared it with me? It was my
introduction to February angling, and I scarce could
recognise my old acquaintance the Wobble itself.
I knew the Wobble in April, in May, and in June.
I did not know it for a deep and desperate brawler.
Where it was wont to linger by the sedges and
talk soft nonsense to reeds and willows, it now
rushed past with angry haste and impatience. Famous pools and reaches, cunning and certain finds
had disappeared. Old stumps, in the shade of which
would lurk a plump trout of a surety, were under
water — promising strongholds, where, when you
bagged the proprietor, his place was occupied a
few days afterwards as regularly as a street crossing
is inherited by a privileged mendicant the moment

the broom is abandoned by the gentleman who
has made a fortune with it. And so I am obliged to
fish as I can, and I am more or less in the dark as
to flies. How, for instance, can I observe the hint I
have read in a book—to compare and to match my
specimens of artificial entomology with the insects
supposed to be disporting over the water? It is
sheer impertinence to offer a trout a midge in a hurricane. And yet the stream is not a bad colour;
on the contrary, it is of a clarified beer hue, the
best complexion perhaps that could be desired for
fly fishing. I endeavour to summon up recollections of wrinkles in the craft. Unfortunately, I
fail to remember suitable precedents. [Again, my
volume of insects is not locally illustrated, there
is nothing in it recommended by the resident authorities on the temper and disposition of the Wobble,
and so I must e'en try what luck will send, and
mount a cast on pure speculation. There is, however, to my mind, but little luck in trout fishing.
If you go wrongly and unskilfully to work at it,
you have your labour and no more for your pains.
In vain did I change fly after fly, and, though I say
it who should not, in the nice conduct of the line
displayed a grace and a dexterity which would not
have disgraced any ancient master, I did not receive the compliment of a single rise. Now I had
come out with high expectations, and had been told
that the advantage of February trout angling partly
consisted in the fact that though the trout might
not be in the best condition they would be most
anxious to taste fur and feathers. Had they not
been deprived of the luxuries during the winter?
Would not the earliest presentation of a new kind of
food be attractive and fascinating to them? Were not
their appetites unspoilt, and their credulity undis-
turbed by recollections of jaw-nicks and fin-rips from
the metal implement of hastily striking anglers?

These reasons, plentiful as blackberries, were urged upon me for the excursion which I had adventured ; but, whatever cause there was for it, no trout showed the slightest anxiety on the first of February, in the Wobble, to avail himself of what I offered.

What I offered—at first. I am a strict fly-fisher. I scruple your spinning business for monsters even. But on the first of February on the bank of the Wobble there arrived for me a " pyschological moment " when the ethical stand-point from which I regarded trout angling for the while sank under me as it were, and I found myself permitting Tom Hackle to bait a single hook on a piece of stout gut for me with—well, with that which ought not to have been in my box carried in the pocket. But what an alteration ensued in the nature of my recreation ! Small and large I caught 'em. These orange pills acted like magic on the hitherto sluggish palates of trout and troutlings. And, as a man when he wearies of being virtuous, becomes very vicious indeed, I lugged and tugged away utterly regardless of consequences. My friends, a pair of moderate pot purveyors, who would think it little harm to net as tream—ay, or to lime it— regarded my operations as Mephistopheles might contemplate the backsliding of Faust. I, who had always a word of contempt for bait anglers, I, who—but why pursue the sorry subject further? I mention my case for a warning and for a caution to others. Trout angling in February is perilous to the due following of trout fishing as a fine art. I sincerely hope I shall never abandon the angling creed in which I have been brought up, in order to make a heavy creel at the sacrifice of an honest conscience.

WHY should we all be subject to the superstition that there is no place but the seaside wherein to recruit from the fatigues and pleasures of London? There is respite and surcease from toil to be had far from the yellow sands, where the angler lies anchored in his punt under the green trees that look into the calm mirror of the Thames. Not to us are borne the sound of vulgar music and the shout of a noisy holiday multitude. It is high noon, and Cliefden woods are as still as though they were painted. The sun is scorching hot, and not a single cloud sends a shadow across the cornfields. The birds will not sing in this tropical atmosphere ; the fish are too warm or too wise, or both, to bite ; and the Master languidly draweth to him a huge jug of something liquid with ice in it. The float is altogether neglected, and the professional assistant, who makes angling his business in life, is drowsily leaning his face on his stout mahogany arms. Presently there are voices and the splash of oars, and a shallop sweeps by impelled by a lady who is all alone in her frail barque. She is clothed in white but wears a nautical hat, and she shoots dextrously under the lee of an ait, where, to all appearances, she plunges into a novel. The voices come from a pic-nic party —three boats in festive procession. They are unprovided with awnings, and it is quite uncomfortable to look at the condition of the pullers. There are half a dozen idle swans lying about who would be easily able to tow a punt were they properly harnessed to it. The lazy brutes do nothing for the privileges they enjoy save to display their proportions, and at

times stick their heads in the river and erect their tails
in the air, as though they were whispering confidential
secrets to naiads, or more properly endeavouring to
find food.   The Pupil proposes to bathe, but the
Master rejects the idea with scorn.   Only across a
meadow of tall grass is the famous lasher of the district, a hole where you might be perfectly drowned did
you not know how to swim.   A shed has been erected
close to it, and apparatus for saving life and for that
ghastly kind of angling which takes place for the still
dumb thing lying so white and motionless amongst the
plumes of the weeds in the gravel when a fatal accident has occurred.   How delicious is the first plunge
into the curling foam of the weir ; and then that turn
over, in which you imitate the movement of the dab-
chick, brings from the shore the applauding notice of
a gentleman in a smock, who has charge of a small
troop of cows.   The swimmer in a small way is a very
vain creature indeed, and observing the simple manner
in which Tim Bobbin is amused, we gambol and frolic through our programme of accomplishments. Alas !
he deems that he should be paid for having patronised the exhibition.   He prefers his request for
beer even at a moment when it is not convenient to
extract the price of the beverage from a pocket.
Behind the shed is a tiny rivulet in which a number of
boys are hunting for bait.   The cows march into it
and stand in the wet with an expression of the most
perfect content in their calm, good-natured eyes. And
the meadow is girded with noble elms and poplars,
over the tops of which the swifts and martins are darting, and from which at off moments there is a quick,
strong flutter, and the sight of a wood-pigeon bolting
from a leafy resting place contrasts in its directness
and purpose with the eccentric weak waggling of a
butterfly who is attempting a zig-zag voyage across
he field.   " Hoy, hoy, hoy," shouts the master to his
errant Pupil, who returns to find the adept impatient

to be home to luncheon, connecting that ceremony with the ordering of the subsequent dinner.

Here is the inn of the sign of "Gog and Magog" at Hookham-on-Thames. It does not look upon the river, it faces the road or the high street, but for all that it is such a retreat as an angler might be well content with. It is, perhaps, scarce as old as the ancient hostelry of Rickholme, but it is thoroughly mellowed by time, and its rooms and passages have the quaint narrowness of the days that are no more about them. Mine host is himself a fisher, who has engaged with pike within the metropolitan district, and a specimen of his prowess leers at you as you await your modest refreshment in the parlour. Our landlady is a gracious mistress, with a very pleasant smile, and a pretty fashion of blushing when spoken to—not through awkwardness or bashfulness, but in a sweet voluntary style. Our library is not extensive, but you do not take up your quarters at the Gog and Magog to pore over books or papers. You can, you are told, read various newspapers for a penny a few doors up the street. Perhaps you want to read one or two newspapers : you find them uncut on a parlour table, and when you have exhausted a certain amount of litera- ture, you cannot discover anyone willing to receive the penny, which at length you deposit on the counter —for gooseberries are sold in the establishment to which the reading-room of Hookham-on-Thames is attached. Both Master and Pupil decide to leave the question of dinner to the mistress of the inn. Well they know from experience that her resources are far beyond what might be expected—it is only necessary for the hungry men to tell her the hour. It is reported that a Civil Service Store contains the most multifa- rious varieties of articles. There is a store at Hookham worth a special visit for the purpose of noting how many samples of incongruous wares may be brought under a single roof-tree. Neckties, bacon, tea, ducks, fish-hooks, nail-brushes, leather, iron, cheap dictionaries, gloves, nets, jewellery, walking-sticks, ink-bottles, stationery, snuff, butter, cigars, marmalade, pocket-knives, toys, Bibles, overcoats, boots, oil-lamps, gunpowder, pills, and live fowl, form part of the stock of this extensive emporium. The odour of it is very curious—quite a novelty in odours. The Master informs a youthful dispenser of needles or anchors, that he hopes to see the proprietor of the store before he, the Master, leaves Hookham. The boy receives this intimation stolidly enough, the fact turning out to be that the person whom the Master wished to shake hands with is not likely to look in of an afternoon on account of his being dead and buried in the neighbouring churchyard for the last six months. And now we wend once more our steps to the waterside, but not with great hopes of fishing. It is only in the early morning and in the evening there is a chance of doing anything. We subside on a plank under the shelter of a railway arch near the ferry, and watch the labours of the jolly boatman who poles the sluggish ferry raft. And within a foot of us is the type of the poorer City clerk, who is having a few days' holiday in a quiet angling manner. He is encased in black, and wears a tall hat, but he is not without cunning in the craft. The Master gives a jealous glance at him as he succeeds in landing small roach much faster than some people could who go to a great deal more trouble and preparation for the purpose. The Pupil decides on defying earwigs, and in having a sleep by the poppies in the wheat. Sleep would come but for the flies, the villain flies. At the moment of conscious going down into the underworld of dreams to the rustling of the corn, the tune of the river, and the chirr chirr-r of the grasshopper, the flies as good as tweak your nose to call you back to the world as it is. The horse-flies are not the worst. It is not a bad plan to put up with the most one of these fellows can do ; after the first nip

you won't mind it ; and somehow or other, the rest of
the tribe appear to think that open hospitality to their
friend ought to insure you from further annoyances,
but the midges are intolerable. They sting or poison
unmercifully, and you are liable, perhaps, by submitting to their attentions, to have a swollen face, or a
pair of cheeks and a profile generally resembling that of
the Irish peasant the day after he had attacked a swarm
of bees with a gridiron. " Hoi ! hoi ! hoi ! "—the signal of the Master, who need never consult his watch to
ascertain when dinner is due. After that meal, capitally
cooked and neatly served, we sit in chairs outside the
room to smoke the pipe of grateful tobacco. Pupil
is much disposed for entire rest for the remainder of
the evening, but the Master peremptorily insists on
the duty of fishing as the night comes on. And the
lagoon into which we drifted as eight of the clock
changed from the church was beautiful exceedingly as
the evening wore on. Our gondola moved with the
stream as we cast for dace with the slender trout rods.
Did we take a large cargo of dace? Were we tired
of hauling them from beneath the lurking shadows of
bank and tree and reed ? Of this nothing shall here be
said but of the wonderful velvet-footed approach of the
soft summer night, with mint perfumes and a lingering
gleam in the golden cups of the lilies, and the slow
conquering of all things by the round, bright moon,
which took serene hold now of river, of wood, and of sky.
But with the Master business is business. A trout has
been heard of feeding at the " lasher." Testimony of
his existence enough to convince the most obstinate
of sceptics has been given at the bar of the Gog and
Magog. Why should not the Master try his angle
upon the thumping trout ? The grave professor casts
from the bridge of the lasher into the water which, in
the moonlight where the swirls and curls and eddies
of foam are, appears to take odd forms, huge twisting
eels, and other uneasy tormented coils, as if there were

H

mysteries and horrors in the tiny Thames Maelstrom.
"That trout, my Master, takes a great deal of fishing."
"Courage, good Pupil, we may yet have him. There,
I thought I felt a nibble." A shiver passes through the
giant poplars, and we find that the dew falls thick as
rain. "Master, had we not best give over; we are
now better than one hour and a half angling for this
reluctant trout?" "Patience, good Pupil, patience."
Anon the chime of midnight is heard, with a tingling
cadence in every note ; and then the Master, trying
a dozen more casts, is content to consider our efforts
at an end. We have despatched our punt to its
destination, and agree to walk the meadow to our
inn. We pass by a sawmill, and in a tree near it is
an owl breathing heavily. He cares not for the
stones pitched near his roosting spot, and snores defiantly after the noise made by the flint amongst the
leaves has ceased.

Cockcrow, did you say? the country cocks, unlike
the foolish fowl of the town, do not begin to bray
until the stars, at any rate, are invisible. But that
strict disciplinarian, the Master, is up at five sharp,
and rouses his sluggish and half reluctant Pupil.
There have been still earlier birds, but they are bank-
fishers, while we have a punt and a professional angler
to ourselves. Some one has noticed that if you see
the first of the morning it seems to be morning number one—the primal smiling infancy of creation ; the
old miracle is repeated for us at every dawn. And a
fancy of the sort occurs to you looking at this bounti-
ful landscape from the river, and hearing the matin
hymns over the grateful corn from the singer who is
told off for the duty of praise. The punt is fixed and
ground-bait cast upon the waters. The fish begin to
bite briskly enough, roach of a not despicable size,
and we have another line differently prepared and
laid out for a jack, angling on its own account. All
of a sudden there is a vicious tug as a dog might give

at the end of a chain at this latter contrivance, and our professional fisherman seizes the rod only to bungle with it, so that the pike has had his breakfast and we our trouble for nothing. We land at nine o'clock with a well-filled basket, and Betsy, the cook of the Gog and Magog, prepares the roach in a manner that causes you to think that roach is a maligned fish when people turn up their noses at it as a delicacy.

Where were we when that tremendous thunder tempest burst over Hookham-on-Thames? It first met us on the stream. We saw it coming from the brazen cloud, and heard it muttering with an odd hum and rumble in the air long before the first blue flash was reflected on the water. How it rained and roared as Master and Pupil are snugly housed in the upper sitting-room of the Gog and Magog, and the Pupil, to while away the hour, stirs up the slumbering echoes of music on a sedate-toned piano! Here, indeed, it was that the Master, starting from a reverie of meerschaum inspiration without notice, trolls a jovial melody. The piano continues to accompany him as first he saw sweet Peggy, and the low-backed car growls horribly in the skies. The Master, having once commenced, is not to be deterred by mere thunder and lightning. His repertoire of half-remembered ditties is inexhaustible, and he has an original adaption from *Rigoletto*, where the cat of the tiles is taken off to such perfection that the Pupil altogether fails to follow it with the limited resources of the instrument. But the storm continues. The landlord and his good lady sit in the bar, and we join them, admiring the grandeur of peal following peal, and shaking the old inn in its shoes. And the tempest then stops as though the stick of a conductor had been raised to bid it cease. The road is sparkling with rivulets and pools of rain, but the sky green-lit. Master, will the weather be good to go a-fishing to-morrow? The Master, from a cloud of fragrant bird's-eye, wags his head Burleighly—it may or it may not. Jolliboys, the landlord, contributes piscatorial information touching thunder. With the morning there is no trace or token of the mighty pother we have had the night before, but the fish are sulky, and a pea-fowl screams from a farm-yard, and swallows hawk low, and before noon there is again an ominous copper-cloud over Cliefden heights, and we have to abandon our angling intentions until another thunder tempest works itself out. That evening we once more besieged the monster trout. We approached him with every sort of engine by which a trout might be induced to leave the water. Our success was not in proportion to our deserts, but you do not go to Hookham merely to fish. Why, there are hundreds of curious matters to be studied in these riparian Edens of the Thames. What will please you most is the general courtesy of the local folk. They are not nearly so spoiled as one might suppose. They are not over obtrusive for backsheesh, and they are sincerely rejoiced when you have something to show for a morning or an evening in a punt. And the Gog and Magog is a comfortable quarter to put up at. It receives not the noisy Beanfeast into its admirably ordered and unpretentious rooms; it gives the cold shoulder to loud obstreperous customers, and a warm welcome, not charged for in a moderate bill, to such placid, equable men as the Master and his humble, honest apprentice.

WHAT time the eel makes of moonless nights for the sea, when the gale of the equinox blow and landladies at the coast feel that their harvest is over, when Parliament is in the provinces and the leaves fall from the trees, the swallows prepare to bid us farewell, for, as the worn German song says, "They dare not stay, they dare not stay, they must away." Some, indeed, like those eager tourists who will not wait for the close of the London season, start off even as early as August. But the martins remain with us much later, and seem unwilling to depart. For a few weeks before the great migration they may be seen congregating about certain spots in our most beautiful landscapes. Round the spire of the grey church or the skirts of the village they swarm in the autumn noon, chasing each other in frolic, now lagging for a second on the wing close to the grass-covered graves, and then with a sudden whisk breasting the dial of the clock beneath the tall belfry. From this you may almost be sure that the birds are not bent so much on hawking for food as expressing their pleasure in the consciousness of life and sunshine. And that low, tremulous twittering that catches your ear from time to time, is it not wonderfully expressive of a joy too full for louder utterance? "Garrula hirundo," writes Virgil, and there are occasions when the black-plumed swift deserves the epithet, but the smaller bird only murmurs, or inwardly pipes a small fluttering note, as he swoops and gyrates through the air. By the pond in the meadow behold them performing a sort of endless ring-dance, sometimes appearing to rest for a second on the water, or sportively following each other—one, two—across the back of the cow which is being slowly driven through the pasture. On the larger meres, in chill October, when the reeds are already stripping, and the lilies have long lost all their lustre, our hirundines are training for their long long voyages. From dawn to sunset they seem to be trying both pace and endurance, and be it known that the swallow is accredited with being able to do not less than 150 miles an hour under ordinary conditions of weather. The birds, however, as a rule, do not like remote or unfrequented haunts. The are attached to the things of human kind, to the cottage and the barn roof, to the common where gipsies squat and geese roam in gangs. They course down the street of the hamlet, and are in constant possession of the exterior of the town-wall, or will perch for an instant with a triumphant impertinence on the very nose of the parish pump. They must be aware by the shortening light, and the warning chills of the frost that powders the grass, and the mortality among the game by which they sustain existence, that they must full soon look for summer in the south. For them the earth must be glad, else they die.

> *Swallow, my sister, O Sister swallow,*
> *How can thine heart be full of the spring?*
> *A thousand summers are over and dead.*
> *What has thou found in the spring to follow?*
> *What has thou found in thine heart to sing?*
> *What wilt thou do when the summer is shed?*

Our Indian summer—what little we have of it—tempts them to postpone the hour of starting, and besides they would really seem to have business to transact in connection with their journey. For it is only then that they gather in hosts. In June and July congresses by the aits of the Thames, and conclaves with jackdaws in cathedral parishes, may be witnessed. But later the swallows have to select guides or managers for their expeditions, and may have to

deliberate as to the quarter of the globe they will fly
to. They hold mass-meetings round the disfigured and
mutilated heath of Hampstead. Every swallow in
London appears to be in attendance on the occasion.
Knots of birds gather at a pool and then make off for
a patch of dusty furze as if to dodge a wintry wind
which whistled across the ill-used wold whenever the
clouds marched past the face of the sun. But no
sooner did the breeze faint off than our swallows resumed business.

The curious belief which Gilbert White seemed to
share that many of the swallows hybernate, has been
now as completely exploded as that the barnacle goose
is a development of the barnacle shellfish. And we
may rejoice at the destruction of the legend. It is not
so pleasant or so fanciful to think that the swallow
sneaks into a hole or a cornice like the ugly bat or
the unsociable bear. There is no suggestion of
torpidity about the swallow. The few loiterers that
are caught in the snow suffer for it in a sleep that
knows no waking. But where do the swallows go when
they leave us? This question has never been ex-
haustively answered. In some charming verses composed by Theo. Gautier in the *Moniteur*, and which
were afterwards cleverly decanted into English by
Father Prout, we have a pretty picture of what the
poet calls a " synagogue " of the birds, assembled for
the purpose of exchanging views as to the several
places they respectively intended to visit.

> Elles, s'assemblant par centaines,
>   Se concertent pour le départ.
> L'une dit, Oh que dans Athènes
>   Il fait bon sur le vieux rempart.
> Tous les aps j'y vais et je niche
>   Aux métopes du Parthenon ;
> Mon nid bouche dans la corniche,
>   Le trou d'un boulet de canon.

Another swallow tells his friends that he has a snug

retreat over a coffee-shop at Smyrna ; a third is a sort
of hermit, who affects a residence among the ruins of
Palmyra and Baalbec ; while a fourth is resolved to
make for the third cataract of the Nile, where there is
a convenient crevice for him in the neck of an ancient
statue. The swallows are, we believe, actually to be
seen in these quarters, and the flight has been frequently
met with on its passage across the sea. The birds are
said usually to fly low on the journey, but they would
be altogether influenced as to this by the wind. They
invariably make for the narrowest straits from point to
point, but yet they must be sometimes so long upon
the wing that, taking into account that there can be
little, if any, insect food over the salt ocean, they must
suffer from hunger and thirst ; for the swallow is a
thirsty soul and is a most valiant trencherman at
minute flies. However, the journey is accomplished
somehow, and we are swallowless until the new year is
born and advanced. White insists that the swifts are
absent quite as early as August, and he appears to have
thought that the most imposing emigrations take place
during that month. He must here have generalized
far too widely from the special observations he took at
Selborne. The larger swallows, by the way, bear a bad
name in Ireland. They are supposed to have each a
single drop of the devil's blood in their veins, and it is
thought ill for the dead when a swifts crosses over the
hearse. Oddly enough, this superstition does not apply
to the smaller birds. The flesh of the swift is supposed
to be poison. In England we have not heard that any
such notions obtain. The swallow ought, indeed, to
be a favourite with every one. He never touches our
fruit, no matter how ripe and luscious the peaches and
the cherries look ; and what more welcome guest to our
shores than that daring pioneer of the proverb ? It is
more than probable that the birds instinctively avoid
putting to sea before a storm. They ought to be experienced meteorologists. They have to regulate their

search for food by the conditions of temperature and atmosphere; indeed, they serve the rustic for a barometer. We may be assured also that they wait to have the wind in their sails, and that it is for this purpose they remain in large flocks day after day near the coast, like Channel passengers who stick at Dover or Folkestone until there is a prospect of their being able to escape the horrors of a rough passage.

WE are dropping up, as the phrase goes here, with the first turn of the tide in a lighter. The lighter is a slow unwieldy craft, having a great lug-sail patched and darned with the most curious variety of rags. We carry oars besides, huge as those at which the companions of Ulysses toiled, and as the wind has died off the harbour we find the unwieldy sculls, which groan in the rowlocks, of service to us on our voyage. The little town of Youghal, with its light-house on the seaward point, and its poor-house on the hill, is still near enough for us to see the sun flashing on the golden cock surmounting the Town Hall, and to hear over the water the sound of a passing bell from a turret from which the same voice has spoken for a hundred years. But soon the current of the tide gains in strength. We sweep along careful to avoid the shoals, Palinurus (*alias* Andy Kilty) care-fully threading his way through the channel. The scene is here calm and tame enough. It is not until we approach the wooden bridge that the beauties of the Blackwater open upon us. And then you enter, as it were, between the portals of the fir-clad hills, and see in the far distance the purple backs of brown moors upon the sky-line, shaped like gigantic whales stranded on a beach. Our appearance is a signal for a flight into the air of a myriad sea-larks, and for the slow, sullen departure of a leash of herons. The latter hunchbacked anglers make directly for the wigwams or settlements they have had from time immemorial in the dark grove opposite the Abbey of Rhincrew, and there they sit perched in state, motionless and ghostly, until the lighter has passed by their native hunting-grounds. Rhincrew Abbey—Rhincroix it is sometimes called—may be associated with Brian de Bois Guilbert ; it was, at least, a retreat and fortress of the Templars. Now, the few parts of it standing are only bound together by the ivy, and the cross-legged effigies of the knights whose swords are rust, show where they were smashed and scattered by the soldiers of Cromwell. By Rhincrew, the little river Toora (good for trout) joins the Blackwater, and glancing up its course you can sight the Castle of Kilnatoora, built by the Earl of Cork, in the reign of Elizabeth, to secure her Majesty's rights and privileges in that remote part of her dominions. The lands round here once belonged to that most wonderful and picturesque of adventurers, the poet, gallant, seeker for the Eldorado, and inventor of tobacco, who, when he came to die and happened not to lay his face to the east according to execution etiquette, remarked to the doomster, " It was no great matter which way a man's head stood so his heart lay right." Sir Walter Raleigh was the owner of thousands of acres of fair ground in the neighbourhood, and it is not too fanciful to conjecture that many of his unfortunate schemes and projects were contemplated and shaped in the woods and wastes of this picturesque locality. It is little changed now from the days when he knew it. There, for instance is a coracle of as primitive construction as anything in a museum devoted to Indian canoes and Indian paddles. Yet the savage who sends it along so easily and dexterously is a very friendly native, and approaching our coal-laden galleon he begs a light for his pipe and inquires of the news from the town. The conversation then continues in Irish, Palinurus, the helmsman, maintaining it with our visitor, who shortly afterwards darts off with the swift and jerky motion of a water-beetle on a lagoon. Our craft nears the quay of Temple Michael, where we remain to discharge a few donkey-loads of cargo, and an

opportunity is given for those who are curious to land
and see the remains of the Convent of Molana, where
a stone statue of St. Molanfide still survives, time,
however, *edax rerum*, having played the deuce with
his worship's nose, mottled his mediæval jaws, and
crippled him in one respect to such a degree that he
has been referred to as rather an off-handed style of gentleman by a picnic joker from Cork.   Alas ! that
where St. Molanfide trod should ever be profaned by
picnicing footsteps.   In the same hallowed region a
real hermit formerly hung out.   The family now in
possession of the property, having a taste for anti-
quities and the fitness of things, started a hermit on a
small salary on the ground, centuries after the real
ascetic had resigned the business and died.   The
venerable recluse wore a beard and a gaberdine, and
was everything, in short, that a hermit ought to be to
all appearances.   He lost his situation, however, for
having been discovered conducting himself rather
Decameronically when he was supposed to be engaged
in spiritual meditations, and as he had no apprentice,
and hermits have gone out with Banshees and foster-
brothers as accompaniments to Irish families, the cell
of Molanfide remains at present probably vacant,
and with no applicants for the situation.   Embarking
again in our lumbering lighter we open the house, and
grounds, and hills of Ballynatray.   The mansion
itself is of the commonplace builder's order of architecture, but neither contracter nor landscape gardener
has had anything to do with the superb slope of those
glorious russet downs, brown from the golden fern,
dotted with hundreds of deer, sprinkled, too, with
green clumps of sheltering trees.   And, hark ! a key-
bugle sounds from a boat near the opposite bank to
summon the echoes to amuse some company on board
her. The last note of the chord has not died into silence
when there succeeds a fairy repetition of it, thin, and sad,
and ineffably sweet and powerful to draw your very

heart and soul, as it were. " Aise wid the bow, Jack, or we'll be down on the weir." What is the use of shaking your fist at the captain for thus rudely breaking the spell laid upon you by an old copper cornet and a couple of vulgar hills? And yet you must look again, and yet again at this lovely scene. That Castle of Strancally reflected in the river, broken bastion and battlement, appears almost to have been placed where it is for effect ; but see beyond it the purple peaks of Knockmealdown. In that remote and abandoned desert lies the Abbey of Melleraye, where the brethren of La Trappe speak no word but in praise of the Lord, and address him only in music warranted lugubrious. Yet you will say it is something for these anchorites to be able to gaze on this glorious panorama from their lofty vantage-ground ; but to them æsthetic emotion is a forbidden indulgence. They have absolutely walled out the view. Strancally was a stronghold of the Desmonds. All sorts of stories and legends are told of the castle. It is built over the deepest part of the Blackwater. It was formerly tenanted by barons as wild as any who ever pillaged the Rhine land and made (apparently superfluous) mortgages of their salvation to the Prince of Darkness. People have dreamed like Whang the Miller and searched here for crocks of gold ; but always some of the traditional interruptions occurred to interfere with the success of the enterprise. It is certain, beyond all cavil or doubt, that a dreadful ogre of a Desmond resided in the castle. The proof that he invariably murdered whoever dined with him is to be perceived in the Murdering Hole which is now quite visible to the naked eye—the hole, that is. When Baron Strancally intended to do for his guest, he had him stuck first between the soup and fish, and then having cleared him out of everything the poor body was cast down a trap which opened into the river. Of how many castles in Ireland, in Scotland, in Germany, is not this pretty little story, illustrative of some of the manners and customs of our ancestors, related? And the testimony invariably adduced for its correctness is the Hole. An interval is now devoted to a luncheon of hot potatoes, whose jackets you peel off yourself. They are toothsome and grateful, washed down with a pint of goat's milk, which happens to be the tipple with which we are provided, for our captain is of a sober turn, and his crew follow his good example. And not far from this we drop anchor for the night. The evening draws on a little cold and misty, but the deck is to be preferred to the saloon of the lighter, where, to use the phrase of our first and only mate, Tom Sullivan, "there's only room for you to stand, sir, on your hands and feet," a declaration which might not have been very intelligible but from the fact of seeing Mr. Sullivan issuing from this cabinet after the fashion in which the serpent was condemned to go upon the earth. By the calendar we had counted on a moon and on so many sights of strange loveliness to be revealed by her to us during the summer night. But the planet only shows in a ragged brazen patch in the sky ; then the rain falls heavily, and the wind soughs and moans as the river lashes white into short tossing waves. A troop of widgeon whistle unseen overhead, and the snoring of Palinurus and his companions soon brings the passenger, not to the ivory gates of dreams, but to that pleasanter No-man's-land, where phantoms do not trouble, and where the weary rest without confronting spectres of memory, of love, of hate, of books, of indigestion, of conscience, or a disordered cerebration.

The tide must be taken an hour before the dawn, and so our slumbers are short enough when we are again called into existence away from the brother of death, to bear a hand in hoisting the big patched sail. But by this the wind has died down, and the stars have come out for a short reign of it, already threatened by a thin streak of red fire in the east.. And as we surge heavily up the stream, the light, with stealthy foot, moves on apace. The orb of the sun wheels up at last, and the noble woods and heights of Dromana, under which we are now slowly passing, thrill with the quickening piping of the awakened birds, while the window-panes of the grey castle itself are turned into flaming rubies and garnets. Early as it is, the Irish milkmaid is abroad, for her chant comes to you distinctly in its wild Celtic cadences. And a poacher is before us in a skiff, who has an engine for securing salmon that you may be assured has never paid licence. Where the morning has broken at this moment in its ample golden effulgence across a high glen or gully, near the top of yonder sierra range, lies buried the eccentric sportsman with his dog, who put such perfect faith in the paradise of the Mohican. And by Dromana is Affane, which you should know is the spot where the cherry was first grown in the British Islands. It was said to have been brought there by Sir Walter, from the Canaries. And it was at Affane also that the famous battle was fought between the Earls of Ormond and Desmond; after which occurred that scene so finely translated into a picture by Maclise. When the victors were bearing the Desmond from the field a prisoner on their shoulders, his enemy of Ormond, the Butler, rode up, and taunted the fallen hero with the inquiry, "Where is now the great Earl of Desmond?" "Where!" was the fierce answer as the wounded warrior, in a last effort, raised himself on his elbow, "where he ought to be, with his foot on the necks of the Butlers." In modern war this fine passage of conversation would be impossible. But Affane has another claim to special notice. Valentine Greatrakes, mesmerist, charlatan, healer by touch, was born in the parish. His memoirs, we believe, in MS., are to this day in the possession of one of his descendants in the neighbourhood. And now, ob-

serve these islands, the haunts of thousands of teal
and duck, the teal spinning from the reeds with
the swift motion of a Japanese top taking wing.
Many of the heavy duck are not yet properly
heavy duck, though they are stronger and bigger
than flappers. On the left bank stretches the ancient deer-park of the Desmonds. It serves for a capital
racecourse at present for the Lismore folk. That little
town with a little church and little houses at the foot
of a little hill is Cappoquin (Capa-chuinn). The
stream bears you right up to it, and there at a little
wharf you disembark without a living person being on
the spot, from which it would seem that early rising is
not regarded as a virtue or a necessity in the
placid burgh. You can, however, secure a comfortable breakfast at Cappoquin, and after seeing
the door riddled with bullets, behind which the
police hid themselves from the boys in '48—Mr.
Stephens, by the way, was reported to have been concerned in the engagement—you can hire an outside
car and voyage close again to the river to Lismore.
The drive is superb at any and at every season of the
year. Lismore cannot be hurried through ; it ought
not at least. The great sweep of the river should be
seen from one of the many jackdaw towers of the
Duke of Devonshire's palace, and the stranger should
procure permission, if possible, to cast his angle on the
waters. After such a voyage a well-meaning tourist
might not blame an Irishman over much for having a
love deep in his heart for a country so beautiful, so
full of memories, quaint, olden, and proud, for at Lismore itself was once a University more renowned than
Salamanca. There seems, however mythical may be
the history of the country when it deals with legends
of former glory and importance, some indefinable expression of melancholy and of tearful having-seen-
better-days sort of aspect in the very landscape, which
causes a queer sympathetic response in the half-abashed

fancy of a spectator. In England you do not observe this. We have the stately homes, the shavenlawns, the trimmed fields, and all the rest of it. In Ireland the stately homes are not many, and whenever they are very stately they are unfurnished or uninhabited ; but nature, and time, and decay have done everything for the hunter in search of the picturesque there. It is diffi-cult after even so short an enterprise as that in which we have ventured on the Blackwater, not to experience a dumb kind of regret that in the Irish scenery, as in the Irish nature, there are notes of pathetic depth, hues of romantic colour, which defy and escape recog-nition or welcome until we meet with the spirit of Irish humour and sensibility and the interpretation of Irish scenery in the Irish music.

PART III

ESSAYS ON SPORT.

REPORTS of accidents in the hunting field and with the gun, are sometimes commented upon as furnishing arguments against following the hounds and shooting. To any one at all acquainted with the great extent and popularity of the sporting world, with the enormous active patronage and support it receives from the middle and upper classes of the country, the wonder and speculation is not that there are so many unfortunate accidents connected with it, but that there are so few. When we take into account, for example, the number of meets arranged for each week over the three kingdoms, and endeavour to obtain some estimate of the average attendances at these pleasant gatherings, we shall then be able to have an approximate notion of the very small amount of risk which the pursuit of the recreation of hunting involves. In point of fact, it would scarce be too much to say that the greatest peril to life and limb through which a gentleman in pink passes through the course of the day occurs when he sits perhaps in his overcoat in a special train, to be in time for the meet. Granting that modern sheep-nets, wire fences, and the hidden iron thread in the hedge have added difficulties and hazards to the chase, there is some reason to believe that the absolute dangers incidental to street-crossing in the City are more real and frequent than those which beset or attend the close follower of the hounds. The death rate from street-crossing is so excessive that if anything in proportion to it could be asserted in connection with hunting, we should have indignant orators and essayists denouncing what they would term the destructive fool-hardiness of the sporting community. Again, as we have hinted, we would suggest that hunting is safer than railway travelling, and that the passengers by an unconsidered excursion, if they only knew it, are often in far greater danger of being killed or crippled than the troops of jovial cavalry who dash along the trail of the hare, the fox, or the deer. On the other hand, it must be said that in hunting, as in everything else, a moderate amount of caution, prudence, and circumspection is protective and serviceable. These qualities are of use in lessening even the danger of accidents in hunting. The man who, not knowing a country, goes with an ugly rush at a big fence, without a thought of a chalk pit at the other side of it, meets with a fate which can surprise no one except himself. Ladies, again, who will mount horses not properly broken for them—who will attempt more than they can perform—will continue to furnish morals and illustrations of the advantages of discretion over valour. Then accidents pure and simple, despite every reasononable precaution, will occur. To say that they supply reasons for the abolition of hunting would be more irrational than to insist that trial by jury should be abolished because a juryman expired in the box during the hearing of a cause, or that the Fire Brigade should be disbanded because one of its members was burned in a patent escape at the combustion of a house. These particulars and exceptional instances point to no general conclusions. And while we steadily deprecate the principles of the mere flash and plunging school of hunting, we are by no means inspired to advocate gap-seeking and crooked ways because of the folly of a few, or the inevitable mishaps which come to others. It is singular enough, however, that the boldest and most careless often escape with far greater impunity than the safe and cautious men. There are some good fellows, by no means shirkers or cowards, who always endeavour,

within fair bounds, to keep an unsoiled jacket or an
unfractured collar bone, and who, nevertheless, possess
a kind of alacrity in falling, independent frequently of
the horses on which they are mounted. They are
simply unlucky ; there is no other word for it.   If there
is only one wire fence in a parish, they will find it out
and come to grief over it, while their wilder or less-
guarded comrades are flying safely across everything
before them.   Then, again, there are physical temperaments unsuited for hunting ; and when we cast up
the probabilities of such temperaments being forced,
or, worse, artificially stimulated, to the pursuit, we find
it difficult to understand how many more serious accidents do not occur.   And again, the present vice of
hunting is not on the side of reckless riding.   There
will, of course, always be in the field a few excitable
and anxious youngsters, but they soon wear off their
excessive and rather worrying enthusiasm.   There
will also be—and we hope the race will never deteriorate — the thoroughly accomplished and bold
straightgoers, who illustrate the due amount of
courage and dexterity, pluck, and skill, requisite to
compose a complete modern sportsman.   To tell
them that they should give up hunting, or carry it on
with hounds and foxes upon three legs, because the
sensibilities of old women of both sexes are hurt
when reading about an accident in the papers, is not
exactly an office for which we should entertain the
least inclination or respect.

   With reference to gun accidents, we have only to
carry over to the sport of shooting many of the fore-
going remarks.   The talk about the intrinsic danger of
firearms is as obsolete as the fear entertained of the
venomous and aggressive qualities of the black beetle.
There was a time when it was almost the proper thing
to do for a lady to shriek at the sight of a gun, as she
would at the awful apparition of a cockroach ; but many
circumstances have tended to render both super-

stitions unfashionable. Guns are now seen everywhere, and ladies are not unwilling to attend Volunteer reviews, where villainous saltpetre is extensively burned, or even to drive to the side of coverts, when the battue is in full swing. It is scarcely necessary to dwell on the decrease also of accidents since the introduction of the breech-loader. With it we have done away with those dreadful catastrophes arising from not drawing the charge to save trouble, from looking into one barrel while loading another, from overcharging, from the gun bursting through shifting of a wad, from an explosion of the powderhorn, and all the rest of it. In fact, the breechloader almost at once, as far as itself is concerned, secures the holder from an accident if he be only moderately vigilant. He is always at the right end of it, and, with respect to other people, there is no temptation for him to leave it about in such a condition as that it could do anyone harm. But yet caution is necessary, even with the breech-loader. It is virtually impossible for a sportsman to be always by himself. He must shoot in company occasionally. Now there are many sportsmen, not in the least nervous or crotchety, who lay down on this score a distinct and definite rule for their own course and guidance, which no amount of persuasion would induce them to infringe. They will only shoot with a certain number of guns, a fixed quantity, under any circumstances. All we can say here is that their scruples or precautions, if not universally imitated, ought to be generally respected. There is, if anything, too much of the practice of having large and scratch parties, thrown together by a kind but thoughtless host, for the purpose of thinning the hares, rabbits, and pheasants. It speaks admirably indeed for the average caution exercised that we read or hear of so few accidents ; but that circumstance does not altogether justify the fashion. It is not necessary to dwell upon the dangers incurred by everything—including brown gaiters—except game, by the addition of an impostor to a shooting party. But, unfortunate for a life insurance company as the presence of a haphazard trigger-puller may be, he is not so perilous a companion as a type of sportsman who, when once he has put up his gun at a bird, must fire, no matter what object intervenes between him and his quarry, though the object be the shooting cap, with the head in it, of his best friend. Now a person of this disposition is incurable, and, knowing his own weakness, should confess it in time. The very nervous sportsman is also a source of annoyance and of danger to all around him. He breaks a line even, to put himself in an imaginary safe place ; he stoops so as not to be clearly seen and in this way is most frequently peppered.

Nothing, not even, straight shooting, is so desirable for a sportsman to learn as how to carry his gun with safety to others and to himself. If the habit is acquired in early life, it is never lost, but gets more perfect by usage and custom. The precautions necessary in going over a hedge, jumping a ditch, handing your weapon for your companions to hold, and during the other various and necessary incidents of an excursion, are observed by the old stager with a sort of instinctive aptitude and correctness. It might also be well borne in mind that the very worst gun ever fitted to a stock shoots wonderfully far when pointed in the direction of a beater or an associate. The distance shot will travel over a stubble to do mischief, and give a startled rustic a slight excuse at least for putting in a claim for " damages," has often caused both mortification and surprise to fowlers. We have no doubt that one of the advantages of shooting as a pastime lies in the very fact of its developing in those attached to it habits of self-control and discipline. As for the idiots who play practical jokes with guns, who pre-

sent them at timid people, and pull triggers in kitchens,
we do not imagine that our words would reach them.
Jokes of the gun-snapping description are now confined to the stable boys or servants who happen to
come across firearms in the household ; but there
is a serious responsibility also entailed upon those
who leave them loaded upon racks, behind clocks,
or at chimney corners. Whatever slight element of
danger may impart a risk to hunting, in shooting
this element is not required, and, in England, at least,
out of place altogether. It is by no means pleasant
to accompany into turnips a gentleman whose ideas
are so far different that he thinks nothing of killing his
partridge by aiming an inch or two to the side of your
ear : what is sport to him may be by no means sport
to you.

Those who assail sport from this standpoint might
advantageously give us the benefit of their bene-
volent impulses in other directions. If we followed
their advice, we should sink or burn our yachts,
though the losses in the pleasure fleet are not even
proportionately comparable to the losses in rotten
and richly-insured colliers. Cricket would have been
long ago condemned—played in suits of armour, if
our tender-hearted advisers had their will, or, as was
suggested in France, with a policeman or gendarme
officially present whenever a round-hand bowler
assailed the wickets. With reference to the hunting
accidents, we have no long-faced moral whatever to
draw. Accidents in the hunting-field are, and will be,
inevitable, and the element of danger—comparatively
slight danger, but still danger, to be overcome by the
exercise of courage, in which exercise a great part of
the pleasure of the sport consists—belongs, it may be
conceded, to the chase. But this nerve-bracing
development of the spirit of daring is worth the
price paid for it. We do not go so far as the enthusiast who declared that the noblest of deaths was

to die in his boots and his scarlet coat ; but there are less picturesque methods of departing this life, and many pleas might be offered in behalf of the eccentric or extravagant taste of the moderate foxhunter who expressed a partiality for mortal concussion over mortal typhus.

PEOPLE who are in the habit of holding as a faith that the pursuit of field sports implies a degradation of intellectual taste, appear altogether to forget what an influence the pastimes of England have had, from the earliest to the latest times, upon many branches of our national literature and art. Take for stance, the various descriptions of hunting and of the excitement of the chase from one division of letters, and the gap will be wide enough to show the loss that would have been sustained if that motive for literary composition had never existed. At the present day a whole school of novelists have sprung up who could easier dispense with hero and heroine than they could with horses and hounds. Indeed, in many cases the horse is the chief character; upon his performances the interest of the story depends, and the pivot upon which the narrative revolves is found to be in the neighbourhood of the racing stable. In other works of a related order, we have breathless records of celebrated runs and famous jumps, with episodes upon bullfinches, and comic interludes upon the mishaps of the parson in the pigskin. Laborious and often clever sketches of the various constituents of the meet, from the hound who is never at fault to the M.F.H. who never stops at anything, are becoming more and more popular at the circulating library every day. And the standard book-world is filled with portraits, which would never have been framed and preserved but for our English custom of hunting. The gallery of fanciful sporting celebrities includes representations of character in connection with the chase as wide apart as those expressed in the pictures of Squire Western and Diana Vernon. The poets are also indebted a thousand times to the horn of the huntsman for materials for verse. The muse of Somerville may be said to have worn hunting breeches, but the laureates of the chase generally may be described as a legion of enthusiasts whose lucubrations smell perhaps stronger of the stable than of the classic lamp. The Quorn, the Pytchley, and the Galway Blazers have had their several bards, who have not failed at least in stout efforts to do emphatic justice to their respective themes. The dramatists also are indebted to the hunting and the racing field for some of the most telling and picturesque devices of their craft. Not long since we had Derbies on the stage, with the exciting spectacle of a horse of tin at the mimic Tattenham Corner, developing, at the finish into a veritable cab hack, about whose real bones there could be no mistake. We have had, too, a stag-hunting scene, with deer and hounds, on the stage of old Drury. The artist also has been in the kennel. The opera itself is indebted again to the chase for brilliant choruses and orchestration, although, of course, the musical impulses excited in Weber have not much in common with the appreciation of dog music felt in the Shires by a connoisseur in the tenors and counter-tenors who are chorussing after the fox.

If we turn to shooting, we shall discover that it has a literature and an art of its own of a most extensive and comprehensive area. No man writes the history of a bag now a days without surrounding almost every bird in it with a certain æsthetic interest. And this is as it should be. It is our contention that the thorough sportsman is never either cruel or stupid. He is observant of nature from habit, and he is educated into a sensibility for her beauties by the force of experience and perhaps of solitariness. To be sure, there are honest fellows, handy enough in the stubble or on the moor, who see nothing in a sunset but a sign to beat home, and who regard a landscape simply for its value as a nursery and retreat for black cock —who view the glories of a pheasant's plumage or the splendours of an autumn wood with the same amount of poetic senti-ment which Peter Bell bestowed on the primrose, or the practical huntsman expressed about violets ; but, on the other hand, there are numbers of sportsmen who, without going into demonstrative raptures, are keenly vibrative—if we may be permitted the phrase —to the Wordsworthian reflex action of the picturesque and the grand in scenery. Our sporting travellers from abroad furnish us with the most trustworthy and striking delineations of the tropical forest, of the Indian jungle, of the arctic snow field. Art is indebted to them and to our resident sportsmen for numberless hints and situations. Many of the most successful of the Landseer paintings derive their effect almost en-tirely from their associations with the pastime of shooting. We might name half a dozen other gentle-men whose works depend to a large extent, for the public attention given to them, upon the business of waiting for wildfowl or stalking deer. And then, if we revert to books—to omit altogether the technical treatises, from the "Gentleman's Recreation" of Nicholas Cox to Stonehenge—we could enumerate the incidental comical, serious, and lyrical allu-sions to the gun and the pointer by the score ; and, with a single glance towards the musical world, as in the case of hunting, we can at least hit upon one of the prettiest songs in the quaint English operetta of " Love in a Village," which is devoted to toasting the merit of the pursuit to which we are re-ferring. But the angler, perhaps, can bear off the palm of supremacy as far as the literary and artistic conse-quence or superiority of his craft is concerned. We are not going to quote the famous Waltonion discussion between Venator, Auceps, and Piscator on the point ; but no doubt the fisherman would tell us of the many brilliant effusions of those who have honoured the diversions by recounting its delights.

Every honest sport honestly pursued is good, not only for physical and moral health, but for the enlarging of an æsthetic sense wherever that æsthetic sense exists. And we have a right, as we have attempted to show, to claim for sport that its prosecution has been valuable in artistic and literary suggestions to an extent neither realised nor appreciated by those who regard every form of athleticism with distrust or dislike. The subject can only be indicated, and cannot be adequately treated within a limited compass. It might be widened, for example, fairly, so as to include the sphere of operations occupied by the Alpine Club, by those who go down to the sea in yachts, and who take to the river in boats. These pursuits have their picturesque and literary values, which have not been neglected or forgotten by Professor Tyndall, Mr. Whymper, and others. We do not claim for sport that it makes an artist or a *littérateur* of a dull man ; but if it does not, it is often, at any rate, the cause of both art and literature in others. In point of fact, physical activity in educated persons generates a temperament favourable to the developement of a talent for descriptive writing, which of course training and practice alone can render available for artistic and set literary designs. We are all well aware of the brilliant amount of fancy to be found in the dining-room after the hunt or shooting dinner, when the story of " Grouse in the Gun-room " has given the signal for each worthy to have his turn at a yarn. In many of these anecdotes we may observe evidence of a faculty for invention which would astonish a toast-and-water advocate for the right of foxes to be free from the long persecution to which they have been subjected ; but this is not exactly the kind of disposition which indicates a capacity for repeating the post-prandial flights in a fashion which will satisfactorily undergo the ordeal of publication.

And now a special word with the artists. We are not disposed to grumble at what the painters and the engravers give us, but we think it is time a protest were entered against certain classes of pictures and prints which have a kind of traditional acceptance as illustrations of various forms of sport. And, in the first place, it may be noted, that many of these productions, especially in connection with hunting, are by no means economical investments. They are not only bad, but dear. They are purchased as decorative furniture at high prices by young gentlemen who without ever having crossed a horse in the field in their lives, think it proper to hang a representation of a steeplechase or a fox's brush in their chambers. They are also, it may be, bought by those who simply take them for lack of better. At any rate, it is evident that they would not be displayed unless there were customers for them; and, to judge from the tariff affixed to their frames, they must undoubtedly be sources of large profit to their merchants. The drawing in the modern hunting print is often almost as bad as that in such an ancient work as the " History of Four-footed Beasts." The hounds appear to be constructed out of the depths of the artist's consciousness, or from an imperfect recollection of a retired beagle. The horses are impossibilities of anatomy, or a group of screws of the most arrant quality. As for the colouring of those carricatures, it is as unlike nature and as untrue to art as the tinting of penny valentines. The grass resembles the hue of badly boiled peas; the horses suggest a mixture of Thames mud and snuff. And yet this sort of thing has a hundred popular varieties in circulation at the present moment. It may be inscribed " At the Meet," " In Full Cry," " The Dogs at Fault," " Taking the Bullfinch," or what not—a pervading note of artistic ignorance distinguishes the series. Then there are the race prints with the toy

jockeys and the giraffe steeds—who is not familiar
with them ? Occasionally in an old inn you may come
across a far superior effort at pleasing the sporting
taste through the medium of pictures. The stage-
coach scenes, for example, were often very cleverly
conceived and executed. There was the cherry landscape, or the gloomy one with snow upon it, and the
breath of the team faithfully depicted upon the canvas
—the last stage, with evening creeping after the
" Highflyer," and the lights of the town twinkling in
the distance ; the departure, the arrival, the attack by
Claude Duval, the upset, the drive through the mist,
and so on. The old sporting artist went to work
with thoroughness and with evident technical study
and attention. He may not be over-accurate as a
draughtsman, but he was demonstratively acquainted
with the points of a horse, and he had a feeling implied in his peculiar branch of work. And so with
many rare old hunting pictures to be met with in
country mansions. These were done, you may be
sure, by an artist on a leisurely visit to the spot—
the good squire in his saddle for his portrait, and his
servants, guests, and companions having a fair proportion of consequence in the group. In our modern
fashion the master of the hounds has all the honours
of a picture to himself ; he is even represented of
heroic size, on a heroic weight-carrier, in a frame large
enough to contain a drop-scene. He is so obtrusive,
indeed, that when hoisted into a position near other
works, the artists bitterly complain that his coat, a
dome of fire, burns out the more delicate hues of their
pictures. Our shooting friends are, perhaps, a little
more fortunate in the mode in which their pursuit is
pictorially illustrated. Deer stalking has certainly received its due amount of attention from the gentlemen of the brush. If anything, we have had almost
too much venison served up on canvas at the Royal
Academy. The stag is, however, a tempting object for

K

a painter. His haunts, his graceful attitudes, the more or less ceremonious ordinations attending his destruction, his surprise, his hauling home, are facts and incidents especially adapted for artistic treatment. He affords opportunities for mornings on the hills, and torchlight in the castle courtyard, and romantic-looking gillies in the heather, luncheon on the brae, and all the rest of it. We shall not find fault with variations of the theme, and only trust that the cunning hand equal to them may long continue to exercise the skill for which it is everywhere famous. Then we have no doubt perhaps a dozen excellent dog painters, gentlemen who can paint the characters of dogs, and whose performances are in their way as sincere works of art as portraits by Holbein or Reynolds. There is no more stupid idea than the classification of animal painting, as an inferior kind of artistic work. We cannot here pause to reason with those who still entertain it ; but we may venture to tell them that the productions they regard as humble from an artistic point of view, require in their proper development an appreciation of humour, a comprehension of dimly expressed sensibilities, a compassionate interpretation of wants and wishes entertained by creatures who live with us, but are not of us, which imply the possession by the artist of that gift which is called genius, which should be respected as it is recognized in Landseer or in Rosa Bonheur, as in Millais or in Delaroche. Our painters of shooting pictures might yet extend the range of their subjects. Partridge shooting, snipe shooting, cock shooting, duck shooting, grouse shooting, not only admit of, but prompt, a thousand methods of interest subsidiary to the central plan. There might be more care bestowed on the subordinate associations of pictures in connection with these several recreations. Turning again to the angler's pastime, we do not find that Piscator is neglected by the artists. He in his fishing boots is tracked by them to pretty "bits" on Welsh streams; they mark him down on Scotch rivers and in Thames punts. He is, as a rule, made rather a convenience than a personality of. He is altogether a mere aid to foam on the water, lichen on the rocks, leaves on the trees. But for all that, he may be well pleased with the honour done to his craft by the artist fraternity. He has also his more special illustrators, who will paint you a fish so accurately that you can smell them—who can colour them so cunningly that as they lie on the painted bank you think they are fading as they would fade in reality. Nay, more, there is your mimetic magician who forms a solid representation of a salmon or a trout, and deceives you into thinking you might have them for dinner by removing them from the basket, into which they are flung with ingenious carelessness. If this sort of thing is not strictly art, it may be useful for student purposes; and we imagine a museum of cases filled with coloured fish statues would be a very interesting and instructive collection. To the yachting artists we need only refer shortly. Not everyone knows how much we are indebted for representations of sunsets on coasts, for pictures of curves of deep water sweeping the base of giant cliffs, for sketches of the tides in storm and calm, to artists who not only go to the sea in yachts, but who paint in pilot coats, and who occasionally find it as hard to draw as the Earl of Dorset did to write, and for the same reason. The practical observation we desire to make here is that we are of opinion that engravers would find it to their interest to cease distributing the rubbish which now caricatures sporting incidents, and to make arrangements for issuing in a moderately inexpensive form works of genuine art, typical of the same kind of sentiment which the ordinary print simply scandalises. We are quite sure that gentlemen would prefer the former, instead of the daubs that only appear to be in the right place when quartered next the pets

of the ballet or the champions of the ring. There is a
growing taste, a growing improvement in the culture as
well as in the patronage of art of every description, and
we should particularly desire to note an advancement
assert itself emphatically and distinctly in these spheres
of sporting interest to which so many of our painters are
indebted, by the discovery of an intelligent eclecticism
on the part of those who patronise illustrations of the
pastimes to which they are attached.

"MANY hares where you were shooting, Mr. Brown?" "Oh yes! I *jugged* a brace every morning before breakfast." Our readers who may have heard or perused this little anecdote will see the application of it at once to the title of our paper. It has been said that every man in his heart believes that he could write a leader for a journal or conduct an opera, although he may have failed utterly at everything else. We have in the sporting world a very extensive tribe of people who are equally convinced that they can shoot or ride, hunt or fish, without ever having proved themselves capable of executing the feats which might constitute even mediocrity. There never was a truer type of a species than Winkle. We have all met him a hundred times. He wears a coat of many pockets, he is learned in the terminology of the craft, he has a perfect armoury of muzzle-loaders and breech-loaders, and he invariably imposes on us at the start. Over a club cigar he slays hecatombs of grouse, and he always breaks his own dogs. Practically his keeper could tell another story, and, if the dogs could speak, the survivors of his kennel after a season might complain that he had not only broken but crippled them. And it is wonderful how he contrives to sustain his reputation in the teeth of discovery by a few who may have tested him. Despite the cynicism attributed to society, society is willing enough to take a pretender at his own estimate. And in such apparently trifling matters as those of sport your shooting-jacket Jeremy Diddler is commonly successful. We call him a Jeremy Diddler, for he obtains the current coin of notoriety for skill under completely false pretences. And have we not the angling blunderer, who hooks himself oftener than any fish, but who is erudite in the literature and in the mendacious possibilities of his pursuit? He has a collection of artificial insects always in his pocket. He tells you he can throw a line into a thimble in the face of a hurricane. He caps your story with an experience that simply leaves you aghast. In his heart he is aware that it is his ordinary fate to whip off his tackle by making a coach-lash at the water. Every tree on the stream he frequents, and every other bush, contains very pretty specimens of a Strand tackle-maker's invention and ability left there by him. His creel is oftener empty than handselled by a single fish; but he smothers the voice of conscience and lies boldly wherever there is nobody to contradict him.

What a surprise it is for us who have listened to the owner of a well-known racing yacht talking of navigation as glibly as the captain of a China clipper —how astonished we are to discover that on board his ship he is the bond slave and obedient passenger of his own skipper at the approach of the slightest difficulty? Instances have been reported of a gentleman exhibiting remnants of sea legs in Piccadilly— not in a white tie, but in the afternoon, as the cavalry man newly joined might display his awkwardness at missing his horse and spurs — who in the Solent becomes as a bilious Frenchman in the chops of the Channel. And the nautical braggart is very difficult to cure. Blue cloth and brass buttons affect him, so to speak, psychologically, and he feels every inch a sailor from the fact of being in yacht uniform. The impostors of the hunting field might be enumerated by the legion. Your hard and straight goer is most frequently both modest and reticent; he leaves his friends, his admirers, or his rivals to speak for him. But the Nimrod who sneaks to hounds through gates, and who never jumps a three-foot fence but with his heart in his mouth and his hand on the pommel, shall make your ears tingle with the records of his courage and audacity.

What is the remedy for the complaint? We scarcely know; and after all, except under peculiar circumstances, our impostors are a very harmless and innocent race. Their self-delusions hurt nobody. This may not be the opinion of a reader whose favourite setter Winkle has peppered, or of another whose trained hunter has had his leg smashed by the blundering of a guest who belonged to the association or body to whom we are alluding. But then our friends should be careful never to accept a vehement sporting talker at his own score. They will assuredly—we had almost written deservedly—suffer for their politeness and their indiscretion. There are few persons, indeed, who go in for sport who cannot find social vouchers for their respective capacities. Some mutual acquaintance has surely seen them shoot, hunt, or fish. To our minds it is really extraordinary what innings in conversation are won by the boasters and impostors of pastime. The circumstance may partly occur from their constant practice in speaking, and from the glibness which custom confers upon our Mendez Pintos in running off their inventions. It is a mistake to challenge their statements. Winkle was diverting when he only claimed to be a shot; but when he endeavoured to realise his conception by assuming the responsibility of a loaded gun, we feel more indignant than amused with him. Our advice to a gentleman who is confronted with a difficulty connected with verbal asseverations on his part that he is an accomplished equestrian or oarsman, when in fact a spirited horse is led up to him by an importunately good-natured host, or he is invited by ladies who have heard him discourse aquatics to row them in a punt, our suggestion would be for him to make a confession of his actual inability to ride or to pull on the spot. Such a course is decidedly preferable to one which may lead to the compulsory execution of the horse or the appearance of the ladies at a Thames inquest; and the sort of people who brag constantly would discover a wonderful interest in telling the truth of an odd time. The sensation would be new to them, and, like a plain chop occasionally to an habitual gourmet.

There are many ways of detecting the sporting impostor before absolutely witnessing his discomfiture or his destructiveness. His partiality for "shop," his passion for ostentatious accoutrements, and his deprecation of others, are all manifestations by which he may be recognised. For he always lacks generosity. He cannot abide hearing another praised. He grows green with jealousy if you have a good word for anyone. He has seen your friend shoot, and thinks nothing of his performance. He has observed him ride, and he is sure he has the hands of a stupid groom, and the nerve of a cock-robin, &c. Now in so much will the sporting impostor differ from the innocent liars. The latter, as the Yankees put it, swap fibs. They have a story turn about, and tacitly agree to believe each other to the utmost limits of credulity, and perhaps a little over the line, when the last bachelor bed pipe is smoked. But the sporting impostor is too small to be liberal in his creeds. He only believes in himself, or desires rather that others should believe solely in him. His crime, or his offence, frequently brings with it its own punishment, but also frequently inflicts certain pains and penalties on his neighbour, or his neighbour's belongings. He runs a constant risk of exposure and ridicule. People whom he has deceived are, very properly, merciless towards him on his break down. They inferentially taunt him on his mishaps; and if he ever again brags, he is stopped, perhaps unceremoniously. But he plays for high stakes, and, as we remarked before, after all, his weakness or his ambition is rather silly than hurtful. His theory of imposition at least involves a homage on his part to the sport in which he pretends to excel. It must occupy a large—proportionately large—space in his mind when he goes through so much to cheat his acquaintances out of an admiration for him in connection with it. He obeys, as metaphysical writers would say, his strongest motive—a theory that would excuse anybody for anything. But, applying it to our sporting impostors, we may be justified in conceiving that their motives for bragging without reason do not upon analysis disclose sufficient criminality for us to visit them with a more definite castigation than that of holding them in mild contempt, and entertaining for them compassion, mixed with some gratitude even, for the amusement their propensities confer upon those who can regard them as objects of social natural history.

But there is what we should term the innocent mendacity of sportsmen. The story referred to in " She Stoops to Conquer," under the name of "Grouse in the Gunroom," at which honest Diggory is told he may laugh, although he is not to smile a recognition of any other anecdote at his master's table, was probably a speculative legend of that harmless order which a certain class of sportsmen are addicted to inventing. We shall never know what the story of " Grouse in the Gunroom " really was. It will remain a mystery, like the Junius puzzle ; and yet it strikes us that the narrative, whatever it was, belonged to the region of fiction rather than of fact. One strong piece of evidence on this score lies in the circumstance that a version of the occurrence, according to the testimony of Diggory and the admission of the Squire himself, had been repeated constantly for a series of years. Whatever ingredient of truth, or outline of reality, had been originally contained in or had surrounded the anecdote, must have disappeared by a process of multiplication, addition, or extension, with which those who have studied the natural history of pet narratives of the same species must be well acquainted. Sir Walter Scott used to speak of giving a tale a cocked-hat and a walking-stick. The *raconteur* of sporting events is an almost invariable decorator of his subject, and it is pleasant custom to change the colour and the form of his theme, and his treatment of it, from time to time, until it often can only be detected as an old friend by its introduction at a particular period of the evening. There is scarcely a sportsman—especially of the old school—who has not his own " Grouse in the Gunroom " story. It is his social property, and the narration or appropriation of it by anyone else is fairly regarded as an infringement of good taste and good fellowship. And being his own—his very own—he can do what he likes with it. We have always sympathised in this connection with the gentleman who narrated an encounter with a shark, and was interrupted by an impertinent listener who wanted to know how it was he drew a clasp-knife from his pocket, when he had just said that he had jumped *in cuerpo* into the water ? " Sir," replied the shark-slayer, " if you know my story better than I do myself, perhaps you had better tell it." The reproof was dignified, and, we have no doubt, effectual. A story told across the walnuts and the wine should never be closely criticised. And still there are men who would analyse every circumstance in the narrative of " Grouse in the Gunroom," in the spirit and in the fashion of the destructive method of criticism. They hear of a wonderful water-jump, the performer does it again over a glass of Burgundy after dinner ; he may be tempted to add a foot or two, or a yard or so even, to the distance ; but the incredulous literalist is down upon him at once. The latter insists he is thoroughly acquainted with the country, &c., &c., and there is no brook of that precise width in the parish ; that that run, at which it was a pride and a joy for ever to be present, of which the papers wrote " Tally-ho " leaders, couldn't have been such great things ! for, look you, as the crow flies, it is only—and so on. We all know this kind of bore—the British sportsman's worst companion. The creature acquires a sort of pointer's nose for this kind of inconsistency. If there is a warp, a flaw, a kink, a weak thread in your spun yarn, he will detect it at once, and, with finger straight as the rudder of the dog we have compared him to when the scent is hottest, he will indicate remorselessly your blunder or your oversight. He makes it his business to count the number of grains in an ounce and a half of duck-shot ; so that, if you venture in a story to kill more widgeon than there are pellets in the charge, he is ready with a crushing arithmetical rejoinder. If you hit a brace of snipe right and left, and knock over a quail with the *other barrel*, you may escape with even the applause of the genial listeners (who are not attending to you at all, but every man waiting for his own chance), but not from the eager personage who triumphantly demonstrates that you are either the enviable possessor of a three-barrelled gun, or the dexterous operator of a feat which Munchausen might have contemplated and shrunk from.

How came first the taste for fiction into sporting anecdotes ? Izaak Walton loved the marvellous dearly. The more startling the legend, the more eagerly did the father of angling swallow it. But he seldom or never ventured on personal records or experiences of an amazing character. He was a humble believer in Du Bartas, but he was chary of lugging on shore an astonishing fish upon his own hook.

The old naturalists rather than the old anglers were prone to ascribe strange qualities, attributes, and faculties to tench or mullet. Cotton never heard a pike bark, nor

found a box of matches (nor a flint and steel) and a pipe
of tobacco in the stomach of any of these creatures. We
believe that with the use and the cultivation of the
artificial fly a superior class of fish anecdotes has been
popular amongst our brethren of the rod. Many a curious
tale of a salmon has hung upon that single horse-
hair by which a fifty-pounder has been played to bank
after a four hours' struggle for existence, during which
he rushed like a bull, walloped the water like a whale
in a flurry, and tried several other manœuvres to
escape which might test the holding power of a sub-
marine telegraph cable. Our theory is that every one
of these courageous contributions to the entertainment
of a festive angling party should be received with
gratitude. The only danger in the publication of
them in books, however, may be that our successors
who may stumble upon a few modern fish stories
in their libraries may be puzzled as to some of
the exceptional habits and dimensions of trout and
salmon in the nineteenth century. The humour
of a thing is often lost with extreme age. The
"Merrie Jests of Dick Tarleton," for instance, are
now intolerable reading. The best wine may be kept
too long. It is almost depressing for us to conjecture that in future ages the jocose exaggerations
of salmoniacal wits may be read *à sérieux*, and that
the mere diversion of angling improvisatores may be
looked upon as the genuine chronicles of careful and
conscientious experts.

Our remote ancestors had not much opportunity for
"Grouse in the Gunroom" tales, though the significance of the phrase "drawing the long bow" would
appear to suggest that as many wonderful shots with
arrows—such as that of Otto the Archer in Thackeray's
version of "Ivanhoe"—were made at fat bucks when
beards wagged over the board in the baron's hall, as are
now made in warm exchanges at rocketing pheasants or
driven grouse. Our far-removed forefathers were cer-

tainly not averse to the legendary strain or drift in connection with the noble art of Venerie. We had extraordinary accounts from them of stags that turned out angels when pursued by impious sportsmen, of demon hounds and headless horses, of Herne with the deer's horns—a myth which no commentator has yet ventured to examine in concatenation with the centaurs of the ancients, or with the taurogriffs or leogriffs depicted on the walls of Nineveh palaces. Our hunting legends, like most of our superstitions, have degenerated in tone and conception. The Ballybotherum fox, who used to read the newspaper, in order to ascertain when and where the hounds would next meet, is a sad descent from the sacred beast that appeared to St. Hubert. The beagles that devoured the witch in the shape of a cat, and that would never afterwards follow anything but mice, are but instances of the low comedy or fanciful element in the current mythology of the chase. The "Wild Huntsman" is as dead as great Pan. He lingered for a long time in Ireland as a deceased member of the Hell Fire Club, compelled for his evil deeds in the flesh to sit upon unhallowed pigskin, and ride over the dark hills and dales with his dumb Styx dogs, upon certain nights. But he has not been heard of for years. If we are now deficient, however, in the more fanciful, weird, and poetic inventions of the sporting world, there is no want of private enterprise in the direction of "possibilities" in the sphere of hunting, shooting, or fishing. We have brought whole continents within the scope of both truth and fiction, as truth and fiction respectively deal with the tiger in India, the elephant, or those monstrous fishes with the locomotive power of steam tugs which are to be hooked in foreign waters. The question of the credulity or incredulity with which travellers' tales ought to be or are received, we shall not at present enter upon. We plead here only for a generous reception for social anecdotes of the "Grouse in the Gunroom" pattern.

One institution is already telling upon these harmless excursions of the sportive fancy. The coffee and the drawing room immediately after dinner have done much to repress the honest bartering of furbished facts or innocent fiction, which took place so regularly on hunting or sporting topics when the port went round the table. But there still remains a refuge in every well-ordered country house for "Grouse in the Gunroom." The smoking den is the Royal Exchange for innocent boasting of deeds with breech-loaders, or for respective recitals of prowess in the saddle or the covert. Every man should have his turn; there exists, for the plaguing of your honest story teller, your Coleridge as well as your Colenso—the irrepressible monologuist and egotist, who, once upon his hobby, never ceases his weariful jog-trot. Perhaps, however, the very pleasantest time and season for snug confidences of the character to which we refer, is when "good-night" has been said all round, and two or three arrant meer-schaumites steal into the most comfortable bachelor bedroom allotted amongst them, and there, for an hour or so by the clock, narrate in fair proportion anecdotes of sporting adventure, until, when the last pipe has been smoked and the last story told, each man goes to his bed, and, like the Roman augurs, all will carefully avoid looking into each other's faces for fear of bursting into laughter.

THE DEVELOPMENT OF THE SPORTING INSTINCT.

IT may be said with much truth that the sportsman, like the poet, is born and not made. In one of Christopher North's flights, the author depicts a youngster angling with a crooked pin in a brook, and tells us that the child was father of the man who could afterwards conquer the stoutest salmon that ever rose to his fly. As a rule the theory so currently accepted, that the genius in the bud gives extraordinary signs of what he will do in the flower, should be regarded with considerable distrust and hesitation. Senior Wranglers and Double Firsts, and other intellectual college lights of the kind, do not invariably turn out either Lord Chancellors or Prime Ministers when they enter upon the real struggle for existence and repute; but the promise of an artistic future in his craft, conceived by Christopher North for his little fisherman to be involved in a humble but enthusiastic commencement, is seldom disappointed, if circumstances are in any way favourable to the encouragement of the inclination. And without this inclination, the most fortunate condition in the world for the production of a sportsman will fail to bring out the qualities of the genuine article. The son of the M. F H. who may be carried from his perambulator into the saddle, and who is almost as accustomed to the music of the kennel as to the song of his nurse, may display a strong distaste and incapacity for everything connected with the associations with which he is in such close and early communion. The country gentleman who presents his lad with a short-stocked gun for a Christmas-box, recollecting his own delight in a similar gift, is at once astonished and grieved to

find that the boy cares no more for it than a Red
Indian would care for a muffin-toaster. When he is
put under the gamekeeper's charge, nothing comes
of it save a listless march at the heel of the person in
velveteen, who wonders how a scion of the family
could have degenerated into perfect indifference on
the subject of game. On the other hand there is the
crack shot of the future, whose propensities begin to
manifest themselves almost as soon as he can walk.
He is the terror of every cat in the neighbourhood,
who suffers dire persecution from the exercise of his
remarkable gift for shying a stone with accuracy and
force. He buys some arrows and a lancewood bow
with his pocket money, and goes about the hedges
and ditches to declare war with those weapons of destruction upon thrushes and blackbirds. At length a
day arrives when he experiences the dear delight of
possessing, unknown to anyone, an old horse-pistol.
To supply provender for this piece of ordnance, it is
as necessary to be as self-denying as an anchorite in
the matter of sweetmeats. The ammunition is procured from the village shop, and the powder has the
bewildering attribute of refusing to go off in nine cases
out of ten, or of exploding at an unexpected moment.
The pleasure of the horse-pistol is, however, rela-
tively greater than any enjoyment subsequently derived from the most superb and finished of breech-
loaders. It is first love ; and it is surrounded with
romantic suggestions from those books of travel or
adventure which usually form the light reading of extreme youth.

Then comes that Christmas-box to which we referred
before—the tiny single gun, with its pretty-twist brown
barrel lying in a snug green-baize cradle, and nestling
against it the mottle-grained mahogany stock and all
the other accompaniments. Now there is no longer a
necessity for concealment or disguise—no feeding with
pocket money that horse-pistol, which has the appe-

tite of the daughter of the horse-leech or of the Wool-
wich Infant; powder and shot are liberally provided
from that domestic arsenal, Papa's "study"—access
to which was strictly forbidden, but an occasional sly
forage among the shelves and drawers of which revealed a ravishing wealth of gun caps and wads.
Should this gun arrive during snow time, woe to those
fearful wildfowl, the starling and the fieldfare ! As yet
we have not acquired that rural accomplishment of
" shooting flying " which Sir Roger de Coverley considered indispensable amongst the qualifications of a
country gentleman. Birds are to be stalked cautiously;
as cautiously as the African hunter watches at a tank
for a lion, so do we from behind a favouring hedge
creep upon the sooty congregation of starling, and
deal death amongst them with a remorseless pot shot.
Then ensues a contention with the cook, a general
feud with the authorities of the kitchen, who make all
sorts of objections to sending sparrows, or starling
even, in a dish to the dining-room ; although the
young sportsman is satisfied that the prejudice against
these birds as articles of food amounts to obstinate
bigotry and ignorance, while he would sooner eat the
thrush of his own shooting than a turkey stuffed with
truffles, or the liver of the fat goose as it is prepared
at Strasbourg.

To turn to another point, are there not boys born
with a good seat, and with delicate as well as firm
hands ? One brother will feel the mouth of his pony
effectually and sympathetically, neither pulling nor
fretting the animal ; the other can never understand
a horse's mouth, and, at the best, will to the end of
his career have only the grasp and the manner of a
rough-rider. And surely. though it is said that the
sight of a handsome, healthy woman upon horseback
is a spectacle worth going some distance to see, it
will be remembered that the picture of an English
boy, such as John Leech drew—with plump cheeks

L

and his clever little rat of a Shetland, with eyes sparkling with fun and excitement—allowed a dash after the dogs, or even a canter to the meet, is an object both pleasant and cheering to contemplate. And it is from these little gentlemen we get the bravest and the boldest riders in the world, the straightest goers, the most unflinching facers of everything but a sneaking and a murderous wire fence.

Another mode by which the instinct for sport is notably developed, is through the young sportsman's humble companion. There is always about a country house an idle, harmless vagabond suspected of poaching, fearing to meet the keeper's eye, although rendering valuable service whenever beaters are required. The youthful fowler soon finds this worthy useful to him, not only in carrying the bag, but in giving hints and suggestions which the regular game guardian will not condescend to offer. This fellow applauds the good shots, and is discreetly silent or loudly apologetic for the bad ones, and his services are easily and cheaply rewarded. He is full of stories and instances of what the master did here with a covey, and there with that rocketing pheasant, and over the way with a woodcock. He very soon inspires the young gentleman with a relish for nobler quarry than starling or thrush, and probably gets him to taste real sport by compassing in the most iniquitous style the maiming or the death of three partridges in a single shot—the feat being performed by firing at the birds as they are running unsuspiciously in the furrow of a field. Nothing is said of the *modus operandi* when these ill-gotten birds are produced from the bag. There is again the old coachman who gossips and encourages the young gentleman of the house to deeds of daring and courage in the saddle; or the young groom, almost a lad himself, who teaches his little master the joys of "larking" over jumps. But the angler's companion is the great dispenser of knowledge in his craft to diminutive aspirants. Every river is haunted by one or more of these fishy pundits, who will readily impart their lore and the *débris* of their fly-books for a trifling consideration to the boy who seeks their retreats. Christopher North's pin-angler might have remained a mere worm-fisher all his life, we may assume, but for his coming across one of the gentry to whom we refer. And fortunate is the angler who in his green and salad days picks up a shabby artist of the complexion we write of! He will learn to cast lightly, and not to waste his time in unprofitable places. He will be the recipient of cunning information and scraps of oral wisdom on piscatorial themes—wisdom such as no book or bookworm knows. He will be duly coached in the mysteries of the business by practical experimental teaching. And his first trout caught with a fly!—his first salmon! We shall not enter into rhapsodies on these incidents, when so many sporting writers have become not only lyrical, but almost hysterical, on the event, and perhaps excusably; the captures undoubtedly mark an era and an epoch in the career of the future operator in Norway, in Scotland, in Canada.

But, from all we have said, we would not have the reader conclude that it is impossible for a man late in life to acquire a taste and a knowledge of sport, and a facility in the branch of it he prefers. The native instinct is the first requisite; but then this may be possessed by many who, until they have arrived perhaps at middle age, have had no opportunity of developing it. A thorough good shot may be spoiled in that hard-working barrister, who sees no chance of indulging his proclivity until he can retire from his profession. Just as men have mastered languages at fifty, or learned to become doctors at the same age, a man may acquire the accomplishment of shooting or fishing, having brought the inherent disposition to the task he puts before him. Tolerable hunting men have gone to the pursuit only when they had passed the grand climacteric; but in no branch of field sports would we expect the real artist and enthusiast to arise, except under early favourable conditions of growth and cultivation. But the sportsmen made, not born, may console themselves with many reflections. If they are neither boastful nor obtrusive, they will receive a hearty welcome amongst the more gifted and fortunate followers of the several pursuits which are intended for the development of recreative faculties, promoting geniality and good fellowship alike amongst men distinguished for an almost inherited proficiency, and others who have to compensate for want of early instruction by an assiduous and intelligent devotion at maturity to the province of sporting interest to which they feel themselves most forcibly impelled.

IT is not given to every sportsman to have £6000 per annum and noble preserves, or such an account at his banker's as will enable him to gratify his tastes for open-air pursuits by winging his way to those happy hunting-grounds, both of the Old and New World. There are hundreds of honest gentlemen in England attached to gun, hound, rod, or horse, who know little of the luxuries of the chase, and who are quite unacquainted with the fashion existing amongst their wealthier brethren of taking their amusements in an imperial and extravagant style. Many of them are, in fact, altogether dependent upon kindly-disposed neighbours for a day's shooting, fishing, or coursing, and, like most people whose opportunities for the special enjoyments they feel impelled to are clipped and limited within a narrow sphere of exercise, the Lacklands experience a zest in following up an odd covey of birds once a month even, which the owner of broad acres may not be favoured with when operating in the richest and hottest corners of his preserves.

Lackland is often engaged in a profession which keeps him to work, within the shafts perhaps of a matrimonial waggon, holding a reasonable cargo of children. Yet he has the sense not to forget that the custom of annual holidays in a lump is not a judicious method of recruiting himself from the fatigues of a dry routine occupation, and so he contrives an occasional dash into the country, during which he may revive and repeat associations of sport and pastime to which an early bent has inclined him. He does not believe in that deceptive theory of unconscious athleticism maintained by people who rush for morning trains, and call their breathless, palpitating spurt a wholesome display of physical energy. He is quite assured that a day's hearty tramp through turnips, marsh, or over hill-side, is worth the most assiduous chamber practice with dumb-bells, or forced marches to an office, suggested by a kind of weak hygienic credulity. And Lackland is not necessarily either a Briggs, a Winkle, or a Tom Noddy. It is quite a vulgar error to suppose, because a man is not accustomed to the services of a gamekeeper in green cloth and gold lace from his youth up, that he must be a bad shot or an ignorant angler. Caricaturists both literary and artistic, and caricaturists neither literary nor artistic, have been constantly treating us to representations of the blunders and the mishaps of what was derisively dubbed the Cockney in the field. This creature of fancy could not distinguish a cock sparrow from a cock pheasant, and he invariably accepted a blackbird as black game. He fired at gipsy children in mistake for rabbits, and he generally blew off his nose and slaughtered his dog by placing a bursting charge in his gun at the end of the book. Whatever remote approach to truth there might once have been in comic sketches of this kind, they now differ as widely from reality as the imitations of drawing-room manners by a music-hall singing clown are distinct from the genuine habits of good society. And it was Lackland who was always set down in the illustrations as the pretentious and incapable fowler or fisherman, as the case might be. This was natural enough, but the notion was carried entirely too far. It may, and indeed it does happen, that a gentleman with only intervals of leisure to enjoy sport makes it a study and a pleasure to master every detail and every etiquette of it, so that when his period of recreation arrives he may be able to enter into it thoroughly. And Lackland may also be able to hold his own with those who are oftener in than out

of gaiters or knickerbockers. He has many a time
stopped the prepared grin on the face of a host who
suspected him of being an impostor simply because he
had no estate, by wiping the eye of the squire in an
off-hand certain fashion, causing that dignitary to surmise that springing coveys of mechanical partridges
must be established in some shooting-gallery of the
metropolis. Many country gentlemen will never
believe that an excellent trout angler may be found in
Pump Court; they assume that, because Lackland
owns no stream, he cannot fish one. But they are
disabused when they discover him exhausting his
permission at the side of the brook by extracting from
it with skill and dexterity the very choicest and
weightiest beauties that swim its waters.

And this brings us to the question of "leave," a
most important question for our friend Lackland and
his tribe. We presume at once that he is a gentleman
as well as a sportsman, and therefore no poacher.
The Lackland specimen who does not hesitate to bribe
a keeper if he can, and to pop over hedges when he
thinks it may be done with impunity, does not belong
to the class of persons to whom we have been referring.
Time there was, we admit, when this sort of thing was
not looked upon with the severity with which it is now
regarded; but it is now a downright breach of honour
and good faith to sneak into grounds without permission of the proprietor, albeit the watcher with the
cudgel has his vigilant eyes obscured by money
dropped into his palm. As a rule Lackland has not very
great difficulty in getting a day off and on in different
quarters, when he may be in a position to produce
proper introductions and credentials. There are of
course churls who preserve game even as misers
preserve gold; there are those who consider—and with
a perfect right—that, except to immediate and intimate friends or to tenants, they should not, even for a
day, accord permission to outsiders to shoot on their

properties. All this Lackland should be provided for. Whenever he contemplates asking the favour, he should be careful to make previous inquiries, not only into the manners and practices of the landowner in that connection, but into the nature of the sport he may be able to secure. For it is a fact that some owners of shooting are boors enough to feel a pleasure in refusing a request which, if granted, would not confer any deep obligation. But they are not ōf frequent occurrence in England. Here, on the whole, a very rational amount of generosity is displayed by proprietors on the subject of leave to Lackland. And generally, where a different disposition is manifested, it is the result of an unfortunate experience of impropriety and selfishness on the part of casual personages who have been allowed for a day the free run of the coverts and fields, with perhaps a few necessary restrictions. There are Lackland fowlers who are perhaps as destitute of courtesy as of property ; having got the leave they have asked for, they kill and slay as ruthlessly as though commissioned for the purpose directly by the poulterer. They are requested to spare thin coveys, and they follow up five birds until the lot is reduced to a bleeding unit. They are desired to keep from pulling at hen pheasants, and they let off only what they miss. Fellows of this pattern often make country gentlemen look on Lackland as Timon of Athens regarded his friends when he took to railing at the world. They will tell you of the man from London—excellently introduced to them —who behaved as we have just detailed ; of that other who stuffed a creel with the under-sized trout he had been warned to return to the stream ; of the third who, informed fully of the special circumstances of harriers and greyhounds being in the neighbourhood, did not hesitate to take advantage of the keeper's absence to load a hamper with hares. With a few recollections of the sort Sir Roger de Coverley himself would turn sour, and never open without impatience a letter requesting liberty to sport upon his estate.

Lackland, of course, is often invited to shoot, and very good use he mostly makes of his time. He is a very glutton to work, and surprises the *blasé* visitors who are going on their annual round of houses by the hearty and honest enthusiasm with which he enters into the pure spirit and fun of sport. What though they lodge him as they lodge unfavoured pictures in the Academy—what though the Lackland be "skyed" as to his bed-chamber, and made to convoy fiddle-backed spinsters to dinner—he nevertheless enjoys himself, by hedgerow and spinney, with an eagerness which the dandies can neither comprehend nor appreciate. He has no affairs on hand to divide his attention with the business the gamekeeper marks out for him. And the gamekeeper, who is not a very venal knave, gets to know and to like Lackland, although he is aware he cannot expect to be heavily tipped by him when the time of departure arrives. Lackland is a fair shot, and never grumbles at where he is placed ; he is civil and polite to Velveteen—who, to do him justice, is not half the mercenary he is painted. If Velveteen is not irreproachable, it is because he is the product of a vicious system, which Lackland at any rate is not responsible for encouraging to a remarkable extent. And Lackland, as he fires away right straightly and merrily, may be inspired with the agreeable poetic fallacy that his host, after all, cannot have more pleasure out of the goods Fortune has bestowed upon him than his guest has in them for the moment.

We feel that we need not say a word as to the mode of dealing with a request of the Lacklands. Besides, every case of "leave" must and will continue to be judged upon its own points and merits. The free-masonry of our craft has done much to establish good fellowship and solidarity amongst its members of every degree ; and by this the sporting Lackland

profits far more than he did in the days when a man would forfeit his life for killing the king's deer, save he happened to be an archbishop, an earl, or a baron on a journey through the royal forest. Sport has become more democratic than it was, and the true sportsman of our time is seldom chary of extending a favour to the Lacklands, unless, indeed, when his liberality has been so persistently abused as to overcome the feeling of generous consideration which we should always expect to find in an English country gentleman.

ALTHOUGH there are some men who entertain precisian views on the exclusion of ladies from the chase, it must be admitted that a well-regulated encouragement for riding to hounds in women who can enjoy the pastime, and who have been properly trained for it, is often attended with great social advantages. We are no admirers of the desperate Dianas in the pigskin. It is not given to the majority of people to witness with unalloyed pleasure the performances of the veteran female highflyer, who will take to the saddle even though her children have taken the measles, and whose horse owes nothing to her sex for consideration or temper. We must also abstain from regarding with special enthusiasm the young lady whose courage is far in excess of her discretion or of her practice, and who will unhesitatingly demand a pilot and guardian over a difficult country, when her notions of equitation are only equal to a canter in the Park or a trot by the covert-side. We know how her disasters embarrass everyone, including the particular male victim of the hour who has been selected as tug or conductor. Then, again, we must lodge an objection against the presence in the field of the lady who flirts, who is not content with availing herself of the natural opportunities for harmless and attractive coquetry offered by the situation, but who is untiring in dragging within her reach a small court of the more weak-minded gentry who are assembled round the master. Ladies of this complexion, too, are often not only (if the phrase may be excused) bones of contention themselves, but the cause of broken bones in others. They encourage fierce enterprises on the part of youths fresh to the

work.   They introduce a spirit of emulation into the
kind of run which, however interesting when depicted
in romances, is often a source of bitter reflection to
some who have been influenced by it to stop at
nothing.   There are, however, hundreds of honest-
minded, healthy, and accomplished English girls,
who, properly escorted, enjoy a day's hunting with
the most complete disregard of matrimonial purposes or designs.   They enter thoroughly into the
spirit and dash of the moment, and, while they
swing along with secure seat and nerves far more
keenly braced and fit for the exercise than half the
stirrup-cupped horsemen about them, they do not give
a single thought to the business which professional
cynics assure us is the supreme motive of every un-
wedded woman's action.   They are, in fact, in the true
sense of the poet's words, quite " fancy free" in the
condition of glowing physical temperament produced
by swift movement, by the keen air, by the sunshine,
by the music of the hounds, by the feeling of using
power in sympathy, by the many sights and adventures
of the course, and the quick succession of views.   The
vulgar error which many men fall into concerning this
subject is as unfair as it is irrational.   We have unhesitatingly indicated the class of spurious Di Vernons
who are the strategic huntresses of heirs and eligibles ;
but Tom Noddy or Sir Carnaby Jinks of the Blues
never fell into a more profound mistake than in thinking
that their figures or their fortunes were matters of
nearly as much concern to the majority of ladies who
ride to hounds, as the duration of the run, or other
specialities of the pursuit of the common fox.

   Chacun à son goût.   Some men do not like their
wives to hunt ; others enjoy nothing better than to see
Madame take her part and her share in the fun.
Other ladies, again, who before marriage were not
only tolerant of hunting, but frequenters, if not of the
hunting field, of the hunt balls, spend miserable days

while their husbands are in the saddle. They are perpetually haunted with visions of cracked skulls, stretchers, and broken limbs. In time, indeed, they get reassured, either through observing that accidents are exceptional, or perhaps from a gradual but inevitable subsiding of fervid personal anxiety. Yet some are never cured of a tendency to ominous anticipations. They suffer so intensely from them, that in extreme cases a man is perhaps bound to surrender his recreation, no matter how attached he may be to it. We say this after full consideration of the different social and even moral problems involved in the question. And for our craft, shall we not assert with truth that the genuine sportsman is gallant and self-sacrificing? The Squire Westerns have disappeared; the old rural Tosspots, who never ceased talking kennel and stable, have passed away. The new school of young, middle-aged, and more than middle-aged hunting men and shooting men, try at least to reconcile and to interest their wives in their pursuits. And, on the other hand, if there are women who cannot overcome their fears on the subject of hunting, or their anxieties on the score of shooting, how many are there who enter heartily and gleefully into their husband's recreations —who, without sacrificing an iota of true delicacy and intelligent refinement, will express and learn to feel a pleasure in the details of the field and the moor! Women of this quality are wise as well as gracious and affectionate by instinct and by culture. And their husbands, for all that attachment to dog or horse so scornfully represented in the Laureate's verses, are pretty certain to value them in such fashion that, if they chose to order the execution of the animal as a mere proof of affection, Mr. Tennyson's objects of comparison would go to the millpond or the knacker's.

Whether a man about to marry ought to tell his wife that he intends to join the Alpine Club, or spend a season or two shooting tigers after the honeymoon, is what might be termed a nice point for reflection. Ladies who would have no objection to hunting, or to their husbands' shooting even in covert with a scratch party, might very well shrink from an alliance with a gentleman who had a taste for getting backwards up the Matterhorn, shinning the ascent of Peter Botte, or potting manslayers which have the moiety of an Indian village in their systems. That, however, is a matter for the lady and not for us. We might find many records indeed, and those of recent date enough, in which ladies have boldly accompanied their husbands into the most difficult and trying regions of sport and travel. These were helpmates indeed. It might be here remarked that in these adventurous co-partnerships the sort of matrimonial separations which Dr. Johnson, in a conversation with General Paoli, anticipated would occur in the woods between husband and wife, do not happen when the experiment is practically tried: " Sir, they would have dissensions enough, though of another kind. One would choose to go a-hunting in this wood, another in that ; or perhaps one would choose to go a-hunting, when the other would choose to go a-fishing ; and so they would part."

This leads us to remark upon the fact that, even directly in the physical practice of sport, ladies have managed to become skilful with the gun and the fishing-rod as well as in the hunting-saddle. Although to take salmon requires more strength of arm than ladies can usually command, trout angling is quite within their scope, and several have grown accomplished in the mysteries of that delicate craft. We confess to a prejudice—if it is a prejudice—against ladies armed in stubble or turnip field. The gaiters have something to do with this sentiment, and the killing of the birds something more ; but no doubt we are open to a charge of squeamishness on the subject. In connection with the title of our paper, however, we are strongly inclined to believe that a young lady firing small-shot at partridges rather deters than attracts serious suitors. If ladies desire to test their accuracy of eye and aim, is there not archery, with its absence of saltpetre, its attractive costumes, its leisurely ways, its imposing, engaging attitudes, and its bloodless results? It only remains for us to say that matrons make a blunder in thinking that sport, as a rule, interferes with the matrimonial prospects of daughters. Judicious and sensible mothers, who have had good social country as well as town associations, adopt other views on the subject, and do not allow either the hunting or the shooting season to pass over without utilizing these occasions for the matrimonial prospects of their daughters, in that fair and legitimate fashion permitted and encouraged by our English manners and habits.

THE CHAMPIONS OF SPORT.

IT was told of the natives of the Balearic Islands that when young they were taught the accurate use of the sling by their parents placing a dinner on the top of a pole, which became the prize of the fortunate lad who knocked it down with his weapon· We do not train our sportsmen or our athletes by measures as severe as this, but we still endeavour, in every department of recreation and pastime, to encourage a wholesome rivalry by badges of merit and certain titular distinctions. Amongst these the name of champion is regarded as one of the greatest rewards that can be conferred for excellence. The term may be said to have become a very excellent one before it was so abominably misused. Originally it stood to signify the hired combatants who did battle for the rights and wrongs of women and others who could not defend themselves by strength of arm. Champions were employed by Charlemagne and by Otto I. in deciding the succession of the empire. Now that all our judicial fighting is done by lawyers, the office of champion in this signification has been abolished; but we have utilized the expression for many modern purposes. As long as the word was confined to its legitimate sphere of application, it brought honour and credit to those upon whom it was bestowed. There is danger, however, that its indiscriminate employment will render it of as little value as the medical diploma of an advertising quack. We have champion singers and a champion painter. The former struggle for precedence by striving to prove superior in discoursing doggerel ballads to music-hall audiences; the latter offers to cover more canvas, and to do it quicker, with oil-colours, than any other man in the world. We have ladies champions of the tight rope, and gentlemen champions of the trapeze ; we have the champion clog-dancer and the champion ballerine ; in fact, the whole motley class of show people have seized upon the phrase, and wear it as a decoration, until its real significance or value is lessened by its staring down upon us from every dead wall. And in other directions the word has suffered from what might be called the historical decay of its primitive associations. The championship of the ring—the champion belt—is a case in point. There were days when it was something to be champion of England. The name brought with it a good deal more than a mere pot-house renown or a Whitechapel notoriety. Now nobody would think of attaching it to any of the spindle-shanked or bloated rogues who cozen " battle money " out of dupes occasionally, and who, at intervals of being hawked or exhibited to fairs by a job-master of mock boxing, start a sham fight under the noses of the police, with as much stomach for real fighting as Bob Acres had in the play. Single-stick championship is also a thing of the past, although some efforts are being made to revive it by those who encourage the "assault of arms" which occasionally takes place in London. On the other hand, we have novel and legitimate claimants for the chieftainship in a hundred modern provinces of sport and athleticism. The running championships are so numerous that it would be difficult to differentiate them without having a list before us. Then there are our friends the oarsmen, both amateur and professional, in whose concern the silversmiths are busy in chasing Brobdingnagian challenge-cups, tankards fit for Magog to drink from, medallions of delicate and complimentary device, and tea-services of domestic suggestiveness. The several championships for sculling, for archery, for croquet, for jumping, for walking—who shall count them ?

It is not given to everybody to be a champion, and

M

the position, we should think, carries with it as many penalties as privileges. Once a champion, you must strive hard to keep your own. The effort must require a tension of both nerve and sinew. The dignity necessitates a compulsory temperance often as severe as that which an anchorite practised. It must be hard indeed for a man to be suddenly deposed from the proud position of first in the game—to have to surrender his medal, his bronze cross, to a daring challenger. In the case of the amateur the situation is not perhaps so trying; but to the professional it must be almost pitiable. In most instances, indeed, the champion meets with consolation for having done his best: but there is so much human nature in the people who have backed him, that they are often ready to believe the worst of the person who has lost their money. These are the disappointed individuals who will tell you that professional champions, are not to be relied upon to compete fairly with each other. We need not say that we do not subscribe to this ungenerous theory, this illiberal innuendo. As a rule, we believe our champion oarsmen are sincerely honest in dealing with the public. The exceptions are few, and are sooner or later found out and punished. In fact here, as in other affairs, honesty is not merely a virtue, it is sound policy. It may be borne in mind that the supremacy in a sport or a game by which the distinction of championship is attained necessitates a discipline of mind as well as of body which contributes to make up the respectable element in character. At first sight the notion may seem a little forced or fantastic, but we are convinced it is true in the main. The rogue or the skulker very seldom takes the lead in a sport. He is almost sure to lack the requisite steadiness and perseverance. He is only equal to spurts and spasms of energy, and, from intemperance or lack of determination, will break down at the assault of a diligent and straight competition. There are knaves in every

pursuit; and, though we admit there is no direct
connection between morality and athleticism or skill—
though we are aware that a first-rate billiard-player may
occasionally smash his cue over his wife's head, and
that a man may jump his own height after having
forged a cheque—there is still in regular conduct a
guarantee for the performance of engagements in sport
considered as a business by professionals, which invariably tends to place the well-ordered in the front of
the special division of pastime to which they are
devoted. The ex-champion has at any rate the consolation of a memory of which he can never be
deprived. There is a sort of halo round him, in his
decay even, similar to that which surrounds the honoured stipendiary of the State who has once sat upon
the Woolsack. The professional ex-champion in the
evening of his days generally seeks the retirement of his
own public-house, and every night in the week receives
a certain homage from visitors for his former prowess.
He also gets the compliment of a special obituary
upon his death, and, if his repute is unstained by scan-
dal, his name remains a toast and a sentiment amongst
the members of the craft to which he was attached.

The ingenuity of champions is a branch of our topic
of which we may say a few words. The amateurs run
the professionals so close in some things, that the former
are often compelled to almost comic exhibitions of
their art in their desire to maintain or to prove superiority. Swimming, for example, is, elementarily
speaking, no very abstruse or difficult exercise; but
when a professor of it takes to his task he will smoke
a pipe for you, perform somersaults, read the newspaper, and even appear to sing a song at the bottom of
the water. Billiards admit of the most startling
combinations and surprises, and a champion or an ex-
champion player, when exhibiting his skill, will
venture and succeed in calculations of cushion force
and elasticity which will astonish the most expert

amateur. This, however, is quite natural; it is what we see in every other social direction. Nobody is above the vanity of displaying his or her excellence, even by extravagant or eccentric demonstrations of it. When these exploits are confined within proper and sensible limits, we regard them with amusement and toleration. When the *tour de force* is either perilous or stupid, we contemplate it in a different temper. But on the whole the feats of professional champions are legitimate and appropriate enough. We should not even quarrel with the subaquatic tobacco-smoker, especially as we suspect his imitators will be a limited quantity, and that the class of persons who may become addicted to reading newspapers under water would not be a serious loss to their relatives or friends if they remained where they were when they had exhausted the contents of the journal. Champions are not responsible for the uneducated audacity of those who are not content with admiring skill, but who endeavour to realise without practice what has been the result of long study and experience. Amateurs should be always careful how to draw the line, or recognise the line that is drawn, between themselves and professionals. In some divisions of sport, however—pulling, for example, or cricket—it is often an open question as to whether the experts or the casuals are the better men ; at any rate there is sufficient doubt as to the result of a trial to justify an *experimentum crucis* in the field or on the river. The divisions between amateur and professional touching championships are yet sharp enough. We can sort them all in distinct catalogues, and the only champion, perhaps, for whom it is difficult to find a reason, either in the department of sport or of warfare, is the extraordinary personage who figures under the title at a Royal Coronation, and who keeps up since the days of Richard II. the custom of challenging anyone in the world who would dispute the right of the sovereign to the throne.

THE romantic title which we have placed over this chapter need not startle any of our readers as a threat of a dissertation to follow upon that province of sentiment which is appropriately monopolised by the poets and fictionists of our day. It may, indeed, be said that there is something disrespectful, if not rude, in using the magic little word in a sense that removes it out of the sphere of the tender affections; but we trust it may not be impossible to justify the employment of the term for the purposes for which we venture to use it. By the "little loves" of sportsmen, we mean their singular attachment to special implements, weapons, appurtenances of their various crafts. When Rawdon Crawley, of "Vanity Fair," was distributing his effects in the event of a certain contingency, it may be remembered that among the articles pathetically referred to in his bill of particulars was a pistol with which he had shot a brother officer in a duel. Similar bequests have been made by gentlemen of Irish nationality who lived in the times of the arbitrament by single combat, and a " saw handle," with as many ominous notches on the stock as a young tourist carries inscribed upon his Alp-staff, was often among the most valued heirlooms in the family of a fighting squire. " Little loves " of this complexion have gone out of fashion, and are not at present held in very high regard—being decently, let us hope, either long ago consigned to the rust of the ironmonger, or placed on the inner shelf of our private cabinet.

The form that our attachment assumes is of a much more harmless pattern. Take, for instance, first the fowler. Who is there belonging to this popular department of British sport who has not "an old gun that he swears by"? It has descended to him by the name of Westley Richards, or Joe Manton, nay of some provincial celebrity whose reputation was always a fast secret out of his own county, but an acknowledged fact within it. The proprietor of this weapon has a history of its performances, not only what it did in his hands, but in those of his father. He resists all attempts to have it "converted" or altered. At most he will permit it to be overhauled before the season opens. Although the conviction is forced upon him that, if only for the convenience of friends with whom he shoots, he must supply himself with a breech-loader and a cartridge belt, on every opportunity of private indulgence he brings his venerable friend from the case where it reposes, and returns from the stubble more satisfied than ever that his opinion of its extraordinary value is a rational estimate. He will tell you how it fits his shoulder to perfection—how it comes to it, as it were, of its own accord. Challenge him to a trial of penetration at a sheaf of brown paper, and, if you want to make him your friend for life, put as small a charge of powder into your gun as will not in the report render him suspicious of a good-natured deception. Even in the case of persons who have abandoned the errors (if any) of the muzzle-loader, and embrace those (if any) of the central-fire, you will frequently detect a lingering regard for the gun with a family pedigree. It is playing havoc with sentiment to part with it. We can conceive no more tender theme for a rhymester, with just a whiff of Pigou and Wilks, or Curtis and Harvey about his muse, than "The Old Sportsman's Address to his Unconverted Gun;" it might be rendered quite as pathetic and affecting as the Arab's celebrated farewell to his horse.

We are afraid, however, that in this practical age there is a tendency to disbelieve in relics. We do not mean that the muzzle-loader as a species of gun, so to

write, is a relic ; but we doubt whether, for instance,
it is generally regarded with that passionate little love
which our ancestors retained so long for the flint lock
of their boyhood. The battle between the flint lock
and the detonator was a battle indeed. But the triumph of the latter was so complete, that the flint lock
was relegated to the museum. There it is still occasionally inspected by the stout old boys of the craft,
with a mournful sympathy and reverence. And it is
a further illustration of the current spirit of scepticism
that with the decay of the muzzle-loader other little
loves have died out. These were trifling affairs, but
they are connected with our subject. Men had powder-
horns that they would not part with for their weight
in gold, and shot-belts of mysterious curve and quality,
associated with so much luck that, taken with a particular game-bag, the whole paraphernalia was surrounded with a fetich value. Nowadays the things and
the superstitions are alike decaying. The gun-room—
study it was often called, on the strength of a legend
that it was used for intellectual exercise or recreation
—was then far more picturesque than it is at present.
Favourite guns, favourite dog-whips, favourite boots,
pictures of favourite pointers, adorned it on all sides ;
it was, in fact, the home of so many little loves and
knick-knacks. The machine for filling your own cartridges is serviceable, no doubt, and the occupation not
uninteresting ; but there was a rough readiness about
the obsolete wad-cutting, a grimy pleasure in pumping
water through the long barrels of the muzzle-loader,
an idle satisfaction in putting a new lash to a dog-whip,
which the conditions and apparatus and customs of
modern sport have rendered it impossible to realise.

Hunting-men, too, have their "little loves," and
very odd, eccentric drifts their fancies often take. A
man will have an undying regard for an old cap in
which he has performed the most perilous croppers in
his career. It has saved him, he is convinced, from

the operation of trepanning more than once.   It is associated with a future steeplechase, with runs of un-exampled length and severity, which came off when this very old cap was new.   The hat does not last so long, and cannot on that account be so easily attached to a history, or permit of a history being attached to it.   The M.F.H. has his little loves in his horses or in his hounds.   The chase is only a means to him for developing the full capacities, faculties, and accomplishments of the kennel.   He is intensely proud of his hounds, of his stud selection of them, and perhaps comparatively indifferent to the affairs of the stable.   On the other hand, some good friend has constantly to keep him straight in the most essential point of his business while he is altogether absorbed in the mounting of himself and of his men.   It is in smaller details, however, that the sort of impulse to which we have been alluding is more markedly displayed.   The hunting-man has a passion for whips—a collection of them, of the most extraordinary variety and number. He would never forgive you for losing one, and thinks it a liberty on the part of his nearest friend to ask for one.   Or his heart is in his clothes.   He loves a scarlet coat (his own) with the love for that colour and garment evinced by the beau-famished belle of a dull provincial town.   He is as particular about his boots as Brummel was about his neckties ; and, as a wrinkle in the wrong place was considered by the latter to involve a dark failure for the day, so in a similar misfortune the badly-fitted hunting-man only half enjoys his run with the Pytchley or the Quorn.   And, as it occurred with the heroic dandies of the Crimean campaign, it often happens that the D'Orsay of the hunting-field is by no means the worst man in it ; and, once he has asserted and exhibited his " little love " for personal and fit decoration at the meet, he is ready and willing to fight and win his way to the front with the roughest and most determined sloven of the lot.

The angler, as becomes his gentle craft, has a hundred little loves. One is his trout-rod—his trout-rod of twenty or thirty years' standing. It is sure to be a spliced affair; so fine and perfect a spring could never be had in screw or plug. He can throw so many yards with it in the teeth of a gale. He never intends to part with it, although he has (and uses) a dozen more modern and convenient implements. Another angling brother has a solemn admiration for, and credulity in, flies of his own manufacture, and perhaps invention, that no argument, including numerous experimental failures, can shake. Only give him the sort of weather and water he wants, and the fish on the rise, and he will back his hook, feathered from the wing of the roc and the dodo, to do more execution than any known or acknowledged insect of angling entomology. He has baits, too, only known to himself, as hideous and eerie in device as the witch soup in " Macbeth." Or his " little love" assumes graver dimensions, and is fastened upon a quiet punt on the Thames and eight hours of unvarying good luck. His whole pastime in its most idyllic branches—idyllic as contrasted with the heroic or salmon division of it— is indeed composed of harmless fancies, inventions, and propensities—in short, of those little loves which we are discussing.

It will be seen that the whole range of these small vanities comprehends nothing either vicious or reprehensible. There is indeed something quaint, instructive, and suggestive in them, as well as the enthusiasm by which they are prompted and nourished; and they are not without their use, not only in imposing a slight check upon hurried reform, but as serving to perpetuate the principle of individuality and independence in recreation, and thereby preventing sport from becoming wearisomely orderly and symmetrical in practice.

BEFORE the flight of the tourists has commenced, there are certain signs and tokens of the season of departure manifest to a social observer, not unlike what the close watcher of the swallow finds in the habits of that interesting bird when it is about to wing its way from us to other lands. In the majority of schemes for excursions we are comparatively little interested. Whether the Kickleburys make up their minds, as usual, to do the Rhine, or more adventurous travellers are tempted into the South Seas, are matters not immediately within our province of discussion. We may only venture to remark that the difficulty of selection tends to increase annually, and a study of the wonderful books of Cook, where the facilities for reaching Jerusalem are set down and measured as definitely as the route to Edinburgh or Llandudno, furnishes at least strong evidence that a holiday-maker cannot fail to enjoy himself for want of variety in opportunities for seeing men, cities, and hotels. Besides, however, the common or ordinary tourists—we do not use the terms in an invidious or offensive sense—there are classes of persons moving about with a specific object who might be called technical uncommercial travellers. Amongst them, for instance, are the people of artistic views, who wish to join sketching parties to the Lakes, and who endeavour to communicate with each other so as to bring their intentions into realisation by a joint-stock process. Then there is the periodical clergyman going abroad who will take charge of a young gentleman during the vacation, and the lady to whom salary is no object who offers to join a family where she might be of use in Switzerland.

Next we come across the programmes of sporting enterprises. Philosophers and critics tell us that a starved imagination is often the most lively and inventive. When Moore composed his " Lalla Rookh," he is reported to have fancied its wonderful glowing pictures amongst the dullest of Derbyshire landscapes; and we know as a pyschological and physiological fact that wretches in the pangs of hunger dream visions of more distracting banquets than Francatelli could devise. In the height of the London season we are in almost an analogous mental state from the perusal of advertisements for sporting expeditions. Many persons truly attached to sport— to shooting especially—may not have the means, or even the leisure for taking a moor for three or four months. They must, through the exigencies of business, only snatch a briefer enjoyment, and in the most economical fashion, consistent with commonsense views on the matter. Hence they begin carefully to examine the possibilities of recreation within their reach. Apparently they ought not to have much trouble in suiting themselves. Vacancies for a single gun are frequent over hundreds of partridge parishes in England. Grouse shooting on a moderate scale is not perhaps so attainable, but still it is offered at very tempting prices indeed, everything considered. Samples of the bags made are quoted with fascinating emphasis, and with a candour which imparts an air of engaging sincerity to the general statement. It is admitted that the roedeer or blackgame may be found not to equal the full expectations of an enthusiastic part tenant. It is not, however, necessary for us to describe the dexterous art with which the owner of a shooting tries to make the best of what he offers in the market. He does nothing more nor less in this way than people in other departments of business who want to dispose of their goods. And the sweeping assertions that have been made as to the average roguery of the sort of announcements to which we are referring, deserve as little attention as most general charges against any class or section of respectable persons in the community. No doubt Scotch swindlers have occasionally entrapped sportsmen into a contract for a season upon moors where nothing but capital exercise was to be had for the day's work. Old stories, of which we shall never hear the end, are reproduced touching the certificated lodge with every convenience which was found without any; the river abounding with salmon which turned out to be as innocent of the fish as the Thames; the warranted dogs that were worthless, and all the rest of it. For these statements there was, and may be, a certain amount of foundation in truth. There are knaves in every calling and under every guise. But if we were to collect the testimony in favour of the other side of the question, we should have an overwhelming balance of evidence in favour of the average *bonâ fides* of sporting assurances. It has before now happened that a man has given a bad report of a moor because he could not give a good account of his own shooting. It is not so easy a matter as it looks in a comic story on this theme to cheat or bamboozle the made-up greenhorn of the facetious novel, who, in ordinary life, looks sharply enough after his rights and his wrongs through the intervention of his attorney.

There are, indeed, sporting expeditions of another order, which we can only regard with amazement in more than one sense. If, however, a party was announced to start for Ireland in order to shoot the famous elk of that country, it would be difficult to entertain much serious compassion for the individuals who would rush forward to join the enterprise. And yet most assuredly excursions quite as—well, as romantic—have not only been promoted, but floated. Here we have at work in one department the same spirit of rather abandoned commercial enterprise,

which in other affairs discovers itself in the guise
of companies for the purchase of a patent for
making short men tall. Advice would be thrown
away upon the class of persons who with their eyes
open walk into fools' traps. In the sporting world
they are not frequent. Despite accepted anecdotes
to the contrary, we maintain that our shooting
friends are prudent enough to take care of themselves, and not to put implicit faith in promises of
an improbable description in connection with their
pastime. Besides, the resources of sport, as a rule,
are under the most reputable guardianship. England, Scotland, and Ireland are not such unexplored
or unknown quarters as to make it easy for any
gang of speculators to fix upon districts on which
they could concoct an elaborate prospectus of misre-
presentations connected with shooting or fishing. And
even of Continental countries, and the world over,
we have sporting data now sufficiently accurate and
extensive to render it hard for an association organised
by Capt. Deuceace to put out a programme of sport
and adventure for the capture of pigeons—or, to use
the rough but expressive phraseology of the turf, for
the skinning of lambs. Yet perhaps we ought to add
a word of warning. The endeavour is not beyond
the courage of the modern tribe of sharp practitioners,
who are ready in a thousand fashions to plunder and
to defraud their neighbours. Nobody of discretion,
or, for that matter, of taste, would accompany a scratch
sporting expedition without making the most cautious
inquiries as to its conduct and origin. There is, of
course, the benefit of society to be had or promised
on such occasions; but society may be too dearly
purchased. For the rest, it is not so difficult to test
almost at once the true nature and character of
a proposed enterprise for shooting elephants before
breakfast and bagging your tiger before tiffin. The
reader who comes across a *carte* of sport of so ex-

tensive and alarming a quality should regard it cautiously and critically. And the writers of these singular bills of fare invariably drift from prose into romance in their very announcements—they are over-picturesque; they overshoot the mark. At the same time, it is of course possible that a sporting expedition on a grand scale may realise everything it places on its placards; on the other hand, it may not, and the duped one has no remedy. We should ourselves incline to the opinion that the most agreeable of sporting excursions would not be those of the most extensive or exaggerated dimensions. They may appear to have in the notion of them something in accordance with the enterprising temper of the age; but we do not wish to see that peculiar spirit of enterprise from which they would seem to be developed enter into the domain of sport at all. It might be a relief to us, suffering perhaps from an excessive competition for moors or stubbles, to have an annual migration of sportsmen bound for Africa or Greenland, brigaded together for campaigns against birds, beasts, and fishes. We should be content to form our sporting expeditions in England, glad as we should be to learn of the success and enjoyment of our brethren of a more adventurous turn. The sporting Cook has yet to arrive, the sporting Gaze who will bring his patrons upon game throughout Europe or America. Even when he comes, we are not sure whether we should have an unreserved welcome for him. When he is, however, called into existence, the fact will be his justification. Here also, perhaps, we may discover an excuse for sporting expeditions as they are. Longfellow says of the —— that he may be for good, by us not understood, and the number of things and of institutions to which we may bring ourselves to be reconciled with on this principle are as numerous and as various as there are vexed questions in the world.

SOCIETY should be grateful for fashionable races. The charges against the Turf that it tends to entirely demoralise its votaries should certainly have set off against them the fact that there are so many occasions of its festivities recognised, as readily as the Opera, as events to be celebrated and patronised by the world of fashion. The races at Ascot or Good- wood are not considered fairly reported unless the millinery displayed upon the occasion is described as closely as the form of the horses; and to read many of the records of the toilet in connection with the Cup Day in the newspapers would at once suggest the theory that the Book of Fashions, or *Le Follet* itself, formed quite as important an element in the studies of a special correspondent as "Ruff's Guide" or the list of famous winners. It is the same thing when we have a boat- race or a pigeon-match demonstratively illustrated in the newspapers. The garb and the conduct of the ladies on the shore, on the balcony, on board the steamer, must be set out in an airy picturesque style. In descriptions of what Mr. Disraeli has designated, with that quaint audacity for which his nicknames are remarkable, "the Tournament of Doves," it is a favourite point to mention the indifference of the female spectators to the extinction of the pigeon, and odious comparisons are even ventured upon to suggest that the ladies present at a blue-rock handicap are as callous to suffering as the dames and demoiselles who saw the gladiator die in the circus, or the bull rip open the miserable screws employed in the national pastime of Spain. But, as a rule, the sporting critics do not mention with severity or reprobation the increasing patronage which the ladies are conferring upon sport in every direction. It is not only a Harrow and Eton cricket-match that is now honoured with the presence of the fair sex; other less celebrated contèsts are beginning to be jotted down by them as exhibitions to be seen or as gatherings to be attended. We confess we regard a movement of the kind with much satisfaction. There never was anything intrinsically wrong, shocking, or startling in boat-racing, horse-racing, or cricket. The manliness of these various recreations by no means included a Spartan roughness or indelicacy, and the only sports extant which perhaps are open to this reproach would be certain pedestrian trials where the running is performed in costumes more suited for Congo than for Fulham.

Sporting picnics are far superior to every other social device of an analogous character. We should perhaps except the originals of the mock-angling representations by artists who attempt to bring fishing and flirtation into a single boat. By sporting picnics we mean the meetings for luncheon in the wood shade, what time it is permitted us to commence thinning the partridge coveys; the junketing on the heather when the doom of the grouse-pack has been ordered; the standing feed on the drag, the waggonette, or the phaeton at the Oaks, at Ascot, at Goodwood; the slighter collation customary at Lord's when the two schools are having it out at the wickets in the presence of everyone in London who is anybody. With reference perhaps to the shooting picnics, we should enter a saving *caveat.* There has been, and there is, a tendency to carry them too far. Not only bad shooting, but shaky walking, lurks at the bottom of a deep Moselle cup, and since the famous collapse of Mr. Pickwick into slumber and a wheelbarrow after cold punch, it is to be feared that more experienced gun practitioners have softened into a desire to return early under the influence of cooling drinks. Of course, where

ladies are present gentlemen are to a great extent free
from this peril or temptation, and, in accordance with
the wholesome and decorous manners of our day, are
cautious to keep well within the bounds that divide
agreeable hilarity from boisterous excitation. Here,
again, is a reason why we should wish to see ladies
share at least as spectators in sport, and we are quite
sure they would be more willing to do so if greater
facilities were offered them for the purpose.

The masculine socialities of sport consist not only
in the friendly freemasonry that should prevail amongst
the craft, and to which we have more than once
adverted, but they might be extended, as they have
been, by communication with our brethren and asso-
ciates in other countries. Four young men pulling
against four other young men in a boat may not have
a strong and lasting effect on the great policies of the
two nations from which the crews hail, and it is very
easy indeed for a writer or a speaker to compose
high-coloured rhetorical confectionary out of such a
theme, but indisputably an affair of the kind, from
the relative importance bestowed upon it, has its
influence for good on the relations between England
and America. So ought the visit of those courageous
cricket clubs who have crossed oceans in order to
show Young Australia how the old land had cultivated
its old pastime. Nor should we be discouraged that
hitherto our yachting overtures in the same way have
not been as productive of peace and fine-fellowship as
might be looked for. Experience is a sound teacher
of the amenities, and we are quite convinced that
jealousy or unreasonable chagrin cannot long continue
to thwart the mutual advantages to be derived from
interchange of civilities between those who own crack
yachts at home, and those who sail crack yachts
abroad.

Genial weather contributes to intensify the socialities of the sports. No blaze of sun is supposed to

N

be too much for a regatta, and a Henley Regatta gives numerous opportunities for these *réunions* on which we have been commenting.   As at Epsom and Ascot, knowledge, of an exact or inexact sort, of the qualities of those who contend for prizes is a very secondary consideration with the spectators.   In a few cases friends of the oarsmen immediately acquainted with them take, of course, a deep and enthusiastic interest in the several results; but the vast majority go in for the pleasing excitement, and an enjoyment of the picturesque and animated scenes to which the regatta gives rise.   This public though ignorant manifestation of the popularity of athleticism is not without a useful consequence.   It encourages the amateur oarsmen to work, even although they may be conscious that their best work can only be duly appreciated by experts.   But then in that particular they have their consolation, as the experts are now multiplying apparently in the ratio of the nails in the horse's shoe in the venerable figure-catch.   Not many years ago, a great deal too many rowing-matches eventuated in legal pulling and hauling, which seldom concluded to the satisfaction of either disputants. Now things are better ordered and managed, and the sentiment of considering sport in a social as well as in a serious aspect will certainly tend to mitigate its accidental animosities, and directly confer many benefits upon its external as well as internal associations.

The socialities of sport differ in kind as well as in degree from the trials imposed on human endurance implied under the term "dining out" in town.   The latter festivities are seldom frank or candid ; they may conceal a motive or a design, or at least they may in the majority of instances be regarded as mere matters of ceremony and form, to which you are asked to contribute your white tie and your conversation, if you have any, in order that your host and hostess may discharge in due form a sort of tax assessed upon them for the privilege of living in society. But the hospitalities of sport are, as a rule, sincere and honest, as the world goes. The people engaged in them are generally of a mind on one topic at least. They are never at a loss for something to talk about. They have fished, shot, or hunted in common. The common pursuit of sport makes them more or less familiar to each other, without much of that preliminary ice-breaking which usually occurs before two Britons will condescend to open their mouths to chat ; and it often happens that persons who have regarded slight acquaintances with the kind of uncharitable disposition in which Lamb cursed a total stranger on chance, discover, on an accidental meeting connected with guns or horses, that their neighbour only requires to be known in order to prove himself a very excellent fellow.

Besides the comparatively private hospitalities of sport, we may refer to the public or county hunt dinners and coursing dinners, which help to such an extent to vary the ordinary round of rural existence, as evidence of the social uses of sport. To be sure, it may be asserted that we are fond of the least excuse for eating in company. Jerrold used to say that if the world were convulsed by an earthquake to-morrow, a number of Englishmen would be certain to find a corner amongst the ruins in which they could lay a table-cloth. But, again, we believe that the jovial entertainments to which we refer are essentially dissimilar to the banquets of state occasion or of gormandising to which the author of the " Caudle Papers " alluded. The hunt dinner has often cleared up difficulties and assuaged animosities, which no amount of official intercourse upon the magisterial bench, no anxious services of mutual friends, could destroy or mitigate—how many agreeable and humorous memories will these gatherings not leave in the fancies of hundreds who have participated in them?

It was at one of these you heard the best song, the
most comical speech, you ever heard in your life ; it
was there you discovered for the first time the talent
for repartee which you never knew you possessed before.   The hunt dinner has become a milder and
more civilised affair than it used to be ; the guests do
not in our days feel a doubt, on mounting to go home,
as to the place where a horse commonly wears his
head. And yet accidents will happen. The fatigue of a
hard run often induces a resort to the stimulus of
another bottle, which is just a bottle too much ; but
the consequence is never so serious as when it involved,
not a peaceable slumber in the hotel where the excess had been committed, but an ignominious bed
under the mahogany, or perhaps an operation of
tattoo on the victim of carelessness by the old practical
jokers of a by-gone era. The coursing dinners have
of recent years become the most numerous of the sort
of convivialities under notice. They are occasionally annual, or monthly, or, better again, informal
meetings, where so many attendants of the coursing-
field agree to turn in for the evening after the events
on the card have been run off. The coursing dinner
is a more democratic junketing than the hunting
banquet. It is also an assembly of what might be
termed all the wonderful appetites. For vigorous
trenchermen, who have infrequent resort to flask or
sandwich-case, who linger not over elaborate luncheons
at hospitable mansions, or at the edge of the wood to
which the ladies come in the afternoon, commend us
to the coursing gentry who watch the hound after the
hare on foot. The anglers, being mostly a solitary
race by the nature of their calling, are not so festive,
perhaps, as their brethren of other sports. But they
have their clubs and their snug nights together also.
They are not, either, as frugal on these occasions as
their venerable master, who appeared to be content
with feeding upon the captives of his own rod and

line ; but we do not think that they ever deserved
that cruel caricature of Seymour's depicting three of
them returning from a river, and falling on a joint
of beef at an inn with the aspect of hungry wolves,
while a horrified landlord hears one Piscator remark
to another, " Eat away, Ned ; 'tis only eighteenpence,
much or little ! "

Hunt-balls are, as everyone knows, both popular
and fashionable with the ladies. They do not attend
hunt-dinners, nor are those institutions regarded perhaps with unmixed satisfaction by married ladies
whose husbands ride to hounds. The balls compensate them for the dinners ; they attract often the
most eligible men in the whole county. And the
same may be said for the regattas, which, we hold,
should never at the seaside be concluded without the
committee making provision for a dance. And this
leads us to the hospitality of croquet. That theme
alone might form the subject of an entire treatise.
The number of pleasant afternoon teas, of lawn-parties,
of luncheons, that croquet has promoted, should render
it a pastime of both interest and consequence to well-
regulated families ; and, as a matter of fact, it is so
considered. No properly furnished country seat is
now without its croquet lawn, and in town people
also contrive to find space for the nice conduct of the
mallet and the due planting of the hoop. And the
hospitalities of croquet are not only agreeable, but
economical. They do not necessitate the upsetting
of domestic routine, or an outlay at a confectioner's, a
stress upon the private cook, a bill for champagne at
(let us hope) the wine-merchant's. The harmless tea-
pot furnishes the most fitting beverage for a social
croquet match. If the occasion should lead ultimately
to a quadrille and waltz in the spring or summer
evening, the circumstance should always be regarded
as a delightful accident. Archery, though in a minor
degree, affords also favourable opportunities for an

interchange of social and amiable courtesies, which are none the less enjoyable for being unattended with elaborate or ostentatious preparations.

We cannot conclude without a word on the hospitalities of yachting. The yachting man is celebrated, and justly so, for his generous practical inclinations. In harbour in the season, his boat is often crammed with visitors, luncheon goes on for ever, sea picnics are his frequent proposals, he is never without a friend and a berth to give him. To such an extent is hospitality a tradition of yachting, that even the odd stingy men who indulge in the pastime consider it necessary to pay homage to the idea at least, by forcing you to partake, in a cheesy cabin, of a sardine and a glass of red ink from Bordeaux, without any provocation on your part. But the stingy men of the butterfly fleet are few and far between. The majority of those who go down to Cowes in yachts are open-hearted to a fault. When you are on board the *Mermaid* with them, nothing within the capacity of her cellars and lockers is denied you ; and the ice-safe and locker of a modern schooner or respectably tonnaged cutter contain resources for creature comfort which would surprise those who are unacquainted with the modern fashion of living on board holiday ships. Indeed, there might be sumptuary laws on the matter introduced for the relief of inexperienced guests. On this topic, however, it is not necessary for us to enter. We only desire to place on record, in a short summary of the incidental hospitalities of sport, a mention of the thoroughly complete method in which generous and good-natured impulses are exercised by the followers of a pursuit which is so exceptionally and characteristically English as that of yachting.

THE world of mere fashion, which turns its back upon matters of sport except when traditional opportunities are presented for picnicking at a boat-race or a cricket-match, might do worse with its time than to spend a little more of it in encouraging the regular series of healthy pastimes which are announced for the season. The sporting world is, however, more or less independent of spasmodic patronage. A man will row his canoe-match, though none be there to see, or be content to pull heartily against the stream into the empty reaches of the Thames. He cares not for the big regattas and the rowdy or the elegant fun of the fair. Though artists depict him too often in sentimental situations, he is more frequently to be noted feathering his oar without any distracting assistant manipulating the tiller. And the wielders of the bat do not practise and work only to exhibit their dexterity before the wicket or in the field when the band is borrowed from the Guards and the marquees are bright with muslin and ribbons. Cricket thus, might be termed cricket *in excelsis,* but, after all, it would not look business enough for the genuine lovers of it. But the ladies are not without their own spring and summer pastimes. When the hawthorn buds appear, archery costumes begin to be looked up. It is to be hoped that the toxophilites will receive an accession of support in the coming months. The science of the bow ought to be more cultivated than it is. The hours before the target on the lawn serve in some degree to restore a colour to cheeks that have paled through late dinners and incessant waltzes. The gentlemen who don Lincoln

green will never, indeed, be asked to form a Spanish-fly
corps for the defence of the country ; but most of them
can handle a gun as well as the lancewood, and
are not the worse in the stubbles for being able to
make centres with an arrow at a garden-party.   And
then there is croquet of course, the level spaces for
which are already being carefully watched after.
Though the fairies have danced on these spots, grass
will grow there, and unexpected knots turn up in the
ground.   And then in the spring the builders are busy
with the butterfly fleet, and the " yachting fixtures " are
placed before us.   The catalogue, read properly, summons up visions of swift schooners, of delicious
mornings under a steady breeze in the *Sea-gull*, of quiet
evening pipes under cover in the *Nautilus*, or on the
deck, of a June night.   For these enjoyments we must
perchance wait ; but in anticipation we can enjoy the
triumphs of our pets, as the various club arrangements
comfort us.

But who is to be envied in the spring, in April
and in May, if not the angler ?   It may be that
he has rather a bad—or say a stiff—time of it,
when the almanac first permits him to fish.   Until
you warm to it, a day with hail in it or a dash of cold
rain on the banks of a river is not invariably a period
of unalloyed pleasure.   The wind in the east does not
deter the courageous sportsman, but he would just as
soon it blew from other quarters.   And there is the
natural beauty of the scenery to be considered.   On
that point we should dread to lapse into an idyllic
vein.   Our readers know all about it, and will be told
again of it, in terms that even outsiders do not easily
weary of.   Your fisher is a perfect glutton for scenery
ever since Walton, his master, taught him the trick of
enjoying it.   And the spring—proper spring, not snow-
spring, but cuckoo-tide—is for the trout-rod the live-
liest season of the year, taking rivers all round.   Even
if that piece of experience be contradicted—and every

sportsman has a born right to contradict his brother in a friendly fashion—angling, we maintain, is pleasantest in spring. Then the waters will probably be neither too high nor too low. The fish, too, are in prime season, and angling for them is sport indeed. And it now begins to grow genial enough to take to the sea, perhaps, with hook and line, to capture the cod, the gurnard, or the more delicate whiting. Sea-fishing is often a chilly pleasure, but it has its own advantages. It is by no means bad fun, for instance, to have your boat attract some roving or resident band of hake. Soon as ever the line runs to its proper depth, which you have duly plumbed with its own lead, you feel a double tug from these insatiable creatures. They are not, indeed, very elegant in proportions, and are but indifferent to eat, but they are wholesome and honest fare enough, and make a brave show in the bottom of your boat.

The country is so delightful in the spring that it is a wonder London brings its residents away from it, even were there no attraction of sport or pastime to engage attention. The garden begins to be more distinct in its bounteous promises. Some of the flowers are out completely, and others are only waiting for a few more warm noons to ripen them into a strange and tender beauty. Poets often exaggerate, but they never yet have said too much about the loveliness of the English spring. And who enjoys it more than the sportsman and the naturalist, who should have within him just a flavouring of the fanciful cultus ? It is a gross untruth to depict the botanist as incapable of sentiment, to refer to the entomologist as a mere beetle-hunter, who wastes his life in missing the entire breadth and width of the world within and the world without us. The naturalist brings the raw material for verse itself to the bard—who, by the way, would often not be a worse bard for attending a trifle closer to what is told him by the observer. We really wish a few of the passionate

admirers of larks and swallows and bees who indite odes
h₂ ⟩⟩   ject of their adoration would now and again
refresh themselves by examining in person the matters
they sing about, and thus perhaps put a little intelligent vitality into the common-form expressions into
which they run.   But we would not have a country
rambler stock his head with the cheap literature of the
naturalist-made-easy, the botanist-in-five-minutes order.
If you can swallow second-hand anecdotes of a frog,
you may ; but the interest it imparts to the sight of
the creature itself is more or less factitious, if not idle.
But it is well to know the names of things accurately.
The number of English ladies and gentlemen in the
country who cannot tell a lime from a beech, an elm
from a larch, is surprising.   And the same with the
distinctions of birds and wild-flowers. They recognise,
of course, a blackbird, or a thrush, or a robin, but the
whole tribe of finches and hedge chatterers of all sorts
are unknown to them.   The primrose, the daisy, the
dog-rose, the violet make up the entire of their vocabu-
lary acquaintance with the flora of the meadows or the
woods.   It gives a real pleasure in a walk to have a
clear notion of these matters, and even the mere ac-
quiring of the proper names leads to a curiosity which
develops itself, perhaps, after awhile, into a pursuit.
Complete ignorance is not bliss in this respect ; and
want of knowledge of the kind we refer to is almost
unpardonable nowadays. If our young country friends
devoted the smallest fraction of the time exhausted
upon the contents of that box from Mudie's which contains the fortunes and misfortunes of eighteen heroines,
to just a passing study of practical botany or natural
history, they would discover a wonderful addition to
the sum of enjoyment to be had from a stroll under
the April sun.

KILLING NO SPORT.

THERE has been, no doubt, a decrease amongst the bush minstrels in the neighbourhood of London, only to be accounted for by overt acts of war upon their kind, and not to be measured by the natural effect and consequence of building extensions and enterprises. And we confess, for one thing, we are glad that the delinquents who have been thinning the finches and bagging the nightingales cannot claim even the remote association with sport that the employment of a gun for these nefarious purposes might confer upon them. We are gratified to note that the race of London or thrush potters has altogether decayed or disappeared. The small birds are the victims of the limed twig and the decoy trap. The fellows engaged in the business are, we are told, of the "rough" pattern. Here we must pause for a moment to comply with a condition imposed upon us by the title of this article. We do not yield to the most fanciful or philanthropic of speculators upon the picturesque beauty, the poetical and absolute utility, of our little friends the song-birds. Everyone should desire to have them rationally protected ; but we confess also that we are not brought to such a view by the fabrications of ingenious reporters who attempt, without hesitation, to describe the most secret thoughts and emotions of a green linnet. There is in children an inherent vice of cruelty, and, in order to check and correct it, it may be fair and reasonable enough to tell them sentimental stories relating to the sufferings of a bruised butterfly, or the pangs of the robin whose nest has been harried ; but adult people ought not to require dramatic fables of the same descriptio bring them to a right mind on a very simple topic. We regard with some distrust the tales of the peculiar tortures inflicted on trapped birds, as well as the various points that are made concerning the cold-blooded inhumanity of capturing a yellowhammer by rousing in his breast the passions of a jealous *prima donna*. The art with which this is done is art over-done. When Mrs. Beecher Stowe gushed over the cir-cumstance of the eggs of the poor peewit being exposed for sale in the beautiful basket-like nest which the bird had constructed for the home of its family, she did not shoot wider of the mark she wished to hit than those who enlarge in detail on the woes of the cock-sparrow suddenly deprived of his hen. The absurdity of the practice may be indicated by pushing the principle of it into unconventional quarters. For example, why not put in a word for the bevy of un-romantic sea-cod confined to an area of comparatively meagre dimensions in the Crystal Palace Aquarium? There are the thousands of imprisoned gold-fish through-out the country, the lobsters coming to market, &c.; but we are never entertained or harrowed with literary exercises on their torments. Our own lives, in fact, would be intolerable if we permitted ourselves a continual consciousness of all our necessary and unnecessary rudeness and injustice, not only to the animal world, but to each other. And there are those who cultivate, we believe, an effeminate ten-derness for the brute creation at the expense of far worthier instincts and dispositions. Insensate, un-intelligent humanitarianism runs into the wildest ex-travagance of stupidity and folly. It is out of its vagaries we have developed the old lady with a room full of cats, and the old gentleman who remembers the terrier in his will. Sensible humanitarianism is not liable to these indiscretions, neither does it fly into a rage at the sight of a foxhunter's coat as the bull does at the flourishing of a red rag. It does not inveigh against the sportsmanlike destruction of game, or keep unceasingly execrating steeplechasing, or discovering the future decline and fall of England in the proceedings of a pigeon-club. Some very good persons, no doubt, may hold their own opinions on these several subjects, and they may be opposed to ours. We can respect them when expressed with coolness and discrimination ; but we prefer to observe them engaged in many of the tasks that are open to such reformers of our time in the sphere of sensible humanitarianism.

The Society for the Prevention of Cruelty to Animals has its work constantly cut out for it. It may be occasionally tempted to go over the line, but it does not as often blunder as might be expected from an association of enthusiasts. So far from desiring it to hold its hand, there are many directions in which one would rejoice to see it more active. The cab-horse requires vigilant attention ; and there is no need to go to Italy for illustrations of brutality to quadrupeds. The support and, at least, moral patronage bestowed by the public on this useful body proves how the community are willing to admit readily the substantial nature of the basis on which it is founded. There are few classes of crimes for which magistrates more peremptorily convict than those which are brought to their notice by the guild to which we are alluding. In fact, it is no exaggeration to assert that a Whitechapelite had much better beat his wife than flog his cat, as far as the punishment which might be allotted to him for either offence is to be considered.

For much-abused grouse-killers, and fox-hunters, and lion-slayers, and anglers, we would assert that no class of persons so cheerfully or so diligently comply with sensible humanitarian conditions as thorough sportsmen and sincere naturalists. The latter, perhaps, may be a trifle over-anxious for specimens, and too ready to encourage the welcome with

small-shot of an illustrious stranger or exotic visitant;
still, on the whole, the pursuit of the naturalist tends
to produce and to develop every sentiment that would
be conducive to the preservation and protection of
our native or accidental fauna.   And the sportsman
has been always warned and instructed on the score
of wanton cruelty.   He has been taught the advantages
and credit of clean shooting; and the inconsiderate folly
of the long, chance shots.   His quarry, at the worst, will
never experience the horrors felt by the unfortunate
gosling under the sanctioned and accredited carving-
knife of the cook.   Sportsmen and naturalists were
among the most eager and persevering advocates of
the Sea Birds Preservation Act; and, no doubt, our
craft has the same disposition for a movement to prevent the complete destruction of singing-birds.   But
the claims for the birds must be urged in sensible,
coherent, and rational form; they do not want advocates to invent legends about them—to ascribe to
them the most tender and complex of human emotions—to stuff them, in short, with as many sentimental conceits and fancies as a young lady
novelist puts into the head of the first heroine she
tries to run through three volumes and Mudie's.
Lady Burdett-Coutts, with natural good taste, avoids
a mistake of the sort we have been endeavouring to
describe.   She leaves her case to speak for itself on
its own merits, with little or no colour or forced attractions.   Hence her letter last year on this topic has
met with more attention than far more elaborate
compositions of the word-painting order.   If people
must have thrilling sensations on the subject of birds,
we recommend them to a study of poultry consign-
ments by rail, or to reflections over the whiteness of
veal.   As for the singing-birds in confinement, a great
majority of them are happy and contented enough,
and would simply refuse their liberty if it were offered
to them.   That matter, however, would open a different

province for discussion from that in which we stand for the moment. We have now in the Wild Birds Act a specimen of protective legislation, capable indeed of much improvement, but still a decided step in the right direction. It is much to be regretted that in the framing of this measure some practical and scientific ornithologists had not been consulted. The schedule of this Act appears to have been written out with the smallest possible knowledge of the subject ; indeed, it manifests a curious ignorance and confusion, even in naming the birds which it is supposed to protect. So carelessly in other respects has it been drawn, that its penal clauses are almost entirely ineffective. However, we must give the measure the benefit and credit of being well intended, and we are moreover promised an amendment of it, in which its more glowing blunders and mistakes will be corrected.

THE ENCOURAGEMENT OF DEMO-
CRATIC PASTIMES.

THERE existed at one time in England what might be termed a system of compulsory education in archery. As early as the reign of the Third Edward, the King commanded, under pain of severe punishment, that the apprentices of London should spend their leisure in practising with the long bow ; an order was made in the reign of Edward IV that every Englishman and Irishman dwelling in England should have a long bow of his own height; and Strutt, quoting an Act of Parliament on the subject, states that, by the provisions of a formal statute, butts should be erected in every township, at which the inhabitants were to shoot up and down upon all feast days, under the penalty of one halfpenny for every time they omitted to perform this duty. And it should be understood that it was not altogether for military purposes that these laws were passed. They had a social aim, inasmuch as they were intended to prevent the people from falling into debasing and enervating recreations ; and it was thought the cultivation of archery would specially contribute towards the repression of a public taste for games of either chance or cruelty. Archery has now become a pastime of rather a fashionable than a popular character ; it would be difficult to get a member of the present House of Commons to propose that a Crown grant should be set aside for its revival ; but perhaps we might discover in past legislation upon the Volunteers parallel for the grave attention once bestowed upon the art in which Robin Hood was so celebrated a proficient. If the Volunteer movement were of no value as a defensive patriotic organization—an hypothesis which we do not entertain—it has been of service as an active agent for the development of physical health, and for supplying a rational means of more or less recreative occupation to many who might otherwise drift into evil courses during off-hours relaxation. Drilling and marching are excellent things in themselves ; an annual experience of camp life, the necessity of temperance for prize-shooting, and various other incidents of an association with the Volunteers, make up a curriculum of perhaps imperfect, but decidedly advantageous training which no sound man will be the worse for being put through.

But we cannot include volunteering amongst our democratic pastimes. By democratic pastimes we mean such games and sports as may be pursued at a comparatively trifling cost, and which do not include the possession of a property or plant, such as would be requisite, for instance, for hunting, shooting, or salmon-fishing. At the head of our democratic pastimes we would place cricket. The cricket-field is becoming every day an established institution in our towns and villages. We have clear and distinct testimony that where a strong interest is felt in the local contests at wickets, where the clubs include almost every caste in the social sphere of our divided community, beer-fever is at its lowest point in the district ; and there is no one who experiences a more direct concern in the affairs of the cricket meeting than the rector of the parish. Healthy athleticism is a foe not only to vice, but to that slovenliness of disposition which, quite as often as the stimulus of sensual propensity, sends the village artisan or rustic to the benches of the pot-house for amusement. We should like to see the fact practically noted by vestries and boards who have invested in them rights over town-fields, and who might frequently, with benefit to the community, make a gift within their powers of playgrounds to the people.

o

Many cricket-clubs are prevented from extension by the assessment of rent for space. Private liberality does a great deal to smooth away the financial difficulties in the construction of a democratic cricket-club. The much-abused landowners are often far more generous in offering ground for cricket or foot-ball than corporations or vestries. And during the cricket season, in many parts of England, may be witnessed scenes over the game suggesting almost the picturesque idealisms of the poets and painters who sang of our island in the olden time, or who placed upon canvas the dance round the Maypole and the figure of Sir Roger superintending the sports of his people. It is no unusual thing, even in our prosaic times, to find in the heart of Bucks, the cricket-field in the very lawn of the squire's residence, and the game shared in by rich and poor ; while, as though in a theatrical group, the old people sit under the shade of the giant beeches to witness the combat of ball and bat. Nor is the good curate's sermon listened to with less attention next Sunday because he defeats, with Etonian vigour, the attempt of honest Hodge upon his wicket, and sends a perilous ball skimming with a red-hot twist in it through the hands of three excited parishioners.

We have referred to the decay of the coarse pastimes—the bull-baiting, dog-fighting, and cock-fighting excrescences of sport. There is, perhaps, scarce any necessity for interfering with the remaining odd exhibitions of these ignorant diversions, so doomed to decay are they of their own nature and by the improved tone of the people. But, in the way of democratic pastimes, it seems to us that in seaport and manufacturing places there is a stronger temptation to indulge in the rougher pleasures than there is in the country or in London. The authorities of a seaport have a great deal in their power as a corrective to brutal amusements, in being able, if willing, to en-

courage regattas. By regattas we do not now understand affairs started as a local speculation for the good
of two crack yachts, the confectioner who undertakes
the ball business and imports the fireworks, and the
crew of a dandy outrigger. Far be it from us to lay a
general charge against regattas, even when they
include the ingredients which we particularise. But
we wish to draw attention to this point, that at these
fêtes the democratic pastimes are not as fairly promoted as they might be. There should be premiums
for rough-and-ready as well as for neat and elegant
rowing. One of the most cheery sights in the world
is a tussle in salt water between two or three ships'
boats, manned by pilots or sailors, who go to work in
a ding-dong heavy fashion, which affords a relief by
contrast to the symmetrical regularity of performances
in an outrigger. At the coast regattas something—a
trifle—might be clipped off the big yacht cups, in
order to establish a fund for the democratic oarsmen,
and the amount would never be missed by the champion craft of the butterfly fleet.

There are other kinds of democratic pastimes which
verge more closely, perhaps, than those we have mentioned upon the province of sport pure and simple.
The humble bank-fisher of the Thames and other
open rivers, for example, with his cheap gear and bait,
can enjoy himself as much as any salmon-slayer in the
Shannon. Coursing may be pursued also in a modest
and moderate style, if he who goes in for it is content
with a couple of dogs and a run for his own amusement, or with a few friends at a private match. And
there is the pigeon-flyer of every grade, not always a
rogue on the look-out for stray birds, but fond of the
fun for its own sake, and only sacrificing for it what he
is very much better without. These "fancies" are not
only harmless, but useful. They inculcate tenderness
to lower natures, and provoke instincts of kindness
and affection which might be dormant in minds un-

awakened by the wisdom of society or the learning of books. We are not, however, about to compose a plea for poor pigeon-flyers. Such a tract might, indeed, be projected, for we believe that humble pigeon-flyers and pigeon-fanciers and bird-fanciers of all sorts are a much abused race, and there are hundreds of people who invariably connect a taste for fantails and finches with short-clipped hair, a velvet coat, and three stolen dogs worn under each arm. A canary or a goldfinch may often have that sort of influence in an artisan's room that has been attributed to the democratic flower-pot. That point, however, may be left for the consideration of the sentimentalist. We only wish to indicate the fact that the various spheres of sport, pastime, and "fancy," include persons, of apparently limited opportunities, who may still have within their reach certain games and diversions of an inexpensive quality. In these the elements of pleasure and of interest are as powerful and keen as they are in the more aristocratic methods of healthy recreation, and there is a sound moral use and efficiency in the attachment felt by almost every able-bodied Englishman of every degree in sport, while at the same time this feeling, when rationally though humbly indulged, contributes to a strengthening of the moral as well as the physical basis of life.

" BUT pray remember, I accuse nobody; for, as I would not make a watery discourse, so I would not put too much vinegar into it, nor would I raise the reputation of my own art by the diminution or ruin of another's." Our readers will probably recognise this sentence, taken from the most popular of all books of sport, and pregnant with a liberality of sentiment which we should like to see more carefully cultivated by the disciples of our various crafts. There would be something excessively ludicrous, if there was not so much that is unfair and unseemly, in the manner in which we occasionally find people taking sides for the special pastime or recreation to which they are personally attached. If they are hunting-men, they are never wearied of exalting their own pursuit over that of the fowler or yacht-owner. They affect to despise the pleasures of shooting as tame and unworthy when compared with that of riding to hounds. They will not admit that there is even an excuse for a sane creature in hiring a moor; and as to fishing, the stupid phrase of Dr. Johnson is for ever on their tongues. The notion of whipping a stream—they always catch hold of the term whipping—appears to them at once comical and weak-minded. And the gentle anglers themselves, on the other hand, are not quite as charitable as their master would have them. They will put "too much vinegar" at times into their discourses. They will institute those comparisons which are odious, and insist that they alone have discovered the *summum bonum* of earthly bliss. Then, again, the yacht bigot, on his sea legs, protests his complete detestation of everything appertaining to a stable or a powder-flask. He will never grant that the fancy of his neighbours is either intelligible or innocent. It is the same through every level of the sporting world, and possibly there are those who maintain that skittles may not only be reduced to a fine art, but that it and bagatelle are the only arts worth practising. Nor is this sort of anti-catholic disposition confined to the natural divisions of sport. The foxhunter of a kind pretends to assume an attitude of scorn towards the harehunter, and has invented an expression to convey an idea of his deportment. A moneyed snob with a 200-ton schooner, fitted up with mirrors like a flash ginshop, sneers at the honest and modest little cutter which a gentleman may prefer to a floating restaurant. Then there is your enthusiast who believes that any rig but one designed by himself represents congenital idiocy on the part of his friends. Anglers will fight about flies, about wind and water, and rods and reels, and gut, and floats, and baits, with extraordinary virulence. They are excited by what the French term the "credulity of advocacy," to such an extent as would in former days have to be settled with their antagonists on the grass before breakfast; but it is really curious, as well as unpleasant, to notice how easily clever and well-meaning gentlemen will contradict each other on points where reconciliation is almost invariably not only possible, but easy. It seems to be now and again forgotten that a gentleman recording an experience of fishing, of travel, of shooting, of natural history, has no object to serve save that of generously sharing his information; and yet other gentlemen will at once dispute his facts, with a singular disregard of caution, to say the least of it. We try to do justice between the disputants and to preserve the peace, but the task is not always easy, and is never agreeable.

It may be remarked, after all, that sportsmen are not worse in this respect than theologians, politicians, or men of science. We have a pretty constant experience of the intensity with which the first maintain their convictions, the second their views, the last their theories. Difference of opinion helps the movement and contributes to the vitality of every department of life. This, of course, is a mere truism. But, to our mind, sportsmen ought to be more charitable than politicians. We have in our fortunate provinces neither Whigs nor Tories, Radicals nor Piebalds. We do not discuss questions of infinite moment or of none. It is not our business to educate the masses, or to speculate on the wisdom of the House. Our task lies in another direction, and does not involve such tremendous consequences or issues. Hence we can afford to keep our temper and to use our judgment. Here we distinctly address ourselves to passionate sporting disputants; we speak also to the hunting-man who thinks little of the angler, to the yachting-man who thinks nothing of either; and we ask them always to remember the golden sentence at the head of this paper. By all means let us have the two or the ten sides of every question concerning us that may turn up. We are always glad to receive hints that may serve as useful data for some time or other formulating definite rules as to the very best means, for instance, of keeping our shooting-boots waterproof, or of killing our superfluous rats. People may desire to be acquainted with the chances of sport in Norway—in Timbuctoo. We are favoured with information on the point by a trustworthy correspondent who has enjoyed himself very much in Timbuctoo, and found the hotels, let us say, as comfortable as any rational sportsman could wish. But another of our good friends who has been at Timbuctoo, perhaps at a different season of the year, writes in the strongest terms to deny that the hotels of that country were even tolerable; while as for sport, he did not come across more than a brace of cassowaries in a month's sojourn.   We are stating merely typical or illustrative cases; but our readers will have no difficulty, we imagine, in perceiving the drift of them.   Then, as to angling, surely a know- ledge of the art ought to render every professor of it discreet in dogmatising, except upon general principles. It is vexatious, no doubt, to be contradicted on some primary point in connection with the pursuit; but silence is the best reply to forward ignorance, and much more effective than an angry explanation.   To break out into abuse is as great a blunder as it was for Doctor Serafino, in the "Golden Legend," to say—

May the Lord have mercy upon your position, you wretched, wrangling culler of herbs !

While Dr. Cherubino replies—

May He send your soul to eternal perdition for your treatise on the irregular verbs !

And we are afraid that sportsmen at seasons indulge in quite as strong language as that of the learned divines at the School of Salerno.

Every man really fond of sport should educate himself into a catholic toleration for it—at least, in all its reputable branches.   He should not allow himself to be prejudiced either by his own bias to a single pursuit, or by an uncultivated bigotry.   The true sportsman should be complete in his tastes and in his instincts.   He should have an appreciation for courage, perseverance, endurance, and skill in every direction of pastime or recreation.   If he does not like fishing, he should comprehend why other men do, and be satisfied, if he fails to understand his friend's devotion to the rod and line, that it may arise from a mental deficiency on his own part.   And for those who have the leisure and the opportunity it is surely well that they should try the round of sport, and be equally ready and willing to employ gun, tackle, horse, or yacht as the season suits.   We might go further, and indite a homily on the advantages of not believing your neighbour a fool because he hunts and you only shoot, or on the virtue of not contradicting a statement without seeing exactly what space it covered. We are certain, however, that the hints we have ventured to offer will answer our purpose. The sporting world in its literary and social aspects ought to be genial and cordial, and not more agitated by the element of dispute or of difference than might be salutary in order to promote the properly tempered circulation of varied or even of opposite opinions.

NOT many years ago there was a prevalent impression, amongst certain writers and speakers, that the English sportsman would have to disappear in the progressive course of things, just as the Red Indian has to vanish at the sound of the settler's axe. The country, as far as shooting, for instance, was concerned, would be reclaimed out of use or interest for the gun. The fens were all to be drained, and left, as the Irish gentleman said of the bog converted into a kitchen-garden, not worth a button—for snipe. The railways would make riding to hounds next to impossible, and it was found that even the telegraph was so far on the side of civilisation, as opposed to sporting, as to do for partridges what the murderous wire fence now does for men or horses. Matters, however, have not progressed at the rate, or in the exact direction, that our opponents prophesied they would. The railways, for example, have done us, on the whole, more good than harm. They have given facilities for reaching centres of sport to persons to whom these desirable quarters had been hitherto inaccessible. The telegraph wires have not yet exterminated our partridges, and, in the opinion of notable naturalists, these birds are inheriting an instinct of avoidance in connection with the posts and wires. We neither rejoice nor grieve that the Lincolnshire fens are not at this moment cultivated beyond the recognition of wildfowl, nor that the Irish moors have not turned out profitable investments for high-farming doctrinaires; but we accept the facts as they are, and conceive that we have at any rate the right as sportsmen to make the best of them. Scotland stands where it did in affairs of grouse, and rather a quickened impulse has been imparted to the management of those broad acres, that would be barren property but for their owners finding their account in satisfying the requirements of those who hire shooting-lodges. The anti-anglers have perhaps occasion for a little sour mirth. Rivers have been poisoned for the rod, which were formerly the haunts of fish, and of those who sought them ; but even here we have our consolation in the circumstance that every day the conviction is gaining ground that the extinction of the salmon, death to the trout, or excessive mortality amongst the rougher and coarser populations of the stream, indicates such a loss and risk to the towns upon its banks, that measures must be taken to secure the waters from a perilous and unsightly pollution. And it may well be said in reference to sport that, though one door may shut, another is sure to open, and progress in civilisation offers a hundred keys for the purpose. American prairies are now within easy distance of us, comparatively ; Canadian rivers are no longer only within the reach of our wealthiest brethren. Africa is no longer a *terra incognita*—at least to the sportsman. For him the most agreeable map is that which literally prints elephants or tigers instead of towns ; and documents very similar in significance are published for him. He is told what he may expect in Abyssinia ; in fact, in 1873, the world is now before him where to choose, and on his journey, gun in hand though it be, he is instructed as to every detail of his enterprise. All this he owes to progress—*i.e.*, to improvement in the means of locomotion—to the literary enterprise and developed taste which brings into open light and discussion the facts and details in which the sportsman is interested.

It is not to be presumed that even a zealous attachment to sport develops a temperament unequal to intellectual expansion. This fallacy has been exposed over and over again, not alone by such exceptional illustrations as might be found in the muscular biographies of men like Professor Wilson, but by the fact patent to anyone who rides, shoots, or fishes, that amongst the confederacies of these several pursuits the average of downright clever fellows (to use a rough phrase) exceeds the proportion of the same species to be found amongst inveterate loungers and stick-at-homes. Sport tends to make even dull people knowing and progressive in more senses than one, and it certainly contributes an influence resembling the force of italics to those who are already neither ignorant nor stolid. The kind of monster summoned up in the brain of those who are too serious to look at a horse except as a beast of burden, when they endeavour to depict a sportsman to themselves, takes the form of the wild enthusiast described by Leigh Hunt, who fed and slept and caroused in the midst of his dogs. Others, of course, have more sensible and moderate ideas on the subject, but still maintain that sport is opposed to progress. In vain you tell them that it promotes and encourages a hundred, nay, a thousand valuable industries and manufactures. Boot-makers, saddlers, as well as gunsmiths, veterinary surgeons, not only profit by these recreative pursuits ; but in these trades, occupations, and professions a perpetual competition is compelled by the exigencies of sport, the advantages of which frequently extend far outside the provinces of sport itself. China clippers may be indebted to yacht racing for model lines, and the fact may serve to illustrate, in a wide and important manner, the question we are discussing.

The rising generation, as the phrase goes, do not at all seem inclined to become educated into a dislike or into a contempt for sport. On the contrary, there is a growing taste for healthy athleticism, not only within public schools and universities, but outside them.

There is just one useful hint which we would venture to give here touching gymnastic exercises and practice. They should not be allowed to degenerate into efforts to vie with the feats of professional acrobats. We do not give this caution without special examples in mind of the pet pupils of ambitious professors having suffered injury from altogether misapprehending the uses and properties of physical culture. However, that is by the way. To return to our theme, it cannot be said that the spirit of the day is opposed to sport or pastime : in every division and province of the recreative sphere there are discoveries of new sources of pleasure, health, and salutary excitement. The old games are revived and kept up with a renovated enthusiasm. Cricket clubs and football clubs multiply every day. Golf insists upon recognition by us, and canoeing has claims on our attention which cannot be ignored. Within doors billiards has been reduced almost to a fine art, and chess and whist are pursued with a scientific earnestness of which our ancestors could have no conception. The only sports, in fact, with which progress has dealt as Stephenson's railway engine would deal with the " coo " are those by whose decay or effacement we have lost nothing, and for the abolition or discouragement of which we entertain no regret whatever. The bull is no longer baited, and the side of the rat-pit has not for some time presented any of the features of a dukery. The ring is an institution of the past, having duly expired by the ripening of the cancerous brutality inherent in its constitution. We do not miss the merely cruel main of cocks, and the coarse dog scuffles are relegated to the districts in which the rough strengthens his native passions for violence by contemplating the ferocity of his pet beast. On the other hand, progress and sport have advanced together upon parallel lines, and we conceive will continue in the same friendly relationship. We must, of course, cheerfully yield any ground fairly claimed from us upon a substantial utilitarian basis. This does not imply that we view with much satisfaction the setting up of wire fences in a hunting country. The part that the wire fence occupies within the scope of the word we have employed to signify improvement and civilisation is at present not obvious, to us at least, and yet we have heard the mischievous man-trap referred to as if it were as useful as the thrashing-machine. What we wish to insist upon is, that honest, healthy, English sports, recreations, and pastimes will be popular as long as our characteristic national life remains to us. We are at the moment so far faithful to the traditions of these venerable crafts and pursuits, that no effort of prig or of precisian has had the slightest manifest consequence in weakening the public conviction as to the necessity and the advantages of physical culture and exercise taken under proper and prudent conditions. The fact is, that those who have made the attempts have failed so signally that their discomfiture has served as a warning unto the unco guid, to whom the sight of a suit of white flannel or a Zingari vest is hateful and detestable. Not only have sports of all kinds, within the fair compass of rational amusement and recreation, obtained an almost complete current immunity from a sort of bedridden criticism formerly in vogue, but, in truth, the followers and practitioners of our pursuits are rather embarrassed by the favourable comments and notices bestowed upon them during special festivals of the year by well-meaning admirers of racing, angling, hunting, or rowing—according as the Derby arrives, salmon-fishing opens, or the windows of the shops begin to flaunt the challenge-colours of Cambridge or of Oxford. However it is not for us to be ungrateful on behalf of sporting interests for the concern displayed in them on the occurrence of momentous incidents, especially when the fact implies an admission of their importance as definite and eloquent as that bestowed upon matters of graver moment.

WONDERFUL for many reasons is the Parliament House of St. Stephen's at Westminster!
In one respect it is an arterial centre, and the beating
of its pulse is felt quite as far as the sound of the tattoo
of that celebrated morning drum so often associated
with the extent of the Queen's dominions ; in another,
its annual return to business may be regarded as
having the most influential consequence upon every
single department and division of English social life.
In March the brown holland has been removed from
the mansions of Mayfair, and there are slight tokens
of the London revival and awakening in the Row.
The lanes and roads will not much longer be fanned
by the skirts of habits of rough-and-ready pattern.
Many of the ladies who will take the place and the
part of belles later on, and who will fascinate hundreds of admirers under the tender glimmer of the
May leaves by their witching equestrianism, may
now be seen rehearsing in the rough as it were, and
with the bloom of the Shires yet lingering on their
cheeks ; for as yet they have not undergone the fatigue
duties of fashion.   Men who are lucky enough not to
be members of Parliament are just opening their campaign against the salmon; but even they know that the
period of escort will arrive for them when Piccadilly
will become inevitable.   He who hunts, however—
if Liberal or Conservative " whip" can touch him not
—continues yet to stick to his work.   The voice
of the gun should cease throughout the land ; already
it is cut off from its chief spheres of operation—
those circles in which partridges moved, pheasants

flourished, and grouse packed. The poulterers' shops still make a brave show enough with the hare, the bunch of snipe, the plover, the teal, the duck; but to an experienced eye they indicate the approach of the amnesty months, when it shall be treason to burn sporting-powder. The snipe have not the brilliant coats they wore in December; the waistcoats of the golden plover are beginning even now to exhibit black buttons; and, though the mallard is still a bird of beauty, somehow or other there is a limpness in his dead attitude suggestive of soft weather, which imparts quite a different aspect to his appearance from that which it wore when the frost was on the wold, and the *canard sauvage* sprang from the fen ditch. And it is also to be observed that the stock of the game-purveyor is eked out with shore birds of dubious table value at this season. But if the shopkeeper suffers in feathers, he makes it up by scales—fish-scales—in February. There you behold the genuine spring salmon, bright as the Harlequin of the pantomime, firm as marble to the finger, red as the dun dawn of a frosty morn where a knife has gashed his fair proportions. You may also be able to distinguish the lean kelt who ought not to be where he is, the noble stout Dutchman, the perfect gentleman from the Shannon or the Blackwater, the monster from the Tay, the giant from the Tweed. Each and all suggest plentiful associations to the enforced exile from the stream. What compost of feathers and fur brought up your forty-pounder, or did he die the death from the drag-net or the treacherous weir? And the trout —those of the beck gleaming with garnets and tinted with topaz; those of the loch or the heavy stream round-shouldered and of duller garb; those from the brook, small, but delicious for breakfast—the prospect arrests the street-wandering angler and that other, no angler, who knows far more of a butter-boat than a coracle, and yet who could tell you at table the

P

nationality (he says) of every salmon that finds its
way into the London market.

Sport on the Thames can scarcely be said to hybernate, but the hardiest will shrink from an encounter with
the sort of nor'-easter that *might* blow in February. Even
here, however, signs of the coming genuine aquatic
season may be observed. The enthusiasts have not
hesitated to keep themselves in some sort of wind, in
utter defiance of the thermometer; but in fine days
even milder oarsmen might venture to don white flannel without much risk of their ears being frozen brittle.
At any rate, we may be sure the boat-builders and
boat-vendors are not idle. In various snug recesses,
in a tender gloom, are whole rows of the brown skiffs
that the pleasure-going Londoner affects. They must
be varnished, they must be cushioned and furnished
generally, for what time the aits are green and the
swallows hawk over the stream. Then will they be
displayed with competitive unction by the Bridge of
Richmond, in all their bravery. And the boats that
have been put on winter duty (we have a fine Sunday
in winter occasionally) are also renovated and vamped
into good looks. They must be made as attractive as
possible for the rakish-hatted water-nymph who later
on will hold the tiller-ropes, while her muscular swain
combines spooning and pulling together. And the
"butterfly fleet" is fast getting ready; the gay craft
must be touched up spick and span for the approaching
regattas; everything must be overhauled and reduced
to order. The period of preparation is one of the
most interesting to the yachtsman; there is nothing he
enjoys more than running down from day to day to
see how the *Nautilus* is being improved or deco-
rated under his directions. And the days draw nigh
when Oxford contends with Cambridge, and the river
may be said, in the bad language of the hour, to be
formally "inaugurated." For the oarsmen we desire
a natural spring—no sudden pouncing back upon us of

early winter again with an iron grip, ironically disguised as February. An aquatic contest in a snow-storm is not comfortable to contemplate, and yet we confess we have so little trust in our climate that we would not put away skates in February, though the primroses were thick and common in Covent Garden.

February is essentially the look-ahead month for London sports and pastimes. Hardy as our friends of the football unquestionably are, iron-cased as their bones seem to be, they will not regret to work upon spring turf, and to do battle with each other out of the smoke of fog and the slush of winter mud. But for this they must yet take their chance. We never know what the Gulf Stream has in store for us, and the hooper swan may still be driven into a Windsor ditch by a violent reaction of Arctic temperament on the part of the season.

There is a feature of the season more or less connected with the opening paragraph of our paper on which we may venture to say a word. A curious essay indeed might be written upon the equitation of the House of Commons. On the whole, the Commons stands an examination in this respect fairly well. Many of the legislators are evidently crack riders, and more at home in the saddle than on the floor of the House. They have been known, indeed, to perform a view halloa at an excited debate, or in the heat of a rabblement motion to shout " Yoicks, yoicks !" as though the hounds were ahead. Other of our representative men evidently come into the Row upon constitutional grounds, hiring a camel from a livery-stable for the purpose, and undergoing the process of being shaken up as a conscientious enterprise requisite for the preservation of health. On Saturday mornings the Cabinet is fairly represented in the Row, and there is a goodly sprinkling on horseback of every other shade of politician in the British Congress. An observer might notice that there is such a thing as a

Radical and a Tory seat in a sense that he never realised to himself before ; that the Cavaliers and the Puritans—as the types of modern society are picturesquely differentiated by Henry Holbeach—proclaim themselves in the saddle as well as on the benches or below the gangway. We shall not pursue the reflection further, but simply indicate the circumstance to our readers, that they may use it in a stroll in the Park when the plump, the clever, or the indifferent hacks perform on the famous brown strip.

There are many subjects of interest besides the clinker glen and the rhododendrons to be studied within the Park, and the course of observation we have suggested may tend to develop a taste for close discrimination which will be found serviceable for application in grave as well as trivial directions. The Lords and Commons at pigeons, the two Houses shooting against each other at Wimbledon, indicate at least that our Assemblies are not indifferent to a sense of generous rivalry in sport and skill, and it is no secret that many of our more distinguished politicians are even adepts on the moor and on the loch.

THE USE AND POPULARITY OF ATHLETIC PURSUITS.

THE real lovers and patrons of sport, who have seriously in mind the sensible culture of athleticism throughout the country, ought not to consider that the special pursuits which they are interested in promoting are to any considerable extent advanced by a spasmodic and abnormal concern in them, which partakes of the nature of a grand spectacle or a great exhibition. It is, however, gratifying to observe that of late the attitude of those who are opposed to the principle of the inherent value of bodily exercise, and of encouragement for it, has been almost deferential to those who differ from them, when we compare it with the deportment which they were formerly accustomed to assume when the question was raised. We have heard very little recently of the statistics of mortality in connection with the Universities and white flannel. Dramatic narratives of possible Senior Wranglers being degraded into mediocre gymnasts ; of boys from whom much was expected missing their degree through practising the long jump ; of distracted fathers finding their sons return from Alma Mater with nothing to show for the money expended upon them but a medal for putting a hammer ; are not now brought forward in connection with school or college sports. A charge was delivered by a highly intellectual journal against the amateur athletes on the score of the vanity with which they must be puffed up in consequence of the notoriety they attain. But this notoriety is an accident, rather than an incident, of a racing match or of an athletic congress. Besides, the statement implies a presumption which requires proof. It is quite possible that men in a University boat feel otherwise than proud of the sort of curiosity they excite amongst the amateur touts at Putney, or of the admiration poured out upon them so liberally in the special literature required to satisfy an exceptional demand. Granting, however, that athletes, oarsmen, and others are not above a sentiment of self-satisfaction in being for a time objects of enthusiasm to the multitude, we fail to see that the circumstance is calculated to do them a lasting moral injury. That, it does them no definite harm, looking at the matter from the most practical point of view, is, we think, plain enough. A legal periodical, in accordance with the temper of the hour, published a list of judicial celebrities who had, before elevation to the bench or advances to the front ranks of the bar, pulled oars in the University eights. The spirit of emulation encouraged amongst them in physical pursuits demonstratively did not deteriorate their capacity for perseverance and resolution in the most difficult and disheartening of professions; nor did the cheers on the river-banks, the wearing of their favours by half London, the discussion of their calibre and style, spoil them for the serious business of life in which they had subsequently to engage.

It is, we confess, with an unreserved pleasure and satisfaction that we notice the daily tendency to a recognition of the use of physical culture manifested around us in the starting of new boating, cricket, and athletic clubs. A short time ago some statistics were published, showing the increase in heart disease, and ascribing the increase to the over mental work and bodily wear and tear produced by the pressure and haste of modern existence. We work our bodies without any notion that they are of delicate construction, and require forethought in rest and in food. A general understanding of athleticism, and of the absolute beauty and fitness of perfect health, would do much, we are inclined to think, to reduce not only the statistics of mortality in any specific direction, but in the average through the entire bulk of our population. So far from there being danger of moral or intellectual detriment from physical culture, it is more than probable that we suffer from the lack of it, even in those provinces of human interest on which our material nature, by a sort of paradox, is supposed never to trespass. Take, for instance, literature. Our poetry, according to the best judges of it, is remarkable for its thin and febrile qualities. It is querulous, languid, forced, and, to use the words of a well-known critic, is suggestive of the atmosphere of a sick-room. It would neither be read by, nor written for, a thoroughly healthy nation. Its over-nervous and over-emotional pictures and revelations are typical of our highly artificial, richly nourished modern fashion of living. It is not only a simile, but a truth, to assert that many of our popular poets would be the better, along with their admirers, for physical training.

Hitherto there has been no large or marked patronage of athleticism in this country. Whatever was done was done by private enterprise and taste. The Government have made a move in having swimming taught in training-ships, the good results of which we suspect might already be fairly estimated by the number of medals distributed to seamen for saving lives at sea by the Committee of the Humane Society. But something more might be ventured upon. It would not be a heavy tax upon the Treasury to set aside a small fund for medals or cups for some of the athletic clubs. A royal or state recognition of institutions of the kind would give a fresh impulse and vitality to them. It is not that they require money or cups to subsidise them, but the effect of " a Queen's plate " extends far beyond its intrinsic worth. One of the Royal Princes would probably not object to take the presidentship of an athletic academy, where the regulations and rules would furnish examples for affiliated associations throughout the country. Most of the great cities have now in working order clubs for gymnastic or athletic training ; but their managements are, for the most part, perhaps not as liberal, as enterprising, or as wise as might be wished. Some are disfigured by an exclusiveness and an extravagance which render them unpopular, save for the odd day when they contrive to get up an expensive celebration of their talents for the amusement of their friends and acquaintances. Others are connected' with distinct establishments, such as those of Oxford, Cambridge, and Trinity College, Dublin. Athleticism should not be confined to any class exclusively, or, rather, to any caste. Its advantages should be so understood that its encouragement should be universal. We are afraid we are not brought much nearer to the end we should desiderate by the periodical popularity of the Oxford and Cambridge sports, although unquestionably these exhibitions are of advantage in illustrating what ought to be a genuine subsisting sentiment, and not a fashionable or a spurious enthusiasm partly promoted by haberdashers and milliners. There are possibilities for establishing athletic sports in London, which are even perhaps more deserving of our attention and support than the Dark Blue and the Light Blue performances over which the world goes mad in two colours.

Although it is not now the custom, as it was some years ago, for ladies to boast of the weakness of their nerves, and to consider it elegant to fall into a hysterical flutter at the sight of a monstrous mouse or an unexpected black-beetle, we have only to glance round us to find that men, as well as women, have established and subscribed to many social practices which are plainly and emphatically inimical to the physical well-being of the race. There

is something ludicrous and pitiable in the enormous
amount of patented preparations sold by druggists,
addressed to those who suffer from ailments which
are simply the result of reckless eating and no exercise. Gluttony, Dr. Farr has just told us, is the vice
of the age. While the believers in an intelligent
athleticism are gaining ground every day, and making
many industrious and eager disciples amongst the
young, there are still hundreds and thousands of
people who utterly ignore the principle that health
is not to be found in the pillbox, and who abandon
themselves to habits of existence which render them
altogether unfit for the performance of the duties
which the claims of business, or even of society,
impose upon them. Indeed, by a curious intellectual
process, the class of persons to whom we refer often
acquire, after a time, a sort of attachment to a bad
digestion. When they can afford it, they take a
positive pleasure in detailing their sufferings to the
polite and sympathetic physician. Women are addicted
to this folly, perhaps, to a greater extent than men—
a consequence partly of the monotonous sort of life
they are mostly compelled to endure ; but the stronger
sex is often not above the weakness of visiting the
doctor in order to flatter a kind of craving for ma-
lingering which attacks persons of unhealthy habits
and of rather limp faculties. Women, as we know,
submit to the tortures of the boot from the shoe-
maker, to the ordeal of the stays by the milliner,
to the hot and heavy helmet of the hairdresser. Yet
there is a decided improvement in these respects of
late. It is not to any fashion of clothing or head-
padding we should put down the startling catalogue
of rickety young girls which may be formed out
of everyone's list of female acquaintances, but rather
to the late dinners, and late hours generally, of
fashionable life, and the neglect of pedestrian exercise. Horse exercise is a capital thing in its way,

and every lady should be able to enjoy it, but it will not make up for an utter disuse of legs save in a waltz in a torrid atmosphere—especially when taken at the sober pace of "The Row." London girls are kept at home, unless they can drive out, on the plea that our streets are not civilised enough for a modest woman to walk through them unmolested; but we suspect that, although an instance to support it might be produced from an occasional police report, that charge is founded upon very limited data. However, even granting there is a difficulty here, it is not insurmountable; and yet it is only poor seam-stresses and shop-girls, on cheap holiday fêtes, who are to be noted enjoying heartily the wholesome dis-tractions of gymnastic movements. Ladies cannot be expected to romp or to play at kiss-in-the-ring, taking a swift preliminary canter before submitting to the salute of their companions; but they would not be the worse for a good brisk walk round Hyde Park, instead of forming sedentary or slow promenading pictures for the criticism of the curious. Country girls who do not mind a tramp from the rectory or the manse to the village, and who can take a fence or a puddle with their stout-shod feet—who are up early and in bed early, and who have none of the feverish and violent delights of the theatre or ball-room—bear the roses on their cheeks, and have an elastic carriage as upright as the graceful posture of Maud the idyllic, not actual, milkmaid herself. The London girl, to be sure, has her season of recruiting—a rush up the Rhine, or a fortnight's dabbling at the sea-shore. She meets everyone at Baden-Baden, and renews the exciting flirtations of June; she reads French novels at Scarborough, and dines at a *table d'hôte* as ceremonious and as unwholesome as a May dinner in Belgravia. She then visits a round of country houses, and would have a chance of recuperating, but that as a rule she will insist on leading a lazy life. She does get better in spite of herself, but misses opportunities of entire restoration, which she is unfortunately unable to appreciate.

It has always been claimed for our men and women that they are more comely and more robust than any other people in the world. This has been attributed to our food, and to the comparative affluence of whole generations of families preventing degeneracy in physique from imperfect or unwholesome diet. The average truth of this assertion might be observed in Hyde Park during the season. There a highly representative cosmopolitan mob is to be witnessed any afternoon of a May or a June week. A peculiar interest was given to observations in the Row a few years ago. The circumstance of the war on the Continent had driven from Paris and New York a whole host of belles and dandies of those cities, and a chance was afforded of contrasting them with their London or English compeers. On the whole, we had decidedly the best of the comparison. The *petits crevés* of the Paris Jockey Club could not be matched for debility and effeminacy with their most inveterate imitators at certain West-end clubs. Strings of them moving arm in arm looked as if the wind of a rattling cricket ball would knock them down. And, though it is perhaps ungallant to say it, where in England will you find girl-cheeks so sallow, girl-eyes so weary, as amongst the numerous French demoiselles whose neat but exquisite toilettes did so much to compensate for their natural deficiencies of figure? If you saw them in the Row or in Kensington Gardens, their nationality was unmistakeable. Now, whether our superiority in this respect will continue is a matter for grave reflection. We are domesticating the French system of cooking largely in London. The papers from time to time have articles abusing the national and natural dietary of the country. The restaurants

—they are all restaurants now—continue to increase their list of made dishes to supply the progressive demand for them. The beef-steak is becoming an object of fashionable ridicule and contempt. The plain joint is regarded as a sort of huge British blunder, of which we ought to feel ashamed. We are by no means advocates for the landlady's mutton chop—for the eternal alternative between beef and mutton in their primitive divisions—for the over-abundance of vegetables, to which culinary justice is never done in our kitchens; but we are of opinion that a good deal of the fashion of ill-health is to be attributed to our young ladies and gentlemen constantly indulging at late hours in dinners of half a dozen courses, containing stimulating spices and other ingredients of the Continental stewpan, which are less amenable to the action of the gastric juice than even a tough beef-steak.

But we are told Young England is, if anything, over-athletic; the public schools are running mad in white flannel, and anxious fathers are in despair because more attention is paid to cricket than to mathematics. The answer usually given to parents of the anti-gymnastic order is to tell them that, as a rule, the good men in college are good men at the bat or the oar, and that the development of biceps never practically seems to interfere with the development of brain, provided always in the latter case there is a basis for the evolution of talent at all. The reply is a sound one; and, so far from our public schools suffering by a mania for muscle, considering the killing pace at which the intellectual work of the world without will have to be ultimately taken by the boy students when men, we deem it necessary that their bodies should be trained for the contest quite as carefully and as industriously as their minds. The worst of it is that, when the university career is over, so many

should entirely abandon the physical culture which
they had commenced at school. We do not mean
that an oarsman in a university boat should be in
training when his name is painted on a door in
Pump Court; but there is no reason why he should
consider his condition of prime health a folly, or
even an excess of youth, which is as much a matter
of indifference to him as the recollection of his Latin
verses. Despite the rowing clubs, cricket clubs, the
Alpine Club, and all the other institutions extant
for the encouragement of manly exercises, we are
still of opinion that their numbers might be increased
with benefit, and not with detriment to the community. Every young man who could at all spare
the time should belong to an association for outdoor
pastime. There are thousands of adolescent loungers
in London, with arms like pipe-stems, and legs like
cedar pencils, who use the privileges of their Saturday
half-holiday over beer bars, and spend their evenings
in reeking music-halls, or in the ill-ventilated billiard
closet of a murky pothouse. It is of such stuff de-
faulting clerks are made. The creature with weakly
frame is tempted into small and large vices. His
conscience grows enfeebled by the perpetual tritura-
tion of fears of detection : he is narcotised and
alcoholised into a miserable tremor of nervousness.
Never will he arrive at that age to say with old
Adam, in "As You Like It—"

> " Though I am old, yet I am strong and lusty ;
> For in my youth I never did apply
> Hot and rebellious liquors in my blood ;
> Nor did not with unbashful forehead woo
> The means of weakness and debility."

He has his prototypes on a different social level.
Although we referred above to the average superiority of the English dandy over the French dandy
in his physical aspect, a search at certain seasons
in the clubs and in promenades would disclose to

us a sad account of British weaklings—an account
which the numbers of their burly brethren would
scarce balance or compensate for. Some of these
gentry have taken to consuming absinthe before
dinner; some (we assure our readers we are writing from deliberate observation) to *stays;* some have
gone as far as paint and powder. These fine fellows
are peculiar products of our own time. We owe
part of their culture to the imperial *régime* in France;
but the modern London fribble, who a short time ago
had his hair down on his forehead like a poodle, as if he
could assist the proclamation of imbecility which
nature has stamped upon his features, revives the
image of Lord Fanny Harvey in the ghastly lines
of the hectic Juvenal who depicted him.

Why should not gymnastics be taught more regularly, not only at ladies' schools, but outside, in
rooms which girls might attend, just as men attend
a swimming club or a rowing club? We should hear
much less of what was formerly called "the vapours,"
but which is now known as hysteria, if young women
could be encouraged to take far more regular exercise
than at present. And why should men of business
confine their "constitutional walks" to either a breathless run almost immediately after breakfast for a train
every morning, or cram the entire necessary physical
relaxation of a year into six weeks or a month of unaccustomed idleness? There are few men so occupied
that they could not find leisure, through a method of
simple athletic hygiene, to avoid frequent recourse to
the family medicine-chest. An Englishman sinks into
fat and into gout with a startling complacency. As a
matter of fact we learn that gout is growing more and
more fatal and frequent. People of distinguished caste
have been quite vain of the number of their relatives
who have had chalk stones, or who have been carried
off by flying gout. It will be a bad time for us when
ill-health becomes a prevalent fashion. It would be

better, in fact, that we had a savage respect for animal health, and returned, in a degree at least, to that primitive notion of the inherent claim of the strong man to power and consequence. There is a lesson of profound national as well as moral consequence in the doctrine of the "Survival of the Fittest," and the recognition of the fittest as the best.

THE death of the old year draws on apace Somehow, as the moment of departure ap proaches, the time past takes a sort of personal figure even in minds of an ordinary and prosaic fashion. The phrases we use, the customs we observe, in connection with the obliteration of a date under which we have written, thought, and lived so long, bring with them many significant reflections to most people.

> " But, oh ! prodigious to reflec',
> A Twalmont, sirs, is gane to wreck."

So writes Robert Burns, in a half-solemn, half-jocular elegy, and the feeling expressed in the lines has been put into a thousand other forms by every singer and teacher whose mission it may be to point a moral, by indicating from book or pulpit the movement of the warning hand upon the dial-face which serves to measure the sum of our days and hours. It is not our function nor our wish, however, to weary our readers with a sermon, nor with a series of appropriate musings carefully distilled from the best published authorities on the subject. We certainly do not envy, either, the task set before many writers through a venerable tradition of reviewing the year "that's awa," for the purposes of, say, a political demonstration. The breath is scarce out of the body of the year when these—we might say clini-cal disquisitions take place. The motto, to speak nothing but good of the dead, is not over strictly observed. The effects, as it were, of the deceased are overhauled with as little remorse or tenderness as a Jew dealer displays when rummaging amongst the articles of an execution sale. There is a temptation

to do this from the mere fact of dallying with an alle-
gory, and so we shall escape at once from that nearly
obsolete ornament of 'rhetoric, and get into plain
prose with our text.

There are diaries and diaries. Such records as
those of Pepys, of Madame D'Arblay, of Horace
Walpole, are not likely to be imitated by the current generation. There is, in fact, in modern life,
little leisure left for chronicles of the kind. Men
such as Dickens and Hawthorne have left us rather
jottings than diaries, invaluable literary legacies,
but only in a small degree partaking of those odd
and intimate confessions which the regular—we
had nearly written professional—diarist used to
whisper to pen and ink, with a consciousness that
when his or her mortal career was closed the whole
incidents of the journey would be bruited for the encouragement or instruction of other wayfarers. There
is a description of diary, however, neither literary,
artistic, didactic, nor Rousseauesque, in which we take
a special interest and pleasure. It is one which, if it
ever come to light when the heir or his solicitors seals
our papers and drawers, we need fear no reproach
upon our memories. It contains no invidious person-
alities, no dreary cynicism, no token as its last chap-
ters are being penned that the lees are in the cup, and
that the milk of human kindness has turned sour.
We refer to a sportsman's diary. In this private
manual you truly fight your battles over again. Of
all things, let it be honest. Supposing in the shooting
department you make a bad bag, and, when you
peruse the headings " Grouse, Black Game, Snipe,
Partridge," what not, every syllable is fraught with
recollections of a miss. We have known men to
shrink from entries against themselves, thus falsifying
what ought to be almost a private conscience. The diary
is an edged tool in this respect. It must be candid ;
it must be sternly, severely truthful. Then, indeed,

it will be found a *vade mecum* of service and recreation. Was it because the birds were wild, or the smoking-room attractive, that so few cartridges went straight on the blank day of blank? If you desire delicacy in notation, imitate a diary such as is now before us. The gentleman to whom it belonged preferred entrusting his weaknesses to hieroglyphics; but they are not so difficult to decipher as a difficult palimpsest, and may be read, as doubtless he often did read them, with, so to speak, half an eye. In the margin, by a sentence containing the laconic admission "shot badly," is an illustration of a meerschaum pipe. In connection with a similar verdict is a neatly executed drawing of a whisky-flask, designed as a tombstone, and inscribed: "PONTO, pointer, ætat 3 years 6 months, died of No. 8 in the head, Ballyslough Bog, Dec. 20, 186—," and so on. We do not suggest or imply that a journal of the same quality should be cultivated or edited upon the same principle, but the notion is perhaps worth making known. It may demand a little ingenuity on the part of the diarist, who, however, need never dread that any indefatigable Lord Braybrooke or other expert will endeavour to interpret his secret or pictorial writing.

Seriously speaking, the diary is of real use in telling a sportsman certain facts as to locality or circumstance which he may have forgotten. For instance, you may enter in it the good finds and the blank draws, until, if your shooting is over the same ground, you will have capital data to suggest a beat to you for a day. And here we might remark that a sportsman keeping a diary will find it of advantage, especially as to wild-fowl shooting, to note the weather on every occasion when he goes out. Reading it in association with the number of birds bagged will be often suggestive of valuable practical hints and wrinkles. As to angling, this point is still more important. If our sportsman is a naturalist, his diary, no matter how concise and condensed, will be frequently of use to him in study. The sporting diary should, however, be as short as is consistent with its being intelligent and intelligible. It need not necessarily be a mere book of entries ; and even when its matter is confined to a simple statement of killed, locality, and disposal, it may furnish the pleasantest reading for its owner, when quietly perused over a cigar, between the lines.

The shooting year is now pretty far advanced. The sportsman's January, to write paradoxically, commences with August. He has been, let us suppose, keeping his diary up to the present. If he has failed in candour, if he has backslided from the principle of making his diary, as we have said before, a private conscience, now is the time for him to amend. To be sure the—well, the mistakes—anent the grouse are perhaps past praying or repenting for. There still remain the wildfowl. The season is one favourable for good intentions and resolutions. The *trottoir* referred to in a certain proverb will not want for repairing material for the month of January at least. We all resolve to do something, learn a new language, pay ready money for clothes, rise earlier in the morning, &c., &c., in honour of the new year. Let our diarists resolve to be accurate in their jottings for four weeks to begin with. The discipline may educate them with sufficient strength of purpose to last until the 12th of August comes round. To our angler who angles, innocent mendacity should also be confined to conversation. He should never put a pike upon paper that he has not fairly put into his creel. A salmon caught only in imagination, and entered as reality in cold blood in a private diary, should haunt a man like a spectre of a fish. Years afterwards, the individual who plays fast and loose with his diary will believe in his own invention. But we are well aware that the average diarist is above the peccadillo to which we refer more in good humour than in anger. He is, perhaps, far more to be trusted than the literary artists who leave voluminous notes and recollections behind them. He has nothing to gain by inaccuracy, and he has no thought of print ahead to deter him from the truth.

NOTES ON SHOOTING

HINTS FOR THE FEAST OF
ST. PARTRIDGE.

IT is highly desirable that those who take part in
this festival should not celebrate it with maimed
rites.   For this purpose a certain class of sportsmen
should bear in mind that birds only are to be hit in
the course of the day.   Neither markers, pointers, nor
setters should be considered under the head of game
by the fowler when afield.   The guests and the hosts
of the house at which a tyro visitor for the First is
entertained should be regarded as so far exempt from
the chances of being slain or wounded, that some care
should be exercised on their behalf by persons whose
guns are liable to unexpected explosions.   The head
of any friend or acquaintance sighted nervously on a
line of fire with the covey is always in danger,
although the young or the untried sportsman may not
think of the fact at the time.   A breechloader can
perforate a common English peasant, engaged to assist
in the great business of the hour, at any distance from
one up to seventy-five or eighty yards.   The effect at
the short range is, probably, instantaneous death ; at
the longer range the result may be simple blinding for
life, according to circumstances over which the sucking or prentice fowler has no control.   Occasionally,
a marker struck at eighty yards may escape with a
mere peppering which causes him to execute a most
diverting *pas seul.*   It might be judicious or charitable
for the inexperienced friend to whom these hints are
offered to ascertain as early as possible in the morning
who are the married men in the party.   To wing an
old bachelor may be awkward, but to bag or cripple
the father of a family is a proceeding about which

there is an air of thoughtlessness and levity. Agreeable reunions on the First have before now been abruptly broken up by the insertion of a small proportion of a cartridge into the leg of the squire himself, who, in an evil and smoking-room hour in town, had invited the operator, who apparently took his host's gaiters for ground game, for a week's shooting. There are few men so fond of shooting that they like to be constantly obliged to look into the barrels of their neighbours' guns. This ought to be kept in mind by the neophyte who, from the mode in which he carries his weapon, appears to think that whoever comes near him is anxious to satisfy himself by personal inspection as to the exact bóre of the loaded piece. Nor is there anything gained, when following your friends over a hedge, by turning the gun on full cock towards the back buttons of their coats. When jumping from the hedge yourself, or sliding down it, there is no object with which wild poultry can be associated, at least, in coming on your feet with your breechloader directed, with a jerk, upon the group of featherless bipeds who are waiting for you to join them.

A partridge to our young sportsman appears to explode into little bits when first flushed, or to resolve itself into a catherine-wheel, like that represented by Leech in his famous picture of Mr. Briggs amongst the pheasants. The delusion, or illusion, however, has so strong an effect on the tyro, that he tries to arrest the transformation as it were by firing at the bird the instant it is off the ground. There could be no greater mistake—as a dog often finds to his cost. It is better not to pull the trigger until the gun is brought fairly to the shoulder, and that manœuvre is inconsistent with the hysterical snap which follows on the spring of a covey from the weapon of the impatient or the excited sportsman. The latter should also remember that he has far more chances of bringing down his quarry at thirty than at ten paces. The partridge will neither burst of his own accord, nor vanish into thin air, if permitted to go a little further. Indeed, he generally retires in excellent order when a wild attempt is made at him at close quarters; but by waiting until he has attained thirty or even forty yards, there is the satisfaction of feeling that, if not missed outright, there is a prospect of his receiving an odd pellet from the charge, which will probably result in his dying in a ditch, attended in his last moments by a weasel or a hawk.

If you are placed next a good shot, contrive as often as possible to fire at the same time that he does. When the bird is allotted to him, look amicably resigned. As a general rule, reverse the spirit of the order in battle to aim low: aim high, for several reasons. The height of a setter from the ground is not much: the human stature is also below the average level of partridges' flight; so that no sportsman-like object can be well attained by sending the contents of your cartridge skimming a couple of feet over the tops of the turnips. Low firing, as understood by our beginner, often consists of simply smashing a mangold-wurzel a few yards off. The mangold does not count in the day's bag. High firing is comparatively a safe proceeding unless the markers are on hazardous elevations. But it is difficult to lay down any specific regulations which would insure comparative immunity from extreme peril for these officials in places where a few of the company are enthusiastically fond of shooting but quite unaccustomed to it. We are almost afraid to venture upon any suggestions to old sportsmen. The veteran is ever and properly impatient of advice. Besides, the man who cannot hit seven partridges out of ten that he fires at on the First is not likely to profit much by our writing. Nothing but steadiness is required for the work. The birds, if approached at a proper hour, will wait to be kicked up, and the old cock ought to be brought down like an old hat to start

with.   Don't take your eye from the bird that catches
it first: have at him determinedly.   The instant you let
drive at him, remember you have a second barrel, and
that a clever practitioner should perform with the right
and left as deftly as a pianist with both hands.   There
is very little credit, indeed, in taking a single bird out
of the lot when the covey is well within range.   It is
quite another matter late on in October, when the
birds are thin and scattered, and when they are wary
and strong on the wing.   On September days, also, if
the weather should be bad (say wet over night and a
high wind next day), partridge-shooting may alter its
conditions completely.   Coveys deprived of the old
birds as soon as possible will be found easiest of
approach.   We believe in "rogue" partridges: single
brutes that will dart under your nose over a hedge, and,
with the rustle of their wings, call up covey after covey
in the fields which you have designed to beat.   There
is nothing for it under such circumstances but to mark
down the flushed lots.

   A good luncheon is generally followed by bad shooting.   Moderate refreshment, of course, is requisite and
useful.   The cigar afterwards (one, and only one) seems
to cool down the excitement, perhaps naturally, conse-
quent upon the first day's campaign.   Forced marches
on this occasion may be also strongly condemned.   To
make a toil of a pleasure is often a vice of an athletic
Englishman.   It may be as well to leave many of the
coveys untouched at the commencement of the season.
There is plenty of sport to be had without a massacre
of the callow innocents who are not much bigger than
quails, and whose tender bodies are as easily riddled
and torn as the carcass of the soft-fleshed landrail.
There are few things more unsportsmanlike than
putting up a partridge nursery, and, when the fledg-
lings flutter separately into the holes and corners of
hedges, marching to them with a cunning old pointer,
or having them poked out with a stick from their

retreats. The contents of the poulterers' shops in London on Monday will, we are afraid, display a sad reckoning on the hooks of partlets cut off in the bloom of youth, before they had time to strengthen on the soil, and were fit to be the quarry of others than chicken-butcher fowlers. There is no skill or fun in compassing the deaths of these infants, and their doom should not be pronounced except upon very much over-stocked ground. Even there the thinning should commence with the lusty and the ripe birds.

A word, in parting, to our friend who enters turnip or stubble for the first time to-day. We most emphatically commend to his consideration the observations at the head of this article. He should have it impressed upon him that once the trigger is pulled it is impossible to recall the charge which goes out upon its mission at the explosion, so that every precaution should be taken antecedent to an act of dog slaughter or markercide as the case might be. Prevention in such circumstances is decidedly better than cure, the extraction of small shot from the human frame being perhaps one of the most uncomfortable operations of surgery to which the living subject can be liable. For the rest, let the young sportsman prattle modestly, if at all, of his exploits. Let his talk not be *perdrix, toujours perdrix,* what time the short interval is allowed before coffee where he is entertained. His deeds should speak for themselves, let us hope not with a tragic, solemn interest, but with a reasonable assertion to a repute for prudence, if not for skill, for an amount of di. cretion which has insured him, at any rate, from the disagreeable consciousness of having to pension a keeper on crutches for the sake of the momentary pleasure derived from firing, where driving up is allowed, indiscriminately into the brain, not of the birds, but of the beaters.

SNIPE SHOOTING.

NO man has studied the art of shooting with due effect until he can with confidence enter a snipe bog and give a good account of what goes out of his cartridge-belt or shot-pouch. And yet it is strange how many experts in the stubbles and clean practitioners upon the moors you will find blundering like Winkle himself when trying to stop the swift flight of that excellent bird upon toast to which this article is dedicated. Snipe shooting, in fact, is a science in itself, and the snipe shot is often a specialist. It has peculiar and varied attractions. For instance, it comes in with the proper weather for sport, when trees are bare and the frost is on the pane. Your best snipe month, perhaps, is December, but as early as October the birds are often thickly congregated in the fens. In the snow you must seek for your snipe by the wet ditches, thawed springs, and running streams.

Last year, when the moors and mountains were wrapped in white, and the bog was frozen so hard that a snipe could no more dig for his dinner in it than he could discount his bill at the Bank of England, I performed a murderous manœuvre in connection with these birds, which at some risk to my character I shall venture to recount. In the very centre of an excellent snipe parish was a single unfrozen patch; the water, in fact, was constantly bubbling through a bed of moss and weed. Near it was a hedge, and here, gun in hand, I waited and watched. Presently a noise in the air more resembling the bleat of a goat than the cry of a bird announces the coming of my quarry. I can see them at an immense height, and down they drop, six of them, until within a few yards of the spring; and then, when their legs are quite visible as they ease them before pitching—well, it was not much to boast of; and the deed was repeated until a total of fifteen couples was made up.

In soft, muggy weather, with no rain, the snipe lie well, and will be found in open and thinly covered ground. It is specially to be noted that snipe have pet quarters which they frequent. Just as there are certain holes in a stream where there always is a fish, and certain other likely-looking reaches where a rise was never got within the memory of angler, so in regard to snipe there are particular haunts which they select year after year, in which they will be flushed when you could not find a feather in their neighbourhood. And I confess it is very difficult to account for the fact. I know of an extensive moor apparently fit in every way for the residence of snipe; I know also that it never pays to walk it: while on its skirts, within range of a constantly travelled high road, you may put up wisps of the birds; and when the wisps have burst around (I use the word "burst" advisedly, as descriptive of the odd globular style in which the congregated snipe spin a few yards from the turf and then scatter as a shell explodes), you may quietly beat over the same place and hit or miss ten or twelve couples. I never could find anything in the soil or situation of this favoured locality to render it so popular with the snipe, but I have experienced a similar thing over and over again. A naturalist no doubt would help me to a solution of the problem.

You will probably miss a great many snipe indeed before you hit one, until you are accustomed to the business. Most persons fire too quickly at a snipe. There is, to be sure, a moment when the snipe appears, at which, if you cover him and pull trigger on the instant consent of eye and finger, you have him as you wanted; but, as a rule, for once you do this successfully, you will twenty times be too late in shooting.

The only occasion when snap firing is to be commended is when a snipe is going straight off from you, because, as he advances even by a yard, his flight becomes more crooked and difficult. It is not hard to pot him in this endeavour to escape you; but, if you want practice for the performance, it is a good plan to have a friend bowl a stone the size of a cricket ball swiftly before you: hit that between twenty and twenty-five yards, and you will improve your hand in for the real article.

In hard windy weather—stormy weather—the snipe are exceedingly wild; but, on the other hand, as they try to head the stiff breeze, you have a fair chance at them. A snipe crosses the wind usually, unless wounded.

You must learn to shoot right and left at snipe. I give a man no credit, when five birds get up within ten yards, if he brings down only one. In executing this little feat dexterously, when done three or four times consecutively, the feeling of self-satisfaction experienced is worth wetting your boots for. Remember that the snipe do not form a " brown," as a covey may; the birds dart aside each on his own hook, so that you must shift your gun considerably when you have pulled the first trigger.

If you condescend to shoot Jacks—I always do— take them easy. Your Jack is a cunning atom of a wildfowl, and will waggle occasionally before your gun like a butterfly in a tempest. But Master Jack can be brought out of the misery of having to live in a bog by watching him steadily for a few seconds, and letting drive at him when he is suspended between one waggle or wriggle and another.

If you are in comparatively strange quarters, and want to know where the snipe are thickest, put on your sentry-box coat, and have a moonlight stroll near the fen, the moor, the bog. Then the bird, so silent during the day unless when roused, is on the alert, squeaking and bleating all over the place. Now you observe where there is most of the squeaking and bleating, and go there the first thing in the morning; you will not regret the preliminary excursion, I can assure you.

Coming on late in the season, the snipe will frequent the turnip-fields, and even potato-gardens in the black reclaimed soil usually contiguous to moorlands; therefore do not omit to search the turnip-fields and potatogardens. Also, if there is elevated ground near your shooting covered with heather, withered ferns, or furze, try it after a rainy night. Snipe often emigrate temporarily to such quarters. Here, too, they will be rather wild, and remember that they will run into the perfectly dry as well as into the damp heather.

I once, and once only, saw a "double snipe," and it was in fern where I was searching for a woodcock I had marked down from a covert. I was quite certain, when he got up without any noise, that he was the cock. I missed him, I am sorry to say, and saw him alight again, after flying, I thought, very differently from any woodcock I ever met with before. On the second occasion I knocked him over, and then found he was the genuine double snipe. The monster was solitary, as monsters usually are, and he is now enshrined in a glass case. However, that is by the way.

Carry a setter with you snipe shooting—an old veteran at it, whose nostrils have not been demoralised in youth by employment upon grouse or ptarmigan. He must know what he is wanted for. Keep him in full diet; he is not required for speed or for range, and an inner coat of fat will be useful to him in the wet and cold he will have to pass through. There is no reason *why* a dog should not be used for snipe shooting; and every well-bred dog will take kindly to it with a little trouble on your part. A pointer is scarcely hardy enough for this business. He is liable to shivers from it, and looks horribly wobegone and unsightly at the end of a frosty day, when icicles are forming on his belly, his eyes are full of tears, and his unfortunate rudder has a crimson tip to it from constantly whisking and rubbing against the reeds of the bog. Mind you, I am not here offering another contribution to that vast pile of erudition which has been lavished upon the great question of Pointer *v.* Setter. Every dog has his day, and for a day's hard snipe shooting commend me to the setter.

Use No. 8 shot for snipe, unless you expect duck about the place, and even then No. 8 is quite effective enough for bringing down a mallard with a properly directed gun up to thirty yards. No. 9, I know, is often employed, but I prefer No. 8. You take your choice; but, with the politeness of a controversial theologian, I urge mine upon you as the best. Wound as few snipe as you can; it is, for many reasons, far more desirable that you should kill your bird outright, and not have to perform the part of butcher upon a miserable winged little fowl, who is ridiculously defenceless-looking when he spreads out his tail at your mercy. Should it be necessary to operate on him, in the name of humanity and sport, don't, as I have seen an ignorant fellow do, take and hammer his head against the stock of your gun, or against your bluchers, and then find him kicking with cerebral convulsions in your bag half an hour afterwards! Press his breast until the bone gives way, and flick his poll at the same time with your finger, and there's a quick end of him—a perfect euthanasia for him.

And now, when you have your snipe, do not keep him over-long hanging in the larder. He should be eaten comparatively fresh, and with the plainest of plain sauce; however, for all this, *chacun a son goût.*

A word to very young sportsmen, snipe shooters included. Don't be nervous when a snipe gets up. Although you feel a kind of shock or fright, bear in mind that a snipe was never yet known to turn upon a fowler and bite him, and that the bird won't, in fact, do anything aggressive to you for firing at him. It may appear superfluous, or even absurd, to put out this assurance ; but who amongst us who knows anything of shooting but can remember scores of men who, at flushing of snipe or partridge, seem as scared as if a bull or a python had to be encountered ?

PLOVER SHOOTING cannot be fairly regarded as belonging to the *haute école* of sport with the gun, and yet it is not without its own peculiar interest, and certainly not without its advantages. The wild-fowl shooter regards it as one of the finest methods of filling a bag; for if you do come across the plover at all, some wholesale work should be effected with the stand. In the earlier part of the season the great flocks or stands of golden plover keep mostly to the mountains and highlands. Here, in ordinary weather, it is extremely difficult to approach them. They have their established " haunts " from time immemorial, frequenting exactly the same spot year after year; but to get near these potting quarters would be as difficult as to surprise the most important outpost of a German army, for the plover would seem to be an admirably drilled bird. You will see the rank and file wheeling through the sky in a vast column, anon breaking into single line, then forming divisions in echelon, moving into solid square, and suddenly dispersing, as though for skirmishing purposes. The only means of having an open at them in the milder period of the year is either to wait for a thick foggy day—a day of mist and drizzle—and then walk in a line of their probable flight, and have them put up by an assistant; or to put yourself behind an artificial or natural ambush, within thirty or forty yards of the patch of stony moor soil on which they are sure to alight every evening.

But there is one thing absolutely indispensable in order to carry the theory of plover shooting into sound and valuable practice. You must have a more or less nice and correct musical ear, and be able to imitate the call of the birds. I have never yet found any shop instrument made to mimic the querulous pipe of the plover of much real service in this business, and for a simple reason enough. The shop instrument is not capable of a variation in tone, and the plover do not always talk to or warn each other in the same fashion. From constant practice and experience I have found that the distinctions in the plover-call, though exceedingly fine and delicate, are marked and plain enough. Within about a fortnight I have bagged over two hundred of these birds, and I attribute more than half my success to the complete manner in which I have deceived the plover by whistling. My custom is never to begin the invitation myself. Very often the "stands" will sail backwards and forwards at an immense height over your head for an hour almost, without speaking a single word in the ranks, save now and again what sounds like a cautious word of command, which does not resemble the usual shrill challenge of the bird. It happens, however, that one individual has strayed from the flock. You see him with flickering wings skirting the purple edge of the mountain, and the moment he gives tongue you must be ready to reply to him. If your answer is satisfactory, he responds, again wheeling in a closer circle to where you are, and then, if you will look up, you will perceive a curious agitation taking place in the host above your head. One by one the members of it begin to chime in with the whistle— plover answers to plover all over the moor. The unfortunate brute whom you have used for a decoy is now perhaps within easy shot, but it will by no means pay you to fire at him. Keep him as it were on hand as long as ever you can ; let him pipe away, and he will attract his brethren in the clouds. They, you will perceive, are gradually descending, and all of a sudden make a simultaneous swerve, and then a dive straight off from you. Whistle as hard as you can, and have your gun on full cock, for the chances are they will be back with a sweep and a rush across your very face.   Here they come with a splash of wings like the tumbling of water.   You blaze right into the advancing line and—kill nothing ; blaze into them when their side is exposed, on the slant, when you see the gleam of their white bellies, and you will have a different account to give of your cartridges.

In frosty, hard weather the plover come into the moist lowlands, and the hills about them, which are not snow-covered like the high mountains.   Here again they have their regular "haunts," which are traditionally certain finds, and you must ascertain where these haunts are before venturing on your campaign.   When in these winter quarters, the birds are far more approachable than when they are on the mountains, and will come to call far more readily. You will not, however, meet them in such vast quantities.   The plover frequently in frosty weather break into small questing parties, and these are mostly on the wing and on the whistle.   If you creep under a hedge near their line of flight, you may have capital practice at them all day long.   Firing at them does not seem to make them wiser in avoiding your whistle-charm.   The only time when your sport at plover is liable to be spoiled in the frost is when the birds mingle with the green plover (lapwing, pewit). Though this wildfowl does not fear propinquity to railway stations, I know no bird, with the exception of the villain curlew, so wary as the pewit.   And the worst of it is that the lapwing is not only wary himself, but the cause of extreme wariness in others. When the green plover join the golden plover, you might as well, to use an Irish phrase, be whistling jigs to a milestone as trying to attract the latter.   And as for imitating the half squeal, half squeak of the lapwing, no mortal lips or mortal throat could attempt that performance with success.   It might perhaps be done with a comb and a piece of paper, but we should not commend these articles as necessary portions of a wildfowler's paraphernalia. The best thing to do when you observe that the pewit and golden plover are packing together is to fire a shot into the allies at any distance, for the mere purpose of making a noise. The pewits will dance, wriggle, tumble frantically, scream, and separate from their cousins. The golden plover will retire in beautiful order and symmetry, and you may have a subsequent opportunity of dealing with them before the squealing nuisances have joined them again. But some of our readers will ask, is not the green plover at this season a good bird on the table? It is not a *bad* bird; that is all I will say for it, and its flesh— what little even there is of it—is in no way comparable to the plump, succulent carcass of the rotund golden plover. If you are anywhere close to the sea in hard weather, you know, of course, that the golden will very often pitch upon the mud-banks. Here they are not to be had until the tide rises; and if you station yourself in a boat in a creek or pill, the flocks are sure to fly low when leaving the ooze. In such places I have met also a small plover exactly the same shape and form as the golden plover, but grey instead of yellow, bronze on the back. I do not know the natural history designation of this bird, but it is by no means to be despised when served upon toast.

Plover require heavy shot. I have fired No. 8 at them with about as much effect as if I had fired a charge of sand. I would recommend No. 5 for this work. Never be in a hurry with your second barrel for plover; when the first is let off, the birds are very likely to wheel round you again, especially if any are running upon the ground wounded. You will thus have the opportunity of taking a more deliberate aim. It is very curious, indeed, how often you might blaze into the thick of a stand without raising a feather, if you do not pull at the proper instant. A second gun and a second fowler will be useful accessories in this sport; but, in the name of good luck and success, do not allow your friend to " call," unless he is able to perform that melodious exercise properly. The plover are driven off at once by a false pipe, and it is very hard to win them back again, if once they have heard a doubtful invitation from the place where you are hiding. It will happen (in snow, for instance) that you may come across a field containing—when you peep over the hedge—all sorts of birds, such as fieldfare, thrushes, buntings. They seem very large, and you must distinguish your proper quarry, the plover, by the circumstance that they run while the others hop. In wild, gusty weather the plover pitch for most of the day in their mountain haunts. If the peasants in the district are in the habit of cutting turf, brushwood, or gorse in the neighbourhood of the haunt, bargain with one of them to act as a stalking-horse for you. I have done wonderful execution in this manner by creeping at the side of an old woman, and letting drive across her venerable back. The birds will often allow a cart or a countryman to come near them, when the sight of a pair of gaiters and a gun-barrel would send them off like lightning. If you can manage to stalk them—and this is seldom feasible, as they are discreet enough to lodge almost invariably away from a hedge or vantage-spot—should you contrive to steal within fifty yards, watch if they are picking and running about, or if they have ceased these manœuvres and are standing still as stones. In the latter case they are watching you, and ready for flight; and I advise a sudden and very obstreperous rush upon them. This has often the effect of surprising them for a few seconds, and then you are fairly within distance. If, on the other hand, the birds go on running and feeding while you approach, you may gradually close in upon them until within range.

ON THE APPROACH TO GAME.

THERE is no sort of game that may not to some extent be stalked. To be sure you do not approach partridge as you might deer, but even with the humbler quarry every sportsman knows a certain system ought to be observed. I am not speaking now of a country where every acre maintains a covey, but of a moderately stocked district. With how many losses, for instance, we purchase the experience of being cautious in jumping from a hedge! We have been beating field after field, we climb on a fence, put the gun on half cock, and whir-r-r, there they go, having sprung before we have got well on our feet. Of course, in time the fowler learns discretion in this respect. It is scarcely necessary here to warn sportsmen from walking in furrows down wind, and yet haste and impatience often suggest this indiscretion. It is, I think, a mistake to lay it down as an invariable rule that birds are wilder 'in thin than in thick covers. I have shot down several coveys in an overfull quarter, and found them lie remarkably close to the most sparsely furnished potato-gardens. But I was sensible enough to make as little noise as possible. Roaring at a dog, calling to markers, whistling encouragement to slow pointers, all tend to render a near approach to birds difficult. They mind whistling, perhaps, least of all sorts of noise; but the silent method of search, with instructions for your four-footed assistants by hand and gesticulation, is always the preferable plan. The same rule applies to woodcock shooting in the open. By the open I mean the heather side of a mountain, as distinguished from the copse. Shouting causes the cock to run, and not to rise, except at awkward distances ; but your beaters may thump and thwack the ferns and gorse as much as ever they like. This has the effect of really "flushing" the bird, while talking and howling frighten him, and warn him into stealing away cunningly.

No matter what may be said as to the chances o easy cross shots at snipe by walking for them down wind, my advice is, don't do it. You will often put up a whole fen full of them in this fashion. Snipe call each other out of danger with remarkable alacrity and emphasis. Wisp bleats to wisp, and, as your footsteps are carried to the squatting longbills, they lose no time in trying to save themselves by flight. The patter of a dog's paws is another signal for their departure. Where the snipe are very wild, tie up your dog alto-gether until you try the ground a second or a third time. In stormy weather it is absolutely fatal to the prospect of a fair snipe-bag to walk down wind. On the other hand, in a gale you may do well enough by approaching them in the teeth of the blast. In frost you will, I am sure, discover your account in shooting up rather than down the streams. I cannot give you the reason—unless it is that the birds are looking up stream—but I am very positive of the fact. Quick rather than slow walking is also to be preferred in snipe-shooting. I believe the birds are occasionally cowed, as it were, by a quick, determined, but not splashing approach. Wild duck you must get at from an ambush, or by marking the flight time, or by studying where the mallards who do not leave the fen at dawn are in the habit of secreting themselves. You need not much care in the latter case about frightening them by voice, or by a shot even. I have known several couples to hide in the reeds within a short stone-throw of a hard-working railway. I have shot many snipe and missed some in a small moor, and afterwards knocked over Mr. Drake and Madame Duck, who were quietly listening to discharge after discharge almost within range. Teal, however, are much more wary. I have just caught a glimpse of or e pretty little head a hundred yards off, peeping from a pool or from the reed-grass. I have understood at once that the sentry was on duty, and that to march straight to the spot would be a signal for other seven or nine to whutter off. A favourite manœuvre of mine in wildfowl shooting, which I have tried most success-fully with teal as well as with plover, has been—if within reasonable approach at all, say two hundred yards—to make a run for it, with gun on full cock, right at them. The effect of this bold stratagem is sometimes everything that could be desired. At any rate, it is better to risk it than to try and sneak over to a flock of teal without shelter when the bird on duty has his eye fixed on you.

In following golden plover or curlew, if you think the latter worth following, of course you must be guided principally by the nature of the ground. Generally speaking, both these fowl are wise enough to avoid places from which you might have a pot shot at them. They will take up their quarters in the centre of a field, for instance, so as to avoid the perils of the hedges, from which a gun might be directed. It often happens, still, that a few birds will stray un-observed from the others within range of the ambush. You do not perceive them, because your eyes are fixed on the larger flock ; but do you not remember how, more than once, when the main stand wheeled aloft, how surprised you were to notice several of the com-pany join them from positions near enough for you to have taken your chance ? Therefore never neglect examining, through your bushes or fences, every part of a field in which you can distinguish an army of plover. It is not a bad dodge, either, to despatch a careful and intelligent help to the opposite side of the place in which you are anxious to do business. Let him not show himself, but let him put up a handkerchief on a stick and shake it over the hedge, and this has often the effect, not of frightening up the stand, but of puzzling them, and perhaps of making them gradually sidle in your direction. At the worst, if it does start them into flight, there is the off chance of their making your way.

The hours of the day, the months, the nature of the soil in the locality, the weather (especially), alter the conditions of approach to game, so that it is exceedingly difficult to dogmatise on the subject. The sound sportsman should always study the problems he is himself accustomed to be confronted with. The punt-shooters have innumerable contrivances for approaching their prey, and very cold and difficult work their expeditions include. I have formed an invaluable alliance, when in pursuit of (edible) sea-fowl, with old ladies, whose occupation it was to collect the weed consumed in a sauce as laver. For a shilling or so I have obtained permission from these ancient dames to convert them to the use of the obsolete stalking-horse. The birds are familiar with them, and go on feeding with quite pathetic confidence while the laver gatherer is stooping to her calling. After a time it is scarcely necessary to say that the value of an ally such as I am describing becomes altogether depreciated. A man with a horse and cart, where horses and carts are employed to bring in seaweed, may be another serviceable aid to the coast-shooter. But you must tell him to drive exactly as he drives on ordinary occasions. If he moves slower, or with a semblance of consciousness in the route he takes, the wary wildfowl smell powder. In very severe weather, snow especially, it is a mere truism to say that birds generally are easy of approach. The same may be observed immediately before any violent change of weather, either for frost or storm, or excessive rain. Birds—plover, snipe, wild duck, partridge, woodcock, grouse, teal—have appeared to me also to be invariably bewildered by heavy fogs. To be sure, the sportsman may be in the same plight to a degree, but he must so far keep his wits about him as to be ready for any off chance that may present itself to him. If you flush a woodcock from the heather in a very close fog, you may be sure, though you have fired and missed him, that he will pitch again not very far off. Partridge, perhaps, do not so much mind the fog; and though grouse seem to shorten their flight, my opportunities for observing them under the circumstance will not warrant me in speaking in italics on the point. I can, however, maintain that snipe are tamed by fogs, and are, when enveloped in the fen cloud, apparently as bothered as a mere Piccadilly lounger would be in the same position.

WHEN the voice of the cuckoo is heard in the land, when leaves are green and birds are nesting, it seems almost like a crime to disturb the gun in its case; but I confess I never could resist the temptation of doing this when what we used to term the May-fowl arrived amongst us. The birds generally put in their first appearance in small flocks in the middle of April, and continued to arrive in greater numbers until the end of the following month. They were to be had close to the coast, on the stones, when the tide was out, and at high water they frequented the neighbouring fen and fields, which the curlew, which they so nearly resemble, were in the habit of resorting to. As new-comers, the whimbrels were not very difficult to approach—indeed, I have walked without any cover within shot of them; but they soon learn to be more cautious. I can call to mind now, one fresh April morning, starting off for a preliminary spin of three miles over a glorious sand. The sea is as smooth as a mirror, and that arrant fish-hunter, the gull, is on the wing, contrasting in graceful movement with the ugly loon, who flops into flight from the soft swelling meadows of the water. Away in the far distance lies a grim plain, known as the Black Rocks, which you enter from an acre of ante-diluvian timber, now reduced to a dark or red pulp; and the clang of the myriad birds on the uttermost verge of the Black Rocks is borne in to you distinctly. You pass the girls coming to market, wearing their shoes in their baskets, as is their custom in these parts, in order to economise the luxuries for prome-

nade through the streets of the town. They have neat
ankles, and ready repartees, and pleasant wishes with
which to greet the fowler who exchanges a genial good
morrow with them. You meet the solitary coastguard with ridiculous jacket and huge telescope, the
gang of dillosk gatherers, the amphibious kind of
farmer riding his " garran " horse on the shingle ; and
then, at last, all alone, you arrive at the region of the
Black Rocks.

The place is studded with pools, and is hard, stony,
and slippery walking. You put up flock after flock of
sandpipers and sea-larks, who come skirling and
whistling round you as though they knew you were
not in quest of them. And the soft voice of the calm
sea grows plainer and plainer, and you begin to distinguish the grey congress of herons, the sooty parliament of cormorants, the hundred and one other
varieties of fearful wild fowl that are lodged at where
the white line marks the surf-point of the coast. And
while you are still only within rifle range, hark ! your
old winter enemy, the whaup, gives a signal, and then
another and another, as who would say, I see him—I
see him ! I see him—see him ! and thereupon the
heavy herons string in bad order towards the open
tide, and the air is clouded with other feathered
bipeds, whose matins or breakfasts have been rudely
interrupted by that scurril, long-billed rascal, whose
conduct almost induces a resort to what Mark Twain
alludes to as profanation, for relief. But be so far
consoled as to believe that the whimbrels, innocent as
they are, will return when the patter raised by the
curlew has ceased. And so you trudge, and slip, and
jump your route outwards and——

Why, there is a whole flock on the ground within
thirty yards of you !

They see you evidently, for, like the golden plover,
they stop moving, and are as motionless as pebbles.
You can't do very much in a shot, for they stand

rather wide apart; and so pick out one, and then be ready with your left when they rise. Move a little nearer! Now! Well, this sort of work is not much to boast of, is it, although you do get a brace? Load again, and behold the whimbrel, foolish as the fat scullion of Sterne, pitch down a few hundred yards off. Give them a short interval to forget the occurrence of the last minute, and you will perceive them moving about each other, as though they were walking stately minuets. And so on and on until the bag is heavy enough, and then quick march, in time for muffin and chop, with perhaps, if the morning be mild enough, a run into and a swim in the sea, to wash from you the flavour of sporting saltpetre.

I would not have you follow the whimbrel into the fen. Our wild ducks are breeding there, and, if you please, I am unwilling that they should be disturbed, with so many cares impending over them at this season. But when evening comes and the water is full, let us to the fields and fallows while we smoke our after-dinner weed. You can be in at the death of the sun and watch the grand funeral the clouds give him, and observe how the song of the lark appears to grow more melancholy and distant when the western wave has folded over the fountain of the light he loves. Or you may do none of these things, but mind your business, and peep cautiously over the hedges of ploughed and bawn lands. You are lucky enough to encounter Tim Lyons, who tells you there is a sight of May-birds at the back of his house. And, indeed, from the yard of the residence of Mr. Lyons (straw roof, style of architecture *mud*iæval, if you will kindly, excuse a jokelet) the April-May-birds are within shot. In fact, you cannot do better than rest your trusty weapon on the top of the hermitage in which the pig lives. Now for it! Tim deserves a sip from the flask for his ministration, and he follows you for the rest of the evening, showing you the favourite resting-places of the birds. It is to be observed that they invariably frequent the same spots year after year, as plover will "a haunt," no matter how many have been shot or fired at in the district.

Your very good friend who is on a visit with you takes another sea-shore walk another evening, and you take to a boat on the water. The boat must be in such a situation as a creek across which the birds are likely to fly. It may be that you may drop a graplin here, and throw out a line for whiting and flat-fish. At any rate, you are pretty certain to get several chances at the April-May-birds, and be careful that you aim well before them.

I have before now confessed to my readers that, though a practical sportsman of more than average experience, especially in wild-fowl shooting, I am a naturalist of the most unreliable ignorance. I have called the birds referred to whimbrels, because I was reminded of my April excursions when reading the Wild Birds Protection Act; and on the strength of several engravings, a copy of Bewick, a pilgrimage to the bird-mummy department of the British Museum, I am satisfied that my April quarry *were* whimbrels. However, I may be wrong—perhaps they were young curlew; if so, I am only sorry I did not shoot more of them, for as a wild-fowl stalker I declare I would shoot a curlew in any place, time, or situation in which I could compass his destruction. The birds I refer to are much smaller than the curlew, higher in colour, and the locality to which I adverted was the south coast of Ireland. My April-May-bird whimbrel made a most excellent dish—quite as succulent as a teal, and no suspicion of fish about him whatever. But, N.B., I am so opposed on general principles to fowling in April under any circumstances, save perhaps in the cause of science, that I would throw over my old pastime and place it under the ban of forbidden pleasures without hesitation, though not without regret. For I have enjoyed these morning and evening rambles in April and in the early May, and I am quite convinced that, as far as my whimbrels (?) were concerned, I selected the proper season for going out to kill something.

CONCERNING BEATERS.

ALTHOUGH I have read numerous essays and dissertations on dogs and guns and the paraphernalia of shooting, I do not think I have ever yet come across a descriptive paper on a necessary adjunct of modern sport—the beater. The beater differs essentially from the gamekeeper proper. He knows little or nothing of the science or art of the pursuit which he follows. He seldom rises from the ranks and gets promoted in his calling. The French soldier may see a marshal's baton in his knapsack, but the beater can never hope to find the promise of a velveteen jacket shadowed in his very limited wardrobe. He is to the superior professionals of his craft as the super at the theatre is to the regular and salaried actor. The beater has a great deal of the vagrant in his composition, and the instincts of a poacher ; only repressed by the examples of punishment which he witnesses, or is compelled to aid in bringing about. He must be an indefatigable walker, and capable of being desperately handicapped with game-bags. To some extent he must be shot-proof. In the course of his career he is almost certain to be peppered now and again by beginners, who take the word "mark" for a signal to pull a trigger, without thinking twice whether any one is in the line of fire ; but the beater is pachydermatous, and will not call out unless his clothes and his hide have been penetrated at short range. He has a complete contempt for thorns and brambles. He will thump the brushwood on a hill-side at an angle of forty-five degrees. His capacity for whisky is enormous, his appetite insatiable ; and yet he will wait at a distance

s

from a luncheon-party without any more emphatic token of voracity than that which may be observed in the pointer, whose wistful jaws involuntarily imitate the motions of mastication which his master may be going through.

The common species of beater is a dull dog as a rule. He has very little to say or to suggest. If he does venture on a remark, his chief, the gamekeeper, considers it *de rigueur* to shut him up at once. He goes about his business mechanically, and with little interest apparently, or enthusiasm When you reflect that perhaps he is aware that every bird you bring down will add to the weight he must carry at the end of the day, you may excuse him for a lack of enthusiasm in your success. Besides, he may be aware that, hit or miss, his wage will not be increased ; his tariff is fixed for him beforehand ; he has nothing to hope for from that generosity which comes of triumph or good luck, and which will put an additional half-crown into the pocket of his superior. The common beater often grows grey in the service. What he does in spring and summer it is not easy to make out. He picks up odd jobs about the farms, but the farmers do not regard him as a willing or a useful hand. He may be observed blinking in the sun outside the door of the village pot-house ; but he is not sociable in his habits, and inside is not received with much favour by the gentry who use the parlour as a place of meeting for brethren who love the occupation of snaring pheasants or of knocking a watcher on the head with a stick. He is not equal to training a dog, and the most that can be expected from him is that he should be acquainted with the topography of a preserve ; but even on this point he is frequently dull, and as likely to lose his way in his own parish as if he were let loose in the prairie or on the pampas.

Of a very different kind is the beater who flourishes where no regular gamekeeper is found. Ireland, for

instance, abounds with idle fellows who are born in
some neighbourhood where there is common, un-
enclosed mountain or moorland, not yet brought under
rent or cultivation for birds. These ne'er-do-wells are
smart and spry to a fault. They are really acquainted
with the best places and the best times for sport ; and,
moreover, to anyone with the least sense of humour,
are the most amusing and diverting rascals in the
world. They are full of bright cunning, often disguised under an air of extreme simplicity. " Oh,
begor, there he goes, sir, wid his feathers knocked out
av him !" was a favourite expression of condolence with
an Irish beater or *sporteen* with whom I first walked
after wild-fowl. The same gentleman, when a snipe
or duck was clean missed, would immediately after the
shot gaze keenly after the bird with an air of the
most serious expectancy, and, changing his look to one
of extreme astonishment when the game was out of
sight, would exclaim, " Well, 'tisn't far he is from us
this minnit, wid somethin' worse than a toothache !"
and so on. The only impostor I ever met amongst
the tribe was an individual once recommended to me
by a gentleman who could not personally vouch for
him. I took him out in a hard frost, and, in consequence of the smoke hanging before the gun, I asked
him to mark carefully where the birds would fall. I
never found him to have the least idea on this score ;
and so on one occasion, having covered a teal, instead
of firing I looked round over my shoulder, and discovered the beater in a stooping posture, with his eyes
shut, waiting for the gun to go off, just as the ladies
do at a melodrama, when a villain draws his pistol to
perforate the hero.

I have encountered several Irish beaters whose
sagacity in the matter of sport would quite rival the
performances of Indian trappers or hunters. They
would never allow you to lose a moment in the day
searching barren acres. Did you want a hare, they

would lead you straight to a form and kick out the
soup for you. They almost invariably had a preference
for bringing you upon woodcock, and never could
understand the excitement of snipe shooting. Many
of these were perfectly candid and independent in
delivering judgment upon your performances. I remember a paragon—now spoiled for his business by
having married and degenerated into a settled occupation—who used literally to tear his hair at a bad miss;
and I have seen him refuse to go out with a persevering officer from the garrison, who considered a
single snipe out of fifteen offers a fair score. To see
Maurice —— beating was a sight to gladden a genuine
sportsman's heart—his smooth ruddy cheeks glowing
with the exercise, his clear blue eyes sparkling with
fun as he thrashed and whacked the heather or the
plantation, the cheerful bellow with which he roared
" Mark !" the satisfaction with which he picked up
your bird and announced the sum total which the last
success amounted to in the bag. There was no sub-
servience or disrespect either about the manner of
Maurice, but he had a constitutional aversion to
blundering fowlers. In fact he would not engage with
them at any price, even when a couple of shillings
might be to him what a guinea would be to a trained
keeper. Of another pattern was Tom Goold—big
Tom Goold—who was born of a cynical turn, and was
suspected of being a Fenian; he certainly wasn't a
fool. The rogue would never bring you where he
thought he would find the walking difficult for himself;
and as for filling the bag, why, that was your affair and
not his. I was obliged to employ him, as he had
charge of a range of mountain on which I had only
occasional permission to shoot, but I punished him by
reducing his tip to the smallest amount I could with
decency bring it down to.

Of Scotland I have no personal experience in
the matter of beaters, but from what I could learn

on good authority the mere gillies there are often
bright, well-informed, and interested in sport, like
their Irish prototypes. I suppose the beater, like
every other creature, is educationally influenced by
his surroundings. I know that with the average
Irish beater, or sporteen, as the country folk call
him, following the gun is almost as much an instinct
or a passion as it is with a setter. Maurice, above
referred to, would not have changed his beating
wattle for the spade or the plough tail but for the
circumstance that the locality in which he flourished
fell by inheritance into new hands, the whole ground
was carefully preserved, a professional gamekeeper was
imported to manage it; and so, Maurice's occupation
being gone, seeing that he could not be worse off than
he was, he "e'en took Peggy"—as Dr. Johnson
remarked every impoverished Irishman does—from
combined motives of economy and desperation. No
doubt in time the species of Irish beater to which
Maurice belonged will universally disappear; but the
class is not yet extinct, and may be hit upon pretty extensively both in the south and west of the island.

To conclude with a few practical remarks. There
is no use in swearing at a stupid beater—it only con-
fuses him. Send him home at once on your own
account, if you see that he knows nothing of his business. Select your own men, if you know the place,
in preference to leaving the matter to a gamekeeper,
who is often either prejudiced or jealous. Perhaps it
is unnecessary to say that, though a beater ought to be
thick-skinned, he is not impenetrable, and his eyes are
as liable to be destroyed by small shot as those of a
poet. A special providence, similar to that which
befriends the drunken man, takes care of him, but
cartridges ruthlessly discharged around him will take
effect if the practice be persisted in. It is a golden
rule to insist on knowing exactly where your beater
is. Make him give tongue from time to time—'tis

cheaper in the end than providing for his family. And if he is energetic, active, and obliging, a little surplus present over and above the common fee will not be regretted, probably, when you next have occasion for the services of the beater, who is happy to the extent of an additional quart of beer procured out of the unexpected dole.

J. OGDEN AND CO   PRINTERS 172 ST. IOHN STREET, LONDON, E.C.

GEORGE ROUTLEDGE & SONS'
RAILWAY CATALOGUE.

Paper Covers.	Limp Cl. Gilt.					Picture Boards.	Hf. Roan.
		AINSWORTH, W. Harrison—					
1/	1/6	Auriol	...	...	...	—	—
1/	1/6	Crichton	...	...	...	—	—
1/	1/6	Flitch of Bacon	...	...	...	—	—
1/	1/6	Guy Fawkes	...	...	...	—	—
1/	1/6	Jack Sheppard	...	...	...	—	—
1/	1/6	James the Second	...	...	—	—
1/	1/6	Lancashire Witches	...	...	—	—
1/	1/6	Mervyn Clitheroe	...	...	—	—
1/	1/6	Miser's Daughter	...	...	...	—	—
1/	1/6	Old St. Paul's	...	...	...	—	—
1/	1/6	Ovingdean Grange	...	...	—	—
1/	1/6	Rookwood	...	...	...	—	—
1/	1/6	Spendthrift	...	...	...	—	—
1/	1/6	Star Chamber	...	...	...	—	—
1/	1/6	St. James'	...	...	...	—	—
1/	1/6	Tower of London	...	...	—	—
1/	1/6	Windsor Castle	...	...	...	—	—

Ainsworth's Novels, in 17 vols., paper covers, price 17s. ; cloth gilt, £1 5s. 6d. ; 8 vols., half roan, £1 5s.

		ALCOTT, Louisa M.—					
1/	2/	Little Women	...	...		—	—
1/	2/	Little Women Married	...		—	—
1/	1/6	Moods	...	...	...	—	—

		ARMSTRONG, F. C.—					
—	—	Medora	...	...	...	...	2/	2/6
—	—	The Two Midshipmen	...	...	2/	2/6
—	—	War Hawk	...	...	...	2/	2/6
—	—	Young Commodore	...	...	2/	2/6

The Set, in 4 vols., half roan, 10s. ; or boards, 8s.

Paper Covers.	Limp Cl. Gilt.		Picture Boards.	
		ARTHUR, T. S.—		
1/	1/6	Nothing but Money ...	—	—
		AUSTEN, Jane—		Cloth.
1/	1/6	Emma	—	2/
1/	1/6	Mansfield Park	—	2/
1/	1/6	Northanger Abbey and Persuasion	—	2/
1/	1/6	Pride and Prejudice	—	2/
1/	1/6	Sense and Sensibility	—	2/

Jane Austen's Novels, 5 vols., paper covers, 5s.; cloth, 7s. 6d.; Superior Edition, cloth, in a box, 10s.

Paper Covers.	Limp Cl. Gilt.		Picture Boards.	
		BALZAC—		
1/	—	Balthazar	—	—
1/	—	Eugenie Grandes ...	—	—
		BANIM, John—		Hf. Roan.
—	—	Peep o' Day	2/	2/6
—	—	Smuggler ...	2/	2/6
		BARHAM, R. H.—		
1/	—	My Cousin Nicholas	—	—
		BAYLY, T. Haynes—		
1/	1/6	Kindness in Women	—	—
`		**BELL. M. M.—**		
—	—	Deeds not Words ...	2/	2/6
—	—	The Ladder of Gold ...	2/	2/6
—	—	The Secret of a Life ...	2/	2/6
		BIRD, Robert M.—		
—	—	Nick of the Woods; or, The Fighting Quaker	2/	—
		BRET HARTE—		
		See "AMERICAN LIBRARY," *page* 23.		
		BROTHERTON, Mrs.—		
1/	1/6	Respectable Sinners	—	—
		BRUNTON, Mrs.—		
1/	—	Discipline	—	—
1/	—	Self Control	—	—
		BURY, Lady Charlotte—		
1/	—	The Divorced	—	—
1/	—	Love	—	—

Paper Covers.	Limp Cl. Gilt.		Picture Boards.	Hf. Roan.
		CARLETON, William—		
1/	1/6	Clarionet, &c.	—	—
1/	1/6	Emigrants	—	—
1/	1/6	Fardarougha, the Miser	—	—
1/	1/6	Jane Sinclair, &c.	—	—
1/	1/6	Tithe Proctor	—	—

Carleton's Novels, 5 vols., paper covers, 5s.; cloth, 7s. 6d.

		CHAMIER, Captain—		
—	—	Ben Brace	2/	2 6
—	—	Jack Adams	2/	2 6
—	—	Life of a Sailor	2/	2/6
—	—	Tom Bowling	2/	2 6

4 vols., half roan, 10s.

		CLARKE, M. C.—		
—	—	The Iron Cousin	2/	—

		COCKTON, Henry—		
—	—	George Julian, the Prince ...	2/	2/6
—	—	Stanley Thorn	2/	2/6
—	—	Valentine Vox, the Ventriloquist	2/	2/6

Cockton's Novels, 3 vols., boards, 6s.; half roan, 7s. 6d.

		COLLINS, Charles Alston—		
—	—	The Cruise upon Wheels	2/	—

COOPER, J. Fenimore—

(SIXPENNY EDITION *on page* 20.)

Paper Covers.	Limp Cl. Gilt.		Picture Boards.	Cl. Boards Gilt, with Frontispiece.
1/	1 6	Afloat and Ashore; a Sequel to Miles Wallingford	2/	2 6
1/	1/6	Borderers; or, The Heathcotes...	2/	2 6
1/	1/6	Bravo; a Tale of Venice ...	2/	2 6
1/	1/6	Deerslayer; or, The First War-Path	2/	2 6
1	1 6	Eve Effingham: A Sequel to "Homeward Bound"	—	—
1/	1/6	Headsman...	2/	2 6
—	—	Heidenmauer: a Legend of the Rhine	2/	2 6
1	1 6	Homeward Bound; or, The Chase	2/	2 6
1/	1 6	Last of the Mohicans	2/	2 6
1/	1 6	Lionel Lincoln; or, The Leaguer of Boston	2/	2 6
1/	1 6	Mark's Reef; or, The Crater ...	—	—

Paper Covers.	Limp Cl. Gilt.		Picture Boards.	Cl. Gilt, with Frontis- piece.
		COOPER, J. FENIMORE—*continued.*		
1	1 6	Miles Wallingford ; or, Lucy Hardinge	2/	2/6
1/	1 6	Ned Myers ; or, Life before the Mast	—	—
1	1 6	Oak Openings ; or, The Beehunter—	—	—
1/	1/6	Pathfinder ; or, The Inland Sea	2/	2/6
1/	1 6	Pilot : a Tale of the Sea ...	2/	2/6
1/	1 6	Pioneers ; or, The Sources of the Susquehanna	2/	2/6
1	1/6	Prairie	2/	2/6
1/	1/6	Precaution	—	—
1/	1/6	Red Rover	2/	2 6
1/	1/6	Satanstoe ; or, The Littlepage Manuscripts	—	—
1/	1/6	Sea Lions ; or, The Lost Sealers	—	—
1/	1/6	Spy : a Tale of the Neutral Ground	2/	2/6
1/	1/6	Two Admirals	—	—
1	1/6	Waterwitch ; or, The Skimmer of the Seas...	2	2/6
1/	1/6	Wyandotte ; or, The Hutted Knoll	2/	2/6

Cooper's Novels.—The Set of 18 vols., green cloth, £2 5s. ; boards, £1 16s.

The SHILLING EDITION, 26 vols. in 13, half roan, £2. Also 26 vols., cloth gilt, £1 19s.; paper covers, £1 6s.

See also page 20.

				Hf. Roan.
		COOPER, Thomas—		
1/	1/6	The Family Feud	—	—
		COSTELLO, Dudley—		
—	—	Faint Heart ne'er Won Fair Lady	2/	—
—	—	The Millionaire of Mincing Lane	2/	—
		CROLY, Rev. Dr.—		
—	—	Salathiel	2/	2 6
		CROWE, Catherine—		
—	—	Lilly Dawson	2/	—
—	—	Linny Lockwood...	2/	—
—	—	Night Side of Nature	2/	2/6
—	—	Susan Hopley	2/	2/6

The Set, 4 vols., half roan, 10s.

Paper Covers.	Limp Cl. Gilt.		Picture Boards.	Cl. Gilt, with Frontis-piece.
		COOPER, J. FENIMORE—*continued.*		
1	1/6	Miles Wallingford ; or, Lucy Hardinge	2/	2/6
1/	1/6	Ned Myers ; or, Life before the Mast	—	—
1/	1/6	Oak Openings ; or, The Beehunter—	—	—
1/	1/6	Pathfinder; or, The Inland Sea	2/	2/6
1/	1/6	Pilot : a Tale of the Sea ...	2/	2/6
1/	1/6	Pioneers ; or, The Sources of the Susquehanna	2/	2/6
1/	1/6	Prairie	2/	2/6
1/	1/6	Precaution	—	—
1/	1/6	Red Rover	2/	2/6
1/	1/6	Satanstoe ; or, The Littlepage Manuscripts	—	—
1/	1/6	Sea Lions ; or, The Lost Sealers	—	—
1/	1/6	Spy : a Tale of the Neutral Ground	2/	2/6
1/	1/6	Two Admirals	—	—
1/	1/6	Waterwitch ; or, The Skimmer of the Seas...	2/	2/6
1/	1/6	Wyandotte ; or, The Hutted Knoll	2/	2/6

Cooper's Novels.—The Set of 18 vols., green cloth, £2 5*s.*; boards, £1 16*s.*

The SHILLING EDITION, 26 vols. in 13, half roan, £2. Also 26 vols., cloth gilt, £1 19*s.*; paper covers, £1 6*s.*

See also page 20.

				Hf. Roan.
		COOPER, Thomas—		
1/	1/6	The Family Feud	—	—
		COSTELLO, Dudley—		
—	—	Faint Heart ne'er Won Fair Lady	2/	—
—	—	The Millionaire of Mincing Lane	2/	—
		CROLY, Rev. Dr.—		
—	—	Salathiel	2/	2/6
		CROWE, Catherine—		
—	—	Lilly Dawson	2/	—
—	—	Linny Lockwood...	2/	—
—	—	Night Side of Nature	2/	2/6
—	—	Susan Hopley	2/	2/6

The Set, 4 vols., half roan, 10*s.*

Paper Covers.	Limp Cl. Gilt.		Picture Boards.	Hf. Roan.
		CARLETON, William—		
1/	1/6	Clarionet, &c.	—	—
1/	1/6	Emigrants	—	—
1/	1/6	Fardarougha, the Miser	—	—
1/	1/6	Jane Sinclair, &c.	—	—
1/	1/6	Tithe Proctor	—	—

Carleton's Novels, 5 vols., paper covers, 5s.; cloth, 7s. 6d.

		CHAMIER, Captain—		
—	—	Ben Brace	2/	2/6
—	—	Jack Adams	2/	2/6
—	—	Life of a Sailor	2/	2/6
—	—	Tom Bowling	2/	2/6

4 vols., half roan, 10s.

		CLARKE, M. C.—		
—	—	The Iron Cousin	2/	—

		COCKTON, Henry—		
—	—	George Julian, the Prince ...	2/	2/6
—	—	Stanley Thorn	2/	2/6
—	—	Valentine Vox, the Ventriloquist	2/	2/6

Cockton's Novels, 3 vols., boards, 6s.; half roan, 7s. 6d.

		COLLINS, Charles Alston—		
—	—	The Cruise upon Wheels	2/	—

COOPER, J. Fenimore—

(SIXPENNY EDITION *on page* 20.)

Paper Covers.	Limp Cl. Gilt.		Picture Boards.	Cl. Boards Gilt, with Frontispiece.
1/	1,6	Afloat and Ashore; a Sequel to Miles Wallingford	2/	2/6
1/	1/6	Borderers; or, The Heathcotes...	2/	2/6
1/	1/6	Bravo; a Tale of Venice ...	2/	2/6
1,	1/6	Deerslayer; or, The First War-Path	2/	2/6
1	1,6	Eve Effingham: A Sequel to "Homeward Bound"	—	—
1/	1/6	Headsman...	2/	2/6
—	—	Heidenmauer: a Legend of the Rhine	2/	2/6
1	1 6	Homeward Bound; or, The Chase	2/	2/6
1/	1,6	Last of the Mohicans	2/	2/6
1/	1 6	Lionel Lincoln; or, The Leaguer of Boston	2/	2/6
1/	1,6	Mark's Reef; or, The Crater	—	—

Paper Covers.	Limp Cl. Gilt.		Picture Boards.	Cloth or Hf. Roan.
		CROWQUILL, Alfred—		
1	—	A Bundle of Crowquills	—	—
		CUMMINS, M. S.—		Cloth.
1	1 6	The Lamplighter... ...	2/	2/6
—	—	Mabel Vaughan	2/	2/6
		CUPPLES, Captain—		Hf. Roan.
—	—	The Green Hand ...	2/	2/6
—	—	The Two Frigates	2/	2/6
		DE VIGNY, A.—		
1/	1 6	Cinq Mars	—	—
		DUMAS, Alexandre—		
1	1 6	Ascanio	—	—
1/	1 6	Beau Tancrede	—	—
1	1 6	Black Tulip	—	—
1	1/6	Captain Paul	—	—
1	1/6	Catherine Blum	—	—
1	1/6	Chevalier de Maison Rouge ...	—	—
1	1 6	Chicot the Jester	—	—
1	1 6	Conspirators	—	—
1/	1 6	Countess de Charny	—	—
1	1 6	Dr. Basilius	—	—
1/	1/6	Forty-five Guardsmen	—	—
—	—	Half Brothers	2/	2/6
1/	1/6	Ingenue	—	—
1	1/6	Isabel of Bavaria	—	—
—	—	Marguerite de Valois	2/	2/6
1	1/6	Memoirs of a Physician, vol. 1 }	—	3/
1	1/6	Do. do. vol. 2 }		
1	1/6	Monte Cristo ... vol. 1 }	—	3/
1	1/6	Do. ... vol. 2 }		
1	1/6	Nanon	—	—
1	1/6	Page of the Duke of Savoy ...	—	—
1	1/6	Pauline	—	—
1	1/6	Queen's Necklace	—	—
1	1/6	Regent's Daughter	—	—
1	1/6	Russian Gipsy	—	—
1	1 6	Taking the Bastile, vol. 1 }	—	3/
1	1 6	Do. vol. 2 }		
1	1/6	Three Musketeers ... }	—	3/
1	1/6	Twenty Years After ... }		
1	1 6	Watchmaker	—	—

Paper Covers.	Limp Cl. Gilt.		Picture Boards.	Hf. Roan.
		DUMAS, ALEXANDRE—*continued*.		
1/	1/6	Twin Captains	—	—
1/	1/6	Two Dianas	—	—
—	—	Vicomte de Bragelonne, vol. 1 ...	2/6	3/
—	—	Do. do. vol. 2 ...	2/6	3/
1/	1/6	Watchmaker	—	—

Dumas' Novels, 18 vols., half roan, £2 13*s*.

EDGEWORTH, Maria—

TALES OF FASHIONABLE LIFE :

1/	—	The Absentee	—	—
1/	—	Ennui	—	—
1/	—	Manœuvring	—	—
1/	—	Vivian	—	—

The Set, in cloth gilt, 4 vols., in a box, 8*s*.

EDWARDS, Amelia B.—

—	—	Half a Million of Money... ...	2/	2/6
—	—	Ladder of Life	2/	2/6
—	—	My Brother's Wife	2/	2/6

The Set, 3 vols., half roan, 7*s*. 6*d*.

FERRIER, Miss—

—	—	Destiny	2/	2/6
—	—	Inheritance	2/	2/6
—	—	Marriage	2/	2/6

The Set, 3 vols., half roan, 7*s*. 6*d*. ; in boards, 6*s*.

FIELDING, Thomas—

—	—	Amelia	2/	2/6
—	—	Joseph Andrews	2/	2/6
1/	—	Tom Jones	2/	2/6

Fielding's Novels, 3 vols., half roan, 7*s*. 6*d*. ; boards, 6*s*.
See also page 21.

FITTIS, Robert S.—

—	—	Gilderoy ...	2/	2/6

Paper Covers.	Limp Cl. Gilt.		Picture Boards.	Hf. Roan.
		FONBLANQUE, Albany, Jun.—		
—	—	The Man of Fortune	2/	2/6
		GERSTAECKER, Fred.—		
—	—	Each for Himself...	2/	2/6
—	—	The Feathered Arrow	2/	2/6
—	—	Sailor s Adventures }	2/	2/6
—	—	The Haunted House }		
—	—	Pirates of the Mississippi ...	2/	2/6
—	—	Two Convicts	2/	2/6
—	—	Wife to Order	2/	2/6
		The Set, 6 vols., half roan, 15s.		
		GRANT, James—		Hf. Roan.
—	—	Aide de Camp	2/	2/6
—	—	Arthur Blane ; or, The Hundred Cuirassiers	2/	2/6
—	—	Bothwell : the Days of Mary Queen of Scots	2/	2/6
—	—	Captain of the Guard : the Times of James II.	2/	2/6
—	—	Cavaliers of Fortune ; or, British Heroes in Foreign Wars ...	2/	2/6
—	—	Constable of France	2/	2/6
—	—	Dick Rodney : Adventures of an Eton Boy	2/	2/6
—	—	First Love and Last Love : a Tale of the Indian Mutiny	2/	2/6
—	—	Frank Hilton ; or, The Queen's Own	2/	2/6
—	—	The Girl he Married : Scenes in the Life of a Scotch Laird ...	2/	2/6
—	—	Harry Ogilvie ; or, The Black Dragoons	2/	2/6
—	—	Jack Manley	2/	2,6
—	—	Jane Seton ; or, The King's Advocate	2/	2/6
—	—	King's Own Borderers ; or, 25th Regiment	2/	2/6
—	—	Lady Wedderburn's Wish : a Story of the Crimean War	2/	2/6
—	—	Laura Everingham ; or, The Highlanders of Glen Ora	2/	2/6
—	—	Legends of the Black Watch ; or, The 42nd Regiment	2/	2/6

Paper Covers.	Limp Cl. Gilt.		Picture Boards.	Half Roan.

GRANT, JAMES—*continued.*

Paper Covers.	Limp Cl. Gilt.		Picture Boards.	Half Roan.
—	—	Lucy Arden ; or, Hollywood Hall	2/	2/6
—	—	Letty Hyde's Lovers : a Tale of the Household Brigade ...	2/	2/6
—	—	Mary of Lorraine...	2/	2/6
—	—	Oliver Ellis : the Twenty-first Fusiliers	2/	2/6
—	—	Only an Ensign	2/	2/6
—	—	Phantom Regiment : Stories of "Ours"...	2/	2/6
—	—	Philip Rollo ; or, The Scottish Musketeers	2/	2/6
—	—	Rob Roy, Adventures of ...	2/	2/6
—	—	Romance of War ; or, The Highlanders in Spain	2/	2/6
—	—	Scottish Cavalier : a Tale of the Revolution of 1688	2/	2/6
—	—	Second to None ; or, The Scots Greys	2/	2/6
—	—	Under the Red Dragon	2/	2/6
—	—	White Cockade ; or, Faith and Fortitude	2/	2/6
—	—	Yellow Frigate	2/	2/6

James Grant's Novels, 31 vols., half roan, £3 17s. 6d. ; boards, £3 2s.

GLEIG, G. R.—

				Hf. Roan.
—	—	The Country Curate	2/	2/6
—	—	The Hussar	2/	2/6
—	—	Light Dragoon	2/	2/6
—	—	The Only Daughter	2/	2/6
—	—	The Veterans of Chelsea Hospital	2/	2/6
—	—	Waltham	2/	2/6

The Set in 6 vols., half roan, 15s.

GOLDSMITH, Oliver—

1/	—	The Vicar of Wakefield ...	—

GRIFFIN, Gerald—

Paper Covers.	Limp Cl. Gilt.		Picture Boards.	Half Roan.
1/	1/6	Colleen Bawn	—	—
1/	1/6	Munster Festivals...	—	—
1/	1/6	The Rivals	—	—

Griffin's Novels, 3 vols., cloth, 4s. 6d. ; paper, 3s.

Paper Covers.	Limp Cl. Gilt.		Picture Boards.	Hf. Roan
		GORE, Mrs.—		
—	—	Cecil	2/	2/6
—	—	Debutante	2/	2/6
—	—	The Dowager	2/	2/6
—	—	Heir of Selwood	2/	2/6
—	—	Money Lender ...`	2/	2/6
—	—	Mothers and Daughters	2/	—
—	—	Pin Money	2/	2/6
—	—	Self	2/	2/6
—	—	The Soldier of Lyons	2/	—

The Set, 9 vols., half roan, £1 2s. 6d.

		GREY, Mrs.—		
1/	1/6	The Duke	—	—
1/	1/6	The Little Wife	—	—
1/	1/6	Old Country House	—	—
1/	1/6	Young Prima Donna	—	—

The Set, in 4 vols., 6s., cloth gilt.

		HALIBURTON, Judge—		
—	—	The Attaché	2/	2/6
—	—	The Letter-Bag of the Great Western	2/	2/6
—	—	Sam Slick, the Clockmaker ...	2/6	3/

Haliburton's Novels, 3 vols., half roan, 8s. ; paper covers, or boards, 6s. 6d.

		HANNAY, James—		
—	—	Singleton Fontenoy	2/	—

		HARLAND, Marion—		
1/	—	Hidden Path ...	—	—

		HARTE, Bret—		
1/	—	The Luck of Roaring Camp ...	—	—
—	—	Poetry and Prose	2/	2/6
1/	—	Truthful James	—	—

		HAWTHORNE, Nathaniel—		
1/	1/6	The House of the Seven Gables...	—	—
1/	1/6	Mosses from an Old Manse ...	—	—
1/	1/6	The Scarlet Letter	—	—

		HEYSE, Paul (Translated by G. H. Kingsley)—		
1/	—	Love Tales	—	—

Paper Covers.	Limp Cl. Gilt.		Picture Boards.	Hf. Roan.
		HOOD, Thomas—		
—	—	Tylney Hall	2/	2 6
		HOOK, Theodore—		
—	—	All in the Wrong... ...	2	2 6
—	—	Cousin Geoffry	2	2/6
—	—	Cousin William	2/	2/6
—	—	Fathers and Sons... ...	2/	2/6
—	—	Gervase Skinner	2/	2 6
—	—	Gilbert Gurney	2/	2/6
—	—	Gurney Married	2/	2/6
—	—	Jack Brag	2/	2/6
—	—	The Man of Many Friends	2/	2/6
—	—	Maxwell	2/	2/6
—	—	Merton	2/	2 6
—	—	Parson's Daughter	2	2/6
—	—	Passion and Principle ...	2/	2/6
—	—	Peregrine Bunce	2/	2 6
—	—	The Widow and the Marquess ...	2/	2/6

Hook's Novels, 15 vols., half roan, £2 ; Sayings and
Doings, 5 vols., half roan, 12s. 6d.

		JAMES, G. P. R.—		
—	—	Agincourt	2/	—
—	—	Arabella Stuart	2/	—
—	—	Black Eagle	2/	—
—	—	The Brigand	2/	—
—	—	Castle of Ehrenstein ...	2/	—
—	—	The Convict	2/	—
—	—	Darnley	2/	—
—	—	Forgery	2/	—
—	—	The Gentleman of the Old School	2/	—
—	—	The Gipsy...	2/	—
—	—	Gowrie	2/	—
—	—	Heidelberg	2/	—
—	—	Jacquerie	2/	—
—	—	Morley Ernstein	2/	—
—	—	Philip Augustus	2/	—
—	—	Richelieu	2/	—
—	—	The Robber	2/	—
—	—	Russell	2/	—
—	—	The Smuggler	2/	—
—	—	Woodman	2/	—

The remainder of the Works of Mr. James will be published in
Monthly Volumes at 2s. each.

Paper Covers.	Limp CL Gilt.		Picture Boards.	Hf. Roan.
		HOOTON, Charles—		
—	—	Colin Clink ...	2/	—
	Ɪ	**KINGSLEY, Henry—**		
—	—	Stretton	2/	—
		KINGSTON, W. H. G.—		
—	—	Albatross	2/	—
—	—	The Pirate of the Mediterranean...	2/	—
		LANG, John—		
—	—	Ex-Wife	2/	—
—	—	Will He Marry Her? ...	2/	—
		LEVER, Charles—		
—	—	Arthur O'Leary	2/	2/6
—	—	Con Cregan	2/	2/6
		LE FANU, Sheridan—		
—	—	Torlogh O'Brien	2/	—
		LONG, Lady Catherine—		Cloth.
—	—	First Lieutenant	2/	2/6
—	—	Sir Roland Ashton	2/	2/6
		LOVER, Samuel—		Hf. Roan.
—	—	Handy Andy	2/	2/6
—	—	Rory O'More	2/	2/6
		LYTTON, Right Hon. Lord—		Cloth.
—	—	Alice : Sequel to Ernest Maltravers	2/	2/6
—	—	Caxtons	2/	2/6
—	—	Devereux	2/	2/6
—	—	Disowned	2/	2/6
—	—	Ernest Maltravers	2/	2/6
—	—	Eugene Aram	2/	2/6
—	—	Godolphin...	2/	2/6
—	—	Harold	2/	2/6
—	—	The Last of the Barons	2/	2/6
—	—	Leila ... ... / The Pilgrims of the Rhine	2/	2/6
—	—	Lucretia	2/	2/6
—	—	My Novel, vol. 1...	2/	2/6
—	—	Do. vol. 2...	2/	2/6
—	—	Night and Morning	2/	2/6

T

Paper Covers.	Limp Cl. Gilt.		Picture Boards.	Cloth Gilt.
		LYTTON, LORD—*continued.*		
—	—	Paul Clifford	2/	2/6
—	—	Pelham	2/	2/6
—	—	Pompeii, The Last Days of ...	2/	2/6
—	—	Rienzi	2/	2/6
—	—	Strange Story	2/	2/6
—	—	What will He Do with It? vol. 1	2/	2/6
—	—	Do. do. vol. 2	2/	2/6
—	—	Zanoni	2/	2/6

Sets of Lord Lytton's Novels, 22 vols., fcap. 8vo, cloth, £2 15*s.*; boards, £2 4*s.* (*See also page* 19.)

MAILLARD, Mrs.—

1/	—	Adrien	—	—
1/	—	Compulsory Marriage	—	—
1/	—	Zingra the Gipsy ...	—	—

MAXWELL, W. H.—   Hf. Roan.

—	—	The Bivouac	2/	2/6
—	—	Brian O'Linn; or, Luck... ...	2/	2/6
—	—	Captain Blake	2/	2/6
—	—	Captain O'Sullivan	2/	2/6
—	—	Flood and Field	2/	2/6
—	—	Hector O'Halloran	2/	2/6
—	—	Stories of the Peninsular War ...	2/	2/6
1/	1.6	Stories of Waterloo	2/	2/6
—	—	Wild Sports in the Highlands ...	2/	2/6
—	—	Wild Sports in the West ...	2/	2/6

The Set, in 10 vols., half roan, £1 5*s.*

MARK TWAIN—

(*See* "AMERICAN LIBRARY," *page* 23).

MARRYAT, Captain—   Cl. Gilt.

The New Edition, with 6 Original Illustrations. (*See page* 19.)

1/	1/6	Dog Fiend	2/	2/6
1/	1/6	Frank Mildmay	2/	2/6
1/	1/6	Jacob Faithful	2/	2/6
1/	1/6	Japhet in Search of a Father ...	2/	2/6
1/	1/6	King's Own	2/	2/6
1/	1/6	Midshipman Easy	2/	2/6
1/	1/6	Monsieur Violet	—	—
1/	1/6	Newton Forster	2/	2/6

Paper Covers.	Limp Cl. Gilt.		Picture Boards.	Cloth Gilt.
		MARRYAT, CAPTAIN—*continued*.	—	
1/	1/6	Olla Podrida	—	—
1/	1/6	Percival Keene	2/	2/6
1,	1/6	Phantom Ship	2/	2/6
1/	1/6	Poacher	2/	2/6
1/	1/6	Pacha of Many Tales	2/	2/6
1/	1/6	Peter Simple	2/	2/6
1/	1/6	Rattlin the Reefer	2/	2/6
1/	1/6	Valerie	—	—

The Set of Captain Marryat's Novels, 16 vols. bound in 8, half-bound, gilt tops, £1 5s.; 16 vols. cloth, £1 4s.; paper, 16s.; 13 vols. (steel plates), cloth, £1 12s. 6d.

				Hf. Roan.
		MARTINEAU, Harriet—		
—	—	The Hour and the Man ...	2/	2/6
		MAYHEW, Brothers—		
—	—	The Greatest Plague of Life ...	2/	2/6
—	—	Whom to Marry and How to Get Married	2/	2/6

These two Works have Steel Plates by George Cruikshank.

		MILLER, Thomas—		
—	—	Gideon Giles, the Roper...	2/	—
		MORIER, Captain—		
—	—	Hajji Baba in Ispahan	2/	—
—	—	Zohrab the Hostage	2/	—
		NEALE, Capt. W. J.—		
—	—	Captain's Wife	2/	—
—	—	Cavendish	2/	—
—	—	Flying Dutchman	2/	—
—	—	Gentleman Jack	2/	—
—	—	The Lost Ship	2/	—
—	—	Port Admiral	2/	—
1/	—	Pride of the Mess	—	—
		NORTON, The Hon. Mrs.—		
—	—	Stuart of Dunleath ...	2/	2/6
		OLD SAILOR—		
—	—	Land and Sea Tales ...	2/	—
—	—	Top-Sail Sheet-Blocks ...	2/	—
—	—	Tough Yarns	2/	—
—	—	The War-Lock	2/	—

Paper Covers.	Limp Cl. Gilt.		Picture Boards.	Hf. Roan.
		POOLE, John—		
—	—	Phineas Quiddy ...	2.	—
		PORTER, Jane—		
—	—	The Pastor's Fireside ...	2/	—
—	—	The Scottish Chiefs ..	2/	2/6
—	—	Thaddeus of Warsaw ...	2/	—
		3 vols., half roan, 7s. 6d.		
		RICHARDSON, Samuel—		Cloth.
—	—	Clarissa Harlowe	2/6	3/6
—	—	Pamela	2/6	3/6
—	—	Sir Charles Grandison	2/6	3/6
		The Set, 3 vols., 10s. 6d., half roan.		
		ROSS, Charles H.—		
1/	—	A Week with Mossoo ...	—	—
		SAUNDERS, Captain Patten—		Hf.Roan.
-	—	Black and Gold: A Tale of Circassia	2/	2,6
		SCOTT, Lady—		
—	—	Marriage in High Life ...	2/	—
1/	1/6	Henpecked Husband ...	—	—
—	—	The Pride of Life... ...	2/	—
—	—	Trevelyan	2/	—
		SKETCHLEY, Arthur—		
—	—	Mrs. Brown on the Liquor Law	1/	—
—	—	Mrs. Brown on the Alabama Case	1	—
—	—	Mrs. Brown on the Tichborne Case	1/	—
—	—	Mrs. Brown on the Tichborne Defence	1/	—
—	—	Mrs. Brown's 'Oliday Houtings...	1/	—
—	—	Mrs. Brown at the Play	1/	—
—	—	Mrs. Brown on the Grand Tour...	1/	—
—	—	Mrs. Brown in the Highlands ...	1/	—
—	—	Mrs. Brown in London	1/	—
—	—	Mrs. Brown in Paris	1/	—
—	—	Mrs. Brown at the Sea-side ...	1/	—
—	—	Mrs. Brown in America	1/	—
—	—	The Brown Papers, 1st Series ...	1/	—
—	—	The Brown Papers, 2nd Series ...	1/	—

Paper Covers.	Limp Cl. Gilt.		Picture Boards.	Cloth.

SKETCHLEY, ARTHUR—*continued.*

—	—	Miss Tompkins' Intended ...	1/	—
—	—	Out for a Holiday	1/	—
—	—	Mrs. Brown on Woman's Rights	1/	—

Mrs. Brown on the Battle of Dorking, paper covers, 6d.

SMEDLEY, Frank E.—

—	—	The Colville Family	2/	3/
—	—	Frank Fairleigh	2/6	3/6
—	—	Harry Coverdale	2/6	3/6
—	—	Lewis Arundel	3/	4/

The Set, in 4 vols., 14s.

SMITH, Albert—

Hf. Roan.

—	—	Christopher Tadpole	2/	2/6
—	—	Marchioness of Brinvilliers ...	2/	2/6
—	—	Mr. Ledbury's Adventures ..	2/	2/6
—	—	The Pottleton Legacy	2/	2/6
—	—	The Scattergood Family... ...	2/	2/6

The Set of Albert Smith's Novels, in 5 vols., half roan, 12s. 6d.;
5 vols., boards, 10s.

SMOLLETT, Tobias—

—	—	Humphrey Clinker	2/	2/6
—	—	Peregrine Pickle	2/	2/6
—	—	Roderick Random	2/	2/6

The Set of 3 vols., half roan, 7s. 6d.

STERNE, Lawrence—

1	—	{ Tristram Shandy, and Sentimental Journey }	—	—

STRETTON, Hesba—

—	—	The Clives of Burcot	2/	2/6

SUE, Eugene—

—	—	The Mysteries of Paris	2/	2/6
—	—	The Wandering Jew	2/	2/6

THOMAS, Annie—

—	—	False Colours ...	2/	—
—	—	Sir Victor's Choice	2/	—

VIDOCQ—

—	—	The French Police Spy	2/	—

Paper Covers.	Limp Cl. Gilt.		Picture Boards.	Cloth.
		WETHERELL, Elizabeth—		
—	—	Ellen Montgomery's Book Case	2/	2/6
—	—	Melbourne House	2/	2/6
1/	1/6	My Brother's Keeper	—	—
—	—	The Old Helmet	2/	2/6
—	—	Queechy	2/	2/6
—	—	The Two Schoolgirls, and other		
		Tales	2/	2/6
—	—	The Wide, Wide World... ...	2/	2/6
		"Whitefriars," Author of—		Hf. Roan.
—	—	Cæsar Borgia	2/	2/6
—	—	Gold Worshippers	2/	2/6
—	—	Madeline Graham	2/	2/6
—	—	Maid of Orleans	2/	2/6
—	—	Owen Tudor	2/	2/6
—	—	Westminster Abbey	2/	2/6
—	—	Whitefriars	2/	2/6
—	—	Whitehall	2/	2/6
		The Set of 8 vols., half bound, 20s.		
		TROLLOPE, Mrs.—		
—	—	The Barnabys in America	2/	2/6
—	—	One Fault	2/	2/6
—	—	Petticoat Government ...	2/	2/6
—	—	The Ward...	2/	2/6
—	—	Widow Barnaby	2/	2/6
—	—	The Widow Married ...	2/	2/6
		YATES, Edmund—		
—	—	Kissing the Rod ...	2/	2/6
—	—	Running the Gauntlet	2/	2/6
		Anonymous—		
—	—	Bashful Irishman...	2/	—
—	—	Dr. Goethe's Courtship	2/	—
—	—	Guy Livingstone...	2/	—
—	—	Lewell Pastures	2/	—
—	—	Manœuvring Mother ...	2/	—
1/	—	The Old Commodore ...	—	—
—	—	Outward Bound	2/	2/6
1/	—	Violet the Danseuse ...	—	—
—	—	Who is to Have It ? ...	2/	—
—	—	The Young Curate ...	2/	—

' LORD LYTTON'S NOVELS.

Uniformly printed in crown 8vo, with gilt backs.
Price 4*s*. each Volume.

Night and Morning.	The Caxtons.
Harold.	What will He Do with
My Novel. 2 vols.	It? 2 vols.
Lucretia.	

Price 3*s*. 6*d*. each Volume.

The Last Days of Pompeii.	The Disowned.
Ernest Maltravers.	Zanoni.
Devereux.	A Strange Story.
Paul Clifford.	Rienzi.
Eugene Aram.	Pelham.
Alice.	

ALSO,

The Last of the Barons, 5/.	The Pilgrims of the Rhine, 2/6.
Godolphin, 3/.	Leila; or, The Siege of Gra-
	nada, 2/.

Sets of Lord Lytton's Novels, 22 vols., crown 8vo, cloth gilt, £4 10*s*.; 11 vols., half roan, £4 3*s*.

Messrs. GEORGE ROUTLEDGE & SONS beg to announce that they have purchased the Copyright of all the Published and Unpublished Works of the late LORD LYTTON, and that they are about to issue an Entirely New Edition of them, in Monthly Volumes, price 3*s*. 6*d*. each.

This New Edition—which will be printed crown 8vo size, from new type, and bound in green cloth, each volume averaging about 400 pages—will be entitled

THE KNEBWORTH EDITION,

And will contain all the Novels, Poems, Dramas, and Miscellaneous Prose Writings of Lord Lytton, forming the Only Complete Edition ever issued of the works of this famous Author.

The first volume, now ready, is "Eugene Aram." To be followed, in June, by "Pelham; or, The Adventures of a Gentleman." With a Portrait of the Author.

WORKS OF CAPTAIN MARRYAT.

An Entirely New Edition of the Works of Captain Marryat, in Monthly Volumes, crown 8vo, bound in blue cloth, price 3*s*. 6*d*. each; printed from entirely new type, with Six original Illustrations by the best Artists. Volumes issued—

Peter Simple.	Frank Mildmay.	The Dog Fiend.
The King's Own.	Midshipman Easy.	Rattlin the Reefer.

ROUTLEDGE'S
SIXPENNY WORLD-WIDE LIBRARY.
(Postage 1*d.*)

J. FENIMORE COOPER.

Afloat and Ashore.
Borderers.
Bravo.
Deerslayer.
Eve Effingham.
Headsman.
Heidenmauer.
Homeward Bound.
Jack Tier.
Lionel Lincoln.

Mark's Reef.
Mercedes.
Miles Wallingford.
Mohicans (Last of the).
Ned Myers.
Oak Openings.
Pathfinder.
Pilot.
Pioneers.

Prairie.
Precaution.
Red Rover.
Satanstoe.
Sea Lions.
Spy.
Two Admirals.
Waterwitch.
Wyandotte.

	£	s.	d.
The Set of the above 28 Volumes, paper covers ...	0	14	0
The 28 Volumes bound in 7 Volumes, half roan ...	1	1	0
Do. do. cloth	0	17	6

The Volumes are sold separately, 3*s.* each, half-bound, or
2*s.* 6*d.* cloth.

Contents of the Volumes :—

Vol. 1. Spy—Pilot—Homeward Bound—Eve Effingham.
  ,, 2. Pioneers—Mohicans—Prairie—Pathfinder.
  ,, 3. Red Rover — Two Admirals — Miles Wallingford—
         Afloat and Ashore.
  ,, 4. Borderers—Wyandotte—Mark's Reef—Satanstoe.
  ,, 5. Lionel Lincoln — Oak Openings — Ned Myers — Pre-
         caution.
  ,, 6. Deerslayer—Headsman—Waterwitch—Heidenmauer.
  ,, 7. Bravo—Sea Lions—Jack Tier—Mercedes.

SIR WALTER SCOTT.
6*d.* each.

Abbot.
Antiquary.
Bride of Lammermoor.
Fortunes of Nigel.
Guy Mannering.
Heart of Midlothian.
Ivanhoe.
Kenilworth.
Monastery.

Legend of Montrose, and
    The Black Dwarf.
Old Mortality.
Peveril of the Peak.
Pirate.
Quentin Durward.
Rob Roy.
St. Ronan's Well.
Waverley.

ROUTLEDGE'S 6*d.* WORLD-WIDE LIBRARY—*continued.*

Sir Walter Scott's Novels, in cloth, 3*s.* each; or half roan, 3*s.* 6*d.*

Contents of the Volumes :—

Vol. 1. Waverley—Rob Roy—Monastery—Kenilworth—Pirate.

„　2. Ivanhoe—Fortunes of Nigel—Old Mortality—Guy Man-
　　　nering—Bride of Lammermoor.

„　3. Heart of Midlothian—Antiquary—Quentin Durward—
　　　Peveril of the Peak—St. Ronan's Well.

EUGENE SUE.

The Wandering Jew.	The Mysteries of Paris.
Pt. 1. The Transgression, 6*d.*	Part 1. Morning, 6*d.*
„　2. The Chastisement, 6*d.*	„　2. Noon, 6*d.*
„　3. The Redemption, 6*d.*	„　3. Night, 6*d.*
Complete in 1 vol., 2*s.*, boards,	Complete in 1 vol., 2*s.*, boards,
or 2*s.* 6*d.*, half roan.	or 2*s.* 6*d.*, half roan.

VARIOUS AUTHORS.

	Paper Covers. *s. d.*	Cloth Gilt. *s. d.*
CUMMINS (Miss). The Lamplighter... ...	0 6	1 0
DE FOE. Robinson Crusoe	0 6	1 0
DE QUINCEY. The Opium Eater ...	0 6	—
FIELDING. Tom Jones. Part 1. ...	0 6	—
Do. do. Part 2. ...	0 6	—
GOLDSMITH. Vicar of Wakefield ...	0 6	1 0
GERALD GRIFFIN. Colleen Bawn	0 6	—
HOLMES. Autocrat of the Breakfast Table ...	0 6	1 0
Do. The Professor at the Breakfast Table	0 6	1 0
IRVING (WASHINGTON). The Sketch Book	0 6	1 0
LAMB (CHARLES). Essays of Elia	0 6	1 0
SMOLLETT (TOBIAS). Roderick Random ...	0 6	—
STERNE (LAURENCE). Sentimental Journey	0 6	—
Do. Tristram Shandy ...	0 6	—
STOWE (Mrs.). Uncle Tom's Cabin	0 6	1 0
SWIFT. Gulliver's Travels	0 6	1 0
VICTOR HUGO. Notre Dame	0 6	—
WETHERELL (Miss). Wide, Wide World ...	0 6	1 0
Do. Queechy	0 6	1 0

ROUTLEDGE'S OCTAVO NOVELS.

Price 6s. each, handsomely bound in cloth.

Under this title, and at the price of 6s. a volume, Messrs. GEORGE ROUTLEDGE & SONS are issuing in Monthly Volumes the best Novels by W. HARRISON AINSWORTH, FRANK SMEDLEY, SAMUEL LOVER, ANTHONY TROLLOPE, CHARLES LEVER, ALEXANDRE DUMAS, and other Authors, each Illustrated by the original Steel Plates and Woodcuts of CRUIKSHANK, PHIZ, MILLAIS, and other eminent Artists. The Illustrations to Ainsworth's Novels by George Cruikshank are the finest specimens of that Artist's work ; and as these books have been out of print for several years, the demand for this New Edition is sure to be very great.

GUY FAWKES. By W. H. AINSWORTH. With Illustrations on Steel by GEORGE CRUIKSHANK.

JACK SHEPPARD. By W. H. AINSWORTH. With Illustrations on Steel by GEORGE CRUIKSHANK.

ROOKWOOD. By W. H. AINSWORTH. With Illustrations by CRUIKSHANK and Sir JOHN GILBERT.

STAR CHAMBER. By W. H. AINSWORTH. Illustrated by " Phiz."

CRICHTON. By W. H. AINSWORTH.

SPENDTHRIFT. By W. H. AINSWORTH.

OVINGDEAN GRANGE. By W. H. AINSWORTH.

MERVYN CLITHEROE. By W. H. AINSWORTH.

THE TOWER OF LONDON. An Historical Romance. By W. H. AINSWORTH. With Forty Illustrations on Steel and numerous Woodcuts by GEORGE CRUIKSHANK. 6s.

LANCASHIRE WITCHES. By W. H. AINSWORTH. With Illustrations by JOHN GILBERT.

WINDSOR CASTLE. By W. H. AINSWORTH. With Portrait of the Author, and Eighteen Illustrations by GEORGE CRUIKSHANK and TONY JOHANNOT, and Eighty-seven Wood Engravings by W. ALFRED DELAMOTTE.

OLD ST. PAUL'S : A Tale of the Plague and the Fire. By W. H. AINSWORTH. With Twenty Illustrations on Steel by J. FRANKLIN and H. K. BROWNE. 6s.

MISER'S DAUGHTER. By W. H. AINSWORTH. With Twenty Steel Plates by GEORGE CRUIKSHANK.

HARRY COVERDALE'S COURTSHIP, AND WHAT CAME OF IT. By FRANK SMEDLEY. Thirty Illustrations on Steel by " Phiz." 6s.

LEWIS ARUNDEL. By F. SMEDLEY. With Forty-two Illustrations by " Phiz."

FRANK FAIRLEIGH : Scenes from the Life of a Private Pupil. By FRANK SMEDLEY. With Thirty Illustrations on Steel by GEORGE CRUIKSHANK. 6s.

ROUTLEDGE'S OCTAVO NOVELS—*continued.*

HANDY ANDY. By SAMUEL LOVER. With Twenty-four Illustrations.

THE COUNT OF MONTE CRISTO. By ALEXANDRE DUMAS. With Twenty full-page Illustrations and a Portrait of the Author. 6s.

CONFESSIONS OF CON CREGAN, the Irish Gil Blas. By CHARLES LEVER. With Illustrations on Steel and numerous Woodcuts by "Phiz." 6s.

THE FORTUNES OF COLONEL TORLOGH O'BRIEN. A Tale of the Wars of King James. By LE FANU. With Illustrations by HABLOT K. BROWNE. 6s.

To be followed by

POTTLETON LEGACY. By ALBERT SMITH.

VALENTINE VOX. By COCKTON.

ROUTLEDGE'S AMERICAN LIBRARY.

Price 1s. (Postage 2d.)

MARK TWAIN.

"Messrs. George Routledge & Sons are my only authorised London Publishers."—*(Signed)* MARK TWAIN.

THE EXTRAORDINARY JUMPING FROG. Copyright Edition.

ROUGHING IT. Copyright Edition.

THE INNOCENTS AT HOME: a Sequel to "Roughing It." Copyright Edition.

THE CURIOUS DREAM.

INNOCENTS ABROAD: Morocco, Italy, &c.

THE NEW PILGRIM'S PROGRESS: Palestine, Egypt, &c.

BRET HARTE.

POEMS: including "That Heathen Chinee," "Jim," and "Dow's Flat."

CONDENSED NOVELS: including "Lothair."

THE LUCK OF ROARING CAMP, and other Sketches. With Introduction by TOM HOOD.

MRS. SKAGGS' HUSBANDS.

Bret Harte's Works Complete in One Volume, 5s.
Crown 8vo, cloth.

EDWARD EGGLESTON.

THE HOOSIER SCHOOLMASTER.

THE END OF THE WORLD.

THE MYSTERY OF METROPOLISVILLE.

NOVELS AT TWO SHILLINGS (*continued*).

By J. F. COOPER.

he Spy.
float and Ashore.
he Bravo.
he Deerslayer.
he Headsman.
he Heidenmauer.

Homeward Bound.
The Last of the Mohicans.
Lionel Lincoln.
Miles Wallingford.
The Pathfinder.
The Pilot.

The Pioneers.
The Prairie.
The Red Rover.
The Waterwitch.
Wyandotté.
The Borderers.

By FIELDING AND SMOLLETT.

FIELDING.
Tom Jones.
Joseph Andrews.
Amelia.

SMOLLETT.
Roderick Random.
Humphrey Clinker.
Peregrine Pickle.

By VARIOUS AUTHORS.

he Night Side of Nature. *Mrs. Crowe.*
icottish Chiefs. *Jane Porter.*
Rory O'More. *Samuel Lover.*
ioldier of Lyons. *Mrs. Gore.*
Who is to Have it?
ron Cousin. *Mrs. C. Clark.*
Each for Himself. *Gerstaecker.*
The Young Curate.
Matrimonial Shipwrecks. *Mrs. Maillard.*
The Two Baronets. *Lady Charlotte Bury.*
Hector O'Halloran. *Maxwell.*
Handy Andy. *Lover.*
Lamplighter. *Miss Cummins.*
Ben Brace. *Captain Chamier.*
The Hussar. *Gleig.*
The Parson's Daughter. *Theodore Hook.*
Guy Livingstone.
Running the Gauntlet. *Edmund Yates.*
Kissing the Rod.
Sir Victor's Choice. *Annie Thomas.*
All in the Wrong. *Theodore Hook.*

Outward Bound. *Author of "Rattlin the Reefer."*
The Widow and the Marquess. *Theodore Hook.*
Emily Chester
Waltham.
Phineas Quiddy.
Lewell Pastures.
Zohrab the Hostage.
Gilderoy.
Black and Gold. *Capt. Patten Saunders.*
The Flying Dutchman.
Clarissa Harlowe. *Richardson.*
Clives of Burcot. *Hesba Stretton.*
Dr. Goethe's Courtship.
Half a Million of Money. *A. B. Edwards.*
The Wandering Jew.
The Mysteries of Paris.
Ladder of Gold.
The Greatest Plague of Life.
The Tommiebeg Shootings.
Horses and Hounds.
A Cruise on Wheels.
Con Cregan. *Lever.*
Arthur O'Leary. *Lever.*

NOVELS AT TWO SHILLINGS.

Postage 4d.

By LORD LYTTON.

Night and Morning.
Ernest Maltravers.
Last of the Barons.
The Caxtons.
Rienzi.
Pelham.
Last Days of Pompeii.

The Disowned.
Leila, and Pilgrims of the Rhine. 1 vol.
Paul Clifford.
Alice.
Devereux.
Eugene Aram.
Godolphin.

My Novel. 2 vols.
Lucretia.
Harold.
Zanoni.
A Strange Story.
What will he Do with I 2 vols.

By ALBERT SMITH.

The Adventures of Mr. Ledbury.
The Scattergood Family.

Christopher Tadpole.
The Pottleton Legacy.

By CAPTAIN MARRYAT.

Peter Simple.
The Dog Fiend.
Mr. Midshipman Easy.
The Poacher.
Jacob Faithful.

The Phantom Ship.
Frank Mildmay.
The King's Own.
The Pacha of Many Tales.

Newton Forster.
Japhet in Search of Father.
Percival Keene.
Rattlin the Reefer.

By JAMES GRANT.

The Romance of War; or, The Highlanders in Spain.
The Aide-de-Camp.
The Scottish Cavalier.
Bothwell.
Jane Seton; or, The Queen's Advocate.
Philip Rollo.
Legends of the Black Watch.
Mary of Lorraine.
Oliver Ellis; or, The Fusiliers.
Lucy Arden; or, Hollywood Hall.
Frank Hilton; or, The Queen's Own.
The Yellow Frigate.
Arthur Blane.

Harry Ogilvie; or, The Black Dragoons.
Laura Everingham; or, The Highlanders of Glenora.
The Captain of the Guard.
Letty Hyde's Lovers.
Cavaliers of Fortune.
Second to None; or, The Scots Grey
The Constable of France.
The Phantom Regiment.
The King's Own Borderers.
The White Cockade.
Dick Rodney.
First Love and Last Love.
The Girl he Married.

By HENRY COCKTON.

Valentine Vox. | Stanley Thorn. | George Julian.